Praise for
Lorraine Bartlett's Books

"Bartlett combines murder, a touch of romance, and a lot of intrigue in this charming story. With a cast of personable characters, and a lively, fast-paced storyline, readers will be enthralled and delighted with this fresh new series."
—*Fresh Fiction*

"Interesting characters, growing interrelationships, plausible reasons for crime and an amateur to get involved in finding the answers—it's like visiting friends and having an adventure rolled into one book after another."
—*Gumshoe Review*

"Ms. Bartlett can be counted on to deliver a fun read, with engaging characters and a tidy plot."
—*The Cozy Library*

"Fun plot, fanciful characters, really fabulous crafts... Bartlett put her art and soul into this mystery."
—*Laura Child, New York Times bestselling author*

"Tori Cannon will grab your heart from page one and the mystery will hook you from the beginning. Bravo to Lorraine Bartlett for creating great characters and a fascinating story."
—*Leann Sweeney, New York Times Bestselling Author of the Cats in Trouble Mysteries*

"Cozy readers will fall for Lorraine Bartlett's charming Lotus Bay mysteries—hook, line, and sinker!"
—*Ellery Adams, New York Times Bestselling Author of the Books By The Bay Mysteries*

PANTY RAID

Tori Cannon and her BFF, Kathy Grant, get together for a girl's weekend of wine, cookies, and laughter, but there's also the specter of a panty pincher hanging around the laundry room of the complex where Tori lives. Kathy thinks they can catch the culprit red-handed in a panty raid!

WITH BAITED BREATH

Tori Cannon and her grandfather, Herb, return from her grandmother's funeral, and it's with sadness that she learns the bait shop and small motel they ran has fallen on hard times. Jammed into one of the motel's units is the body of one of Herb's customers, his mouth filled with spikes. The victim had no enemies, except for maybe the rich woman who wanted to level his eyesore of a home. But he also had a daughter who's resentful her father wasn't a major force in her life, and some friends who were anything but friends. Tori's friend, Kathy, arrives to help spruce up the property, and the two of them find themselves mixed up in the petty jealousies and deadly consequences that murder entails. Can they save the bait shop and find a murderer or will they, too, sleep with the fishes?

Books by Lorraine Bartlett

The Victoria Square Mysteries
A Crafty Killing
The Walled Flower
One Hot Murder
Recipes To Die For: A Victoria Square Cookbook

The Tales of Telenia (Adventure-Fantasy)
Threshold
Journey
Treachery (2015)

Short Stories
Love & Murder: A Collection of Short Stories
Panty Raid: A Tori Cannon-Kathy Grant Mini Mystery
Blue Christmas
An Unconditional Love
Prisoner of Love
Love Heals
We're So Sorry, Uncle Albert

Writing as L. L. Bartlett

The Jeff Resnick Mysteries
Murder On The Mind
Dead In Red
Room At The Inn
Cheated By Death
Bound By Suggestion
Dark Waters

Short Stories
Evolution: Jeff Resnick's Backstory
When The Spirit Moves You (A Jeff Resnick Mystery)
Bah! Humbug (featuring Jeff Resnick)
Cold Case (A Jeff Resnick Mystery–the inspiration for
        Bound by Suggestion)

Spooked! (featuring Jeff Resnick)
Abused: A Daughter's Story

Writing as Lorna Barrett
The Booktown Mysteries
Murder Is Binding
Bookmarked For Death
Bookplate Special
Chapter & Hearse
Sentenced To Death
Murder On The Half Shelf
Not The Killing Type
Book Clubbed
A Fatal Chapter

Panty Raid

A
Tori Cannon-Kathy Grant
Mini Mystery

* * * * *

With Baited Breath

A
Lotus Bay Mystery

by
Lorraine Bartlett

 Polaris Press

Dedication

To my Mum
Valerie Bartlett
who started me reading mysteries.

TABLE OF CONTENTS

Panty Raid 1

With Baited Breath 25

Recipes 243

About the Author 247

FROM THE AUTHOR

Thank you for joining Tori and Kathy on their first adventures. As a bonus, I'm including their mini mystery, Panty Raid, as part of this edition of With Baited Breath. I hope you'll enjoy it and their longer story on Lotus Bay.

My thanks go to Judy Beatty, Linda Kuzminczuk, Janice Dince, and other members of the Lorraine Train street team-chjjjjjj for proofreading, and Frank Solomon for layout and design of this print edition.

The Lotus Bay Mysteries are set in Western New York, by the great Lake Ontario. Be sure to check out my website to learn more about Tori and Kathy and the other books I write.

www.LorraineBartlett.com

Panty Raid

A
Tori Cannon-Kathy Grant
Mini Mystery

Classmates. That's what they'd been at SUNY Brockport (otherwise known as State University of New York at Brockport).

Kathy and Tori. Best friends for four wonderful years. Then, upon graduation, they'd drifted out of each other's lives. Email kept them connected, but jobs and distance—albeit not that much—had kept them from daily, face-to-face contact.

"Let's do lunch" happened at longer and longer intervals until it became just a Christmastime thing, so Kathryn Grant was surprised when she glanced at the caller ID on her cell phone to see the call was from Tori Cannon on a Thursday evening in late May.

"Kathy?" the voice on the other end of the wireless connection asked tentatively.

"Oh, my God! Tori, is that you?"

"It's me all right."

"What a wonderful surprise," Kathy said and sat back in her chair in the manager's office at the Batavia, NY, Hampton Inn. "To what do I owe the pleasure?"

"We're coming up on a holiday weekend. I know I'm asking you kind of late, but Billy's out of town this weekend and I wondered if you'd like to come here for a girl's weekend."

Kathy's lips quirked upward. "You mean a sleepover—like when we were roommates back in college?"

"I can't bake like you can, but I know a great bakery that does. And getting a bottle of wine isn't as hard as it was back in those days."

Kathy's smile widened. "Fattening treats, wine, and staying up half the night talking—sounds like heaven to me."

"Come for a day or two. We can talk, shop, talk, eat, talk, and maybe discuss the future."

The future? Now that was a scary topic.

"Aw, Tor, I'd love to. But my circumstances don't exactly allow me that kind of freedom. To get a day off around here—let alone two—means calling in favors. I've just started a new job and I'm low man on the totem pole."

"Would you be willing to impose upon them? I really could use your expertise."

"Me? Expertise?"

"In your line of work, you come across a lot of weird stuff. Maybe you could advise me on a problem I've been having."

"Weird is the word all right. What's your problem?" Kathy asked.

Tori gave a mirthless laugh. "Things have been disappearing around my apartment complex. The cops here have no interest in petit larceny when they can bag a speeder going forty in a thirty-five mile zone less than half a mile away. The town loves that kind of income, but it doesn't help me."

Kathy could believe that. "Okay, I'll see if I can get coverage for tomorrow night. I'll email or text you as soon as I know."

"Great. It was wonderful talking to you."

"You, too!"

They rang off and Kathy slid her phone back into her slacks pocket. Something was up. Tori was the most laid-back, competent person Kathy had ever met. That she needed help with something—anything—was unusual, and the fact that she'd invited Kathy for the weekend and that Billy, the guy she'd been living with for the past three years, was away, was suspicious, too. But maybe that was part of the reason she'd wanted to get together—to bear her soul knowing Kathy would listen without judgment. And what had she said about her apartment complex—that things had been disappearing? Hopefully between the two of them, they would soon find out the cause. But right now Kathy needed to find coverage—oh, and on a holiday weekend! She might have to sweeten the offer by offering to give up her next day off. Of course, the chance to connect with Tori for more than a couple of hours would be worth it. Lately she'd felt the pang of loneliness herself.

Tori had been and still was the best friend Kathy had ever had. Though they weren't as close as they'd once been, no way did Kathy want to refuse her friend's request for assistance. If nothing else, she could give Tori at least an entire evening of her undivided attention.

Kathy opened an email, addressing it to two of her subordinates, and began to type. She just hoped she was a better negotiator than her fellow employees.

Tori—short for Victoria—Cannon looked at herself in the antique oak mirror that hung on the wall between her bedroom and the apartment's bathroom. She'd bought it at a yard sale the summer before. It had been covered with six layers of different colored paint and had taken her the better part of a week to strip and refinish it. Now the golden oak had been restored to its former glory, and though the reflective coating on the back of the glass wasn't in tip-top shape, it pleased her. She needed another such project to work on, something to keep her mind off her current situation, which was being alone after she and Billy had had yet another fight and he'd decided to take a few days off from the relationship, heading down to Florida to visit a buddy with a big boat and lots of spare cash. It didn't bode well for their future, but then Billy had pulled this stunt before and had always come back to her. Only, with each departure and arrival the welcome home was less enthusiastic, and sometimes Tori wondered what the heck she'd ever seen in the guy.

But in the meantime she had other things with which

to concern herself. Her students' end-of-term tests were just two weeks away. Those tests were the bane of this high school English teacher's existence. She'd been instructing sophomores and juniors for seven years, but the satisfaction she'd once felt at being part of the profession had begun to wane. She loved the kids who had a thirst to learn, but with each passing year she saw fewer of them. The brats who passed through her classes came armed with cell phones, sneers, and seemed to be on a quest to disrupt each carefully planned lesson.

Kathy had changed jobs way too often these past few years. She might not be making as much money, but the last few times Tori had spoken to her she'd seemed happier. She was stressed, but happy with her decision not to climb up the various motel chains' corporate ladders. She preferred a hands-on approach rather than become a paper pusher. Tori admired her for that, feeling like a coward that she didn't possess the same kind of courage to give up her safe but unhappy life for the chance of something better—or maybe just something different. Her contract came due in August of the following year. She'd probably sign it because...what else besides teaching was she good at?

Tori glanced at her watch and realized the dryer in the laundry room downstairs had stopped some five minutes before. Damn! Grabbing her keys, she snatched up the empty laundry basket she'd left by the door to the hall. She pulled the door closed behind her and locked it before heading down the stairs.

The communal laundry room was warm and humid. The washer was grumbling and the dryer was tumbling, but no longer were her clothes inside it. Her lingerie and nightgowns now sat in a crumpled heap on top of the dryer. She had counted each and every item before putting them in the washer and did the same when returning them to the basket. Four, five, six. Damn! Another pair of her panties had gone missing.

Fists clenched, she had a mind to stay in the laundry room and confront the person whose clothes now tumbled in the dryer and shout, *"J'accuse!"*

And so she sat there for what seemed like forever, fuming. The dryer stopped at the 45-minute mark, but no one appeared. It was at minute 51 when the grumpy older woman from Apartment 3 showed up with an empty plastic laundry basket in hand.

"Hi, Marie," Tori said, trying to sound cheerful. Somehow she doubted Marie was the panties thief. They had to be way too many sizes too small for her.

The woman grunted a hello and headed for the dryer.

"By any chance did you take my clothes out of the machine before you put your own clothes in?"

"No."

"Because I seem to be losing some of my clothes on a regular basis."

"I didn't take them, if that's what you want to know," the woman said flatly.

"Oh, I wasn't accusing you."

Marie glared at her, then turned back to the dryer.

"Did you see anyone in the laundry room when you came down before?"

"No."

"Has anyone messed with your laundry lately?"

"No!" Marie said with annoyance.

Tori picked up her laundry basket and forced a smile. "It's always nice talking to you, Marie."

Marie didn't react to her sarcasm, and began folding her towels.

Tori left the laundry room and trooped back up the stairs for her apartment. At the rate she was losing underwear, she was either going to have to go commando or start buying them by the gross.

The sun had begun its swing to the west when Kathy
Grant pulled into the apartment complex's parking lot
and cut the engine. She stared at the cookie-cutter buildings. She'd lived in an apartment like this just a year earlier and she'd hated it. Her last move landed her in half
a house out on Route 5. What she wanted was to buy an
old house—a big old house that she could turn into a bed
and breakfast. She couldn't even hope to buy a stately
home—in any state of disrepair—and turn it into a lovely
inn until her inheritance came through in another eighteen months. Until then it was a pipe dream, she reminded herself. But what was life if you couldn't dream?
One day she was sure she would be an innkeeper. She just
had to find the right property at the right price, fix it up,
and fill it with lovely antiques. For that, her anticipated
inheritance was going to be far too small.

Time marched on, and way too quickly.

Kathy grabbed her purse, duffle, and a plastic grocery
bag from the passenger seat and got out of the car. As she
walked up to the building's entrance she noticed quite an
abundance of catnip growing around the well-trimmed
boxwood. Had Tori planted it for her kitty, Daisy? She
nipped off a piece to offer the cat upon her arrival and
stepped up to the door.

She'd only been to Tori's apartment one other time,
and was still surprised there wasn't more security. The
door opened to a shared lobby and anybody could enter
the building, which housed four apartments. She pressed
the buzzer under the metal mail slot for Apartment 4 and
seconds later the door to the upper apartment on the left
opened. "Hey, you're a sight for sore eyes," Tori said, grinning broadly.

"So are you," Kathy said and laughed before heading
up the stairs. Tori stepped inside and Kathy followed.
They paused to give each other a hug before Kathy pulled

back and brandished the plastic bag hanging from her wrist. "I baked."

"You always bake. What is it this time?"

"Your favorite—chocolate chip-oatmeal cookies."

"Aw, you shouldn't have—but I'm glad you did."

"It's how I relax. And I brought an offering for Daisy, too."

Tori smiled. "You got that outside my door, didn't you? You can't believe how much catnip grows around here—it's unnatural. I snitch a few leaves every time I come in. The maintenance man keeps yanking it out, but it's the gift to cats that keeps on growing."

"I've got a patch for my guys behind my back door, too."

"Daisy! Daisy!" Tori called and a plump tabby came running into the living room.

"Look at you," Kathy said, bending low and crushing the leaves between her fingers. The cat stood on her hind legs, her purr going into overdrive. She took the leaves from Kathy's fingers, leaving them wet with slobber.

"Oh, my. I'm going to need to wash my hands."

"You can do it at the kitchen sink. Meanwhile, I just made a fresh pot of coffee. We can drink it and stuff ourselves with your cookies. Follow me."

Kathy dumped her duffle and purse and followed Tori through the small living room and into the kitchen. It, too, was compact with only a round Formica table and four chairs clustered around it. She looped the plastic bag over the back of a chair before marching over to the sink, where she squirted a generous supply of hand soap onto her fingers, working it into a frothy lather, and then rinsing. Grabbing a couple of paper towels, she dried her hands, before discarding the toweling. Then she marched over to the table where she withdrew the Tupperware container and set it on the table while Tori gathered cups and plates from a cabinet above the granite counter. She set the table, got out milk and sugar, then poured the coffee and joined Kathy.

"I'm sorry I could only get tonight off. It's a holiday weekend and everyone thinks they deserve a day away from work, but not me."

"That's okay. Are you happy there?"

"I love the work. I wish I was working in a different venue, but then I've bored you with that subject far too many times."

Tori smiled, but it soon faded. "At least there's something you enjoy. Right now my life feels so small."

"How come?"

"Billy, mostly."

Kathy nodded. She'd never liked the guy. He wasn't good enough for Tori, but then nobody was. Still, she'd had her share of man trouble and wasn't about to judge Tori's choice when it came to a partner.

"We don't need to go there," Tori said, selecting a cookie and taking a bite. She chewed, swallowed and smiled. "Why is it your cookies always taste better than mine?"

"It's my secret ingredient—the same one my Grandma Nancy put in all her baked goods."

"Love," Tori guessed.

Kathy laughed. "You got it."

Tori shook her head. "I'm sorry the old gal's gone."

"Don't go there. You'll have me in tears within a second," Kathy warned. She sipped her coffee and glanced in the living room where Daisy had flopped in a happy daze. "So what's been happening around here that's so mysterious?"

"Theft," Tori said simply.

"What have you lost?"

"My underwear."

"From the laundry room?"

Tori nodded.

"Sounds like a pervert."

"From what I've heard, the really skeevy guys like soiled underwear so they can sniff it when they they..." she paused. "... pleasure themselves."

"Ugh!" Kathy said and shuddered. "But your guy seems to like clean underwear."

"I guess it's a guy who's stealing them," Tori said. "But how can I be sure?"

"Are there any other women your size in the building?"

Tori shook her head. "But if I keep eating these cookies, I'll soon be the size of one of my neighbors." That said, she picked up another cookie and began to nibble on it.

"What about in the other buildings?"

"I can't say I've paid attention to those neighbors. I mean, I come home from work, make supper, get on the Internet, and then go to bed."

"Same routine when Billy's here?"

"Pretty much. He works nights, remember?"

Billy was a bartender, which was how Tori had met him. She wasn't the kind to bar hop, and had been out with a bunch of her teacher friends for a girls' night out when the group had decided to patronize an Irish pub in the Park Avenue area of the city. Tori had always gone for working class guys, while it was Kathy who'd ended up with the more cerebral type. Tori's father was a businessman, but she'd always seemed to identify more with her hard-working grandfather, who ran a bait-and-tackle shop on Lotus Bay an hour from the city. And she'd made no bones about the fact that she felt more at home with her grandparents than her parents. They had that in common, too. Tori at least still had her paternal grandparents; Kathy's were long gone.

"Has anyone else noticed anything missing?" Kathy asked.

Tori shrugged. "My one neighbor, Marie, isn't the chatty type. The bottom two apartments are rented out to guys. I've never run into them in the laundry room. I'm pretty sure one of them takes his laundry to his mother. He'll go out on a Sunday with a big garbage bag full of stuff and come back hours later with the same bag—not that I spy on my neighbors or anything. I just like to look out the window—especially on snowy nights."

"And thank goodness we haven't had any of them for a couple of months," Kathy put in. She took another sip of her coffee. "What about the storage lockers?"

Tori looked thoughtful. "I hadn't thought to see if ours had been tampered with. It's got a padlock on it."

"When was the last time you looked?"

Again Tori shrugged. "Must have been months ago— when I put the Christmas decorations away."

Kathy drained her cup. "Why don't we go have a look?"

"Why not?" Tori agreed. She, too, drained her cup and rose from her seat. She grabbed her keys from a rack on the wall. "Come on."

Kathy followed her friend across the living room and down the stairs to the shared laundry room, which was quiet, with nothing in either the washer or the dryer. A door straight ahead led to another room. Like the outside door to the building, it wasn't locked, either. Tori switched on the light before she entered.

"Our locker is over here," she said, but stopped. "What the—"

Kathy looked around her. If there was a padlock hanging from the hasp, it was long gone. "I take it Billy's the only other person with a key."

"That's right."

"Could he have forgotten to lock it last time he was down here?"

"He doesn't have much in here. There'd be no reason

for him to come down here. God knows he'd never do laundry."

Tori opened the door and inspected the contents. The boxes had obviously been tampered with, as garland and strings of Christmas lights were haphazardly hanging from opened boxes that had been shoved into the space. Tori stood on tiptoe and moved the contents around on the top shelf.

"Oh, damn! It's gone."

"What's gone?" Kathy asked.

"A bottle of sherry. I was going to give it to my grandma next time I made it to the bay. I put it in here because I didn't want it cluttering up my kitchen."

"How long ago was that?"

"Same time as the Christmas decorations. I really do need to get off my butt and visit my grandparents. They're not getting any younger."

"Could Billy have taken it?" Kathy asked.

Tori shook her head. "Billy? Drink sherry? Not in this lifetime."

"Isn't your grandmother a diabetic?"

"She only has a glass of sherry on special occasions."

"Maybe we should go to Home Depot and get another lock," Kathy suggested.

"I guess," Tori said.

"We should do it now—before we break open a bottle of wine."

"I could use a drink about now," Tori admitted. She closed the door. "Let me go get my purse and we'll head to the store."

"Should we get something to eat while we're out?" Kathy suggested.

"I was thinking of ordering a pizza."

Kathy's expression soured. "I feel like I live on pizza. That's all the night crew at the motel ever orders in."

"What sounds good to you that's easy to make?"

"Let's hit the prepared food section at Wegmans. They have everything," Kathy suggested, "and we can nuke it."

"Any time I don't have to cook is a good day," Tori said.

They left the storeroom, closing the door, and headed out to the lobby, then back to the apartment for their purses. They had lots of hours to talk about the panty thief. For now, their mission was clear. Get a new lock and get something either decadent or comforting to eat. No doubt about it, they had their priorities straight.

The grocery store was bustling with holiday weekend shoppers stocking up on hotdogs, hamburgers, buns, and cold salads from the deli counter. Tori and Kathy walked up and down the aisle, carefully perusing the plastic containers filled with ready-to-eat foods the grocery store had made. "We could get mac and cheese," Tori suggested.

Kathy shook her head. "Good as they make it, I survived on a little too much of it the first couple of years after college. It got so I almost forgot what meat tasted like."

"They have really nice julienne salads."

"Are you in a diet mood?"

"Not with those cookies you made still sitting in my kitchen," Tori countered.

They reached the end of the cooler and started back down again. "Pot stickers are good," Kathy suggested.

"Okay, we could get them and at least two more things. We did say we'd stuff ourselves."

"How about one of these little quiche Lorraine's? I haven't had quiche in about a million years," Kathy suggested. "And then to balance it out, we could split one of those salads, because that would counteract the fat in the quiche and the pot stickers."

"And the cookies, too?"

"Probably not, but that's the cross we have to bear."

"Sounds like a plan," Tori said. She got the salad while Kathy got the quiche and they headed for the check-out counter.

"I've been thinking about your panty poacher."

"And?" Tori asked.

"What time of day do you usually do your laundry?"

"In the evenings."

"After work or on the weekends?"

"Both. What are you thinking?"

"We should stake out your laundry room tonight."

"That would be kind of difficult, since there's nowhere to hide," Tori said.

"You don't seem to think your thief is one of the residents, so it must be someone who's entering the building, stealing your panties, and then leaving again."

"Are you suggesting we sit in my car or something?"

"We could try it. The lot outside your apartment isn't exactly well lit, so we shouldn't be seen."

"You're right, and that's one of my chief complaints about the complex."

It was their turn to check out, and they pooled their resources, paying in cash. Tori carried the bag out to the car.

"How does this guy even know when I'm doing laundry?"

"The dryer exhaust," Kathy said simply. "He can probably hear it."

"You're right. I hadn't thought about that. What if I put a load in, we go sit in my car, and then the guy doesn't show up?"

"At least you'll have clean laundry," Kathy pointed out.

They got in the car and Tori started the engine. Dusk was still a couple of hours away when they arrived back at her apartment complex. They trudged upstairs and put the appetizer in the microwave. Kathy got out plates, bowls, and cutlery, while Tori pulled out the toaster oven for the quiche. "Break out the wine and we can feast on the pot stickers while we wait for the quiche to heat through."

"Sounds good to me," Tori said, and soon after they were ensconced in chairs in the living room, sipping wine while Daisy lolled at Tori's feet, purring with glee.

"So, what time do you think I should put in the first load of laundry?" Tori asked.

"What time do you usually do it?"

"About nine"

"Good. It ought to be dark by then." Kathy glanced at the clock on the wall. "We've got a little more than two hours to wait. That ought to give us plenty of time to eat."

"What if our guy doesn't show up tonight?" Tori asked, cutting a pot sticker in half with her fork.

"I'm sorry I can't be here more than just tonight, but you're no slouch. You can lay in wait for the guy tomorrow, or the night after, or the night after that."

"And do what while I'm waiting?"

"Pull out your e-reader and read."

"Except that my e-reader glows in the dark. That would give me away for sure."

"Listen to the radio and hum?" Kathy suggested.

Tori laughed. "Yeah, I could do that."

Darkness had fallen by the time Tori grabbed the laundry basket full of towels from the back of her closet, ready to start the sting. Meanwhile, Kathy gathered up the glasses, wine, and cookies for sustenance while they waited in the parking lot in Tori's car.

Once the washer was chugging along, they retreated to the parking lot. Upon their return from the grocery store, Tori had selected a parking space where they could watch the front of her building to see anyone who entered. They settled in for what they hoped would not be a long wait.

"I've only got enough dirty clothes for two loads," Tori told Kathy, once she'd refilled their wineglasses.

"Who says you can't wash clean clothes?"

Tori shrugged and sipped her wine. "I don't think I've ever done this before."

"Done what? Been on a stake-out before?"

"No, drunk wine in the front seat of my car."

"So you have been on a stake-out?" Kathy asked, her tone light.

"Well, no. Hand me a cookie, willya?"

Kathy passed the container. "I've never been on a stake-out, either. It looks really boring when they do it on TV; that's why we have wine and cookies."

Kathy sipped her wine, but then leaned forward, squinting as she looked through the windshield. "Hey, someone's coming."

Tori leaned forward, too. Sure enough, a figure moved in the shadows. It carried a bag. They ducked down in the seats as the figure passed.

"It's a guy," Kathy whispered.

"Yeah," Tori agreed, but he's going to the Dumpster, not my building."

"Scratch one suspect."

"Maybe not. He could be throwing away evidence. Let's see what he does."

They watched the man as he retraced his steps, heading back to his own apartment building, then sat back in their seats and resumed sipping.

"Do you ever think much about the days when we used to hang out?" Tori asked.

"All the time," Kathy said. "It seems like my job is my life. Sometimes I wish I could step back in time ... back to when anything seemed possible. Back to when I didn't have to work nights and weekends in a job with no real future."

Tori nodded. "But at least you've got goals and made plans. When I think of the future, long-term, I don't see Billy in it."

"Oh, I'm sorry."

"When you think about it, it's kind of odd that we ever got together. Taking a breather right now is actually a good thing. Maybe absence really does make the heart grow fonder. We'll see."

They were quiet for a while, sipping wine—crunching cookies—just being comfortable in each other's company. Tori finally broke the quiet. "This is kind of like Thelma and Louise."

"Except they were criminals—we're the good guys, or gals," Kathy suggested. "And, we'd need a convertible. I don't know about you, but I want a car that's going to survive a rollover." She paused. "Then again, I'm driving an aging Focus, so what the heck do I know about car safety?"

Tori smiled. "I'm sure your Grandma Nancy would have preferred you drive a tank. That way the rest of the world would keep out of your way."

"She was protective. Maybe overly so, but I turned out all right. Didn't I?"

Tori nodded. "You're okay."

"Just okay?" Katie asked.

"Better than okay."

Kathy drained her glass. "Okay."

Movement on the sidewalk outside another of the buildings caught Tori's attention. "Look," she said, and Kathy leaned forward, too. "Sorry," Tori apologized as it became evident that the figure walking along the sidewalk outside her building wasn't a man, but instead was an elderly woman. Her stooped gait registered the years she'd walked on the planet. "False alarm."

Still, the woman turned at Tori's building and entered.

"Are you sure?" Kathy asked.

"What do you mean?"

"Do you know that woman? Does she live in your building?"

"No."

"Then, you can't dismiss her as a suspect."

"Oh, come on. Why would an old lady want to steal my underwear?"

"Ah, that's the question," Kathy said. She made sure the screw cap on the wine bottle was tight before setting it on the floor mat, then turned to put the Tupperware container, no-longer filled to the brim with cookies, on the back seat. She opened the car door.

"Where are you going?" Tori demanded.

"To get a better view."

Kathy got out of the car and a puzzled Tori followed.

"You can't think—" Tori started, but Kathy shushed her into silence.

They moved up the sidewalk along the building so that they were directly opposite Tori's building. The woman stayed inside for only a minute or two before she came back outside. She held something in her hand.

"Oh, no," Tori groaned.

"Oh, yes," Kathy said. "Come on. We've got to follow her."

"Why? She couldn't possibly—"

"Tori—think outside the box."

"I hate that expression."

"So do I, but sometimes it works," Kathy said, already on the move. She took the lead and Tori reluctantly followed, trailing the woman two buildings down, where she entered. They were only a few paces behind, and stepped inside the building in time to see the door to Apartment 1 close.

"Now what do we do?" Tori hissed.

"You have to knock the door and confront her."

"And what do I say?"

"I don't know. Fake it."

"Fake it?" Tori demanded. She swallowed hard before she strode up to the door and forced herself to rap three times on the steel security door.

For several long seconds nothing happened, but Tori could have sworn she was being eyeballed via the peephole. Then at last the door opened on a chain. A woman much younger than the one they'd followed appeared. "Yes?"

"Hi," Tori very nearly squealed. "My name is Tori Cannon. I live in the building two doors down." She gestured toward Kathy. "And this is my friend Kathy. We ... we—" and then she ran out of things to say.

"We were wondering about the other lady who lives here," Kathy piped up.

"My mother?" the woman asked.

"Yes. You see, we followed her back here after—" And that's when Kathy ran out of things to say.

"After she visited the laundry room in my building," Tori finished.

The woman's brow furrowed. "What are you saying?"

"It seems that your mother is a panty pincher," Kathy said.

The woman's face twisted into a malevolent glare. "What?" she demanded.

Tori swallowed. "Well, for the past couple of weeks, someone has been stealing my underwear. At first I thought it must have been some kind of pervert, but then tonight we staked out the laundry room and ... well, we saw your mother go in and come out with some of my undies."

"Are you insane?" the woman asked, her voice tight with anger.

"I don't think so," Kathy said. "Could we speak to her?"

"No!" the woman said, and was about to shut the

door when a voice behind her called out.

"Susan, who's at the door?"

"A couple of nuts, mother," the woman said tersely.

"May we please speak to your mother?" Kathy implored.

"No!" the woman said angrily.

"Susan!" the older woman called again, and appeared right behind her daughter.

"Hello!" Tori called. "Can we talk to you?"

"Susan, don't be so rude. Open the door," the older woman commanded.

The chain was removed and the door thrown open.

"Hello!" the older woman called brightly. "I'm Mary; and you are?"

"Tori and Kathy," Tori said, jerking a thumb in Kathy's direction. "We were wondering what you were doing in the laundry room a couple of doors down."

"Getting material," the older woman said with pleasure.

"Material?" Kathy asked.

"Material?" her daughter asked with a curious glance over her shoulder.

"Yes," Mary said with a broad smile.

"What do you need material for?" Tori asked.

"For my product, of course," Mary said, as if it made perfect sense, which it did not.

"What do you make?" Kathy asked.

"Catnip mice," Mary explained. She waved a hand, beckoning them inside. They followed the old woman as she trotted across the immaculate living room. In the corner of the room was a very hairy cat bed, where an elderly cat slept. Beside the little bed was a fabric tube made of purple lace."

"I recognize the cloth on that toy—it used to be my underwear!" Tori exclaimed.

"You must be mistaken," Susan said firmly.

"Mary, do you always get your material from the other dryers in the complex?"

The old woman smiled. "Where else am I going to get it? Susan won't let me drive to the fabric store anymore. She took away my car keys."

"Mother!" Susan implored.

"I grow my own catnip," Mary said proudly. I've planted it in front of every one of the apartment buildings. It's a hundred percent organic—no pesticides. Then when it grows tall enough, I pick it and dry it in my bedroom."

"You do?" Susan demanded.

"Yes. I've got sheets of cardboard under my bed. It dries out quite nicely on it. Of course it takes a couple of weeks. My first crop this year is now ready to be made into catnip toys. My other daughter, Linda, brings me pillow stuffing she gets at yard sales, and I make the catnip toys and sell them in her booth in a craft store the next town over."

Tori's mouth dropped open. "Made of my underwear?"

"Good Lord, Mother!" Susan practically wailed. She turned her anguished eyes toward Tori. "I am so sorry. I don't know what to say—how to apologize."

"Perhaps a trip to the fabric store might be in order," Kathy suggested. "If you got her a couple of fat quarters of fabric, it would stop her visiting the laundry rooms around the complex."

"I'm so sorry," Susan told Tori. "I'll be happy to replace whatever it is she's taken."

"Well, I did have a bottle of sherry that's gone missing."

Susan turned on her mother. "Do you know anything about that?"

"I found it."

"Do you mind if I ask where?" Tori asked.

"In a closet. The door was open. I figured if it wasn't locked, nobody cared about what was inside."

"Mother, you're not supposed to drink alcohol. It'll mess up your medications."

"I only have a little drop at night—after you go to bed. And it's strictly for medicinal purposes."

Tori held up a hand. "You don't need to replace it. I just want her to stop taking my things—and anything else she's been helping herself to from the rest of the laundry rooms in the complex."

"Be assured, I'll be keeping a much closer eye on her," Susan said firmly.

"Do you have cats?" Mary asked, happily.

"Well, yes," Tori answered. "We both do."

"Then perhaps you'd like one of my toys. Maybe you'd tell your friends about them and where to get them, too."

Tori looked at Susan, as if to get permission. She nodded. "I think that would be very nice."

"Yes, thank you," Kathy chimed in.

Mary bustled off toward what they assumed was one of the apartment's bedrooms.

Susan looked like she wanted to cry. "I don't know what to say. I'm so, so sorry about this. My mother is usually no trouble, but lately she's been showing some signs of dementia, that's why I had her come here to live with me. She's a bright, happy soul and she's always loved to sew. I must admit I didn't pay much attention to where she was getting her crafting supplies. I assumed my sister was giving her everything she needed."

"That's okay. We completely understand," Kathy said soothingly.

Soon Mary trotted across the carpeted floor to stand in front of the open door once more. "These are two of my newest creations." She held them up for them to see. They were made of pale green nylon and fringed with white lace. She held one in front of her nose and inhaled deeply.

Oh no! Tori thought. *Someone really is sniffing my underwear!*

Mary handed a toy each to Tori and Kathy. "Please tell your friends about them."

"Oh, we will," Kathy promised, and Tori felt like giving her best friend a kick in the ankle.

"Again, please accept my apologies," Susan said sincerely.

Tori nodded. "It was nice meeting you."

"Likewise," Kathy called as they backed out of the apartment.

The door closed behind them, and they heard an exasperated Susan wail, "Mother!"

They hurried out of the building and headed back for Tori's car to retrieve the wine, glasses, and what was left of the cookies.

"Well, that solves that," Kathy said, smiling.

"And though I'm out six pairs of panties, at least Daisy has something new to play with," Tori said as they headed back to her apartment building. Upon closing the door, they retreated to their former position, put the glasses, bottle and cookie container on the coffee table, and collapsed on the couch and chair.

"Well, that felt great," Kathy said. She grabbed one of the wineglasses and the bottle and poured.

"Hey, what if that wasn't your glass?" Tori asked.

"Have you got a communicable disease?" Kathy asked.

"Not as far as I know."

"Me, neither," Kathy said and shoved a glass toward her friend. She poured another for herself and then raised it in a toast. "To us."

"To us," Tori agreed, and drank deeply.

"I enjoyed that," Kathy admitted. "It was an adventure. Wouldn't it be fun if we had more adventures just like that?"

"You mean like solving crimes or something?" Tori asked, incredulous.

"Why not? You're right; we could be the Thelma and Louise of good guys right here in Western New York."

"That's the wine talking," Tori said.

"So what if it is?" Kathy asked and laughed. "Tor, it's too bad you're married to your job. I think if you and I put our heads together we could do anything. Just anything!"

"You want me to give up my job? A sure thing for—for what?"

"I don't know. I'm just saying that if the opportunity ever arose for us to do some kind of project together, there's no one else I'd rather do it with—there's no one else I'd trust to be my partner."

"High praise," Tori said and raised her glass. "Why not?"

Kathy raised her glass, too. "So, instead of blood sisters, we are now officially wine sisters."

"I think you may have had a little too much to drink."

"And I'm just happy we solved your problem. Go forth tomorrow and replace your panties," Kathy said and laughed.

"Very funny, but I think I will." Tori took another sip of her wine and sank back farther in her chair. "Do you really think we could one day go into business? What would we do? I don't have any real skills. All I can do is teach."

"And you don't consider that a skill?" Kathy demanded.

"Oh, sure, but beyond tutoring, how could I apply it to another vocation?"

Kathy brandished her nearly empty glass. "Now is not

the best time to ask me that question. But I'm sure if the opportunity presents itself, we'll be ready."

"But how will we know it's an opportunity?"

Kathy smiled. "We'll know. Until then—" she raised her glass in a toast, "let's drink to it."

And so they did.

With Baited Breath

A
Lotus Bay Mystery

ONE

Tori Cannon looked over the scarred Formica table and into her grandfather's watery eyes. "It was a beautiful service," she commented idly, not knowing what else to say to the old man who had just buried his wife of fifty-one years.

He shrugged. "It would have been better if more of our family had bothered to attend."

"Mom and Dad were there," Tori said, and lifted her cup, taking a sip of the tepid coffee within it. She really did prefer tea.

"They had to get to the airport," Herb Cannon muttered bitterly. "They couldn't even stay an extra day to sit and talk?"

"Aunt Janet and Uncle Dave were there, too," Tori said, thinking about how empty the church had seemed, remembering how the pastor's voice had echoed over their heads. The sun hadn't even bothered to make an appearance on that unseasonably cold rainy day in June.

"They hightailed it out of the gathering afterwards faster than jack rabbits."

"It was nice of the Ladies Circle to have a reception," Tori commented. They'd sent the leftovers—dozens of home-baked cookies—home with Herb. It was a good thing he had a big chest freezer in the shop, but would he want to store all those tasty little treats along with the frozen bait he kept for his customers? At one time, Cannon's Bait & Tackle shop had been *the* place for fishermen to stop on Lotus Bay. Those days had long since passed.

"I've made a decision," Tori said, knowing the old man was going to fight her on it.

He glared at her.

"I'm coming to stay with you."

He shook his head. "I don't need a caretaker. Hell, I was the one who took care of your grandma all these years. And I'm not so old that I *need* a keeper, either."

"Who said you needed either? I just thought—"

"I know what you thought, and I say no!" he said emphatically. He grabbed his cup and rose from his seat, moving stiffly across the crowded kitchen to the counter where he warmed up his coffee.

"It's not forever," Tori said, looking around the room. Grandma, for all her generosity, her quick smile and kind heart, had been a packrat. She hadn't quite made it to being a hoarder, but she'd been close. "I thought I might help you sort things out."

Herb leaned against the counter, looked around the room, and then took a sip. "Well, I guess I could use your help with that. Her precious treasures are just junk to me. But what are you going to do with it all?"

"I thought about renting a Dumpster."

"I ain't got money for that," Herb said.

"Who said you had to pay for it? I was—"

"I don't take charity."

"Who says it's charity? I was going to give it to you for your birthday."

"My birthday is three months away."

"Then you'll get your gift early," she countered.

Herb shook his head. "You've got your job. I can't expect you to—"

"I'm a tenth grade English teacher. You know I have summers off." She hadn't yet told him that she'd lost the job. The district's voters had decided to cut teacher positions and the arts instead of putting a dent in the sports programs. Great for the jocks, not so good for everyone else.

"You must have made plans," he said.

"I'd planned to hang out here and help you take care of Grandma."

Tori's grandmother had been grossly overweight and suffered with complications from diabetes. Five days earlier, she'd suffered a massive stroke and died three days later. It was sudden, and for her, painless. It wasn't quite so painless for Herb, who'd been caring for her since he'd retired from his day job some seven years before. Together, the couple had run the bait shop and a small motel, the latter of which had been closed for almost a decade. The partially boarded-up building was now an eyesore and a sad memory.

Herb had bought the business soon after he and Tori's grandmother had married. While he'd worked a day job, her grandmother, Josie, had raised their two children and run the shop. They'd sent their two children to college, and both had made it clear they had no interest in the business, but Tori had always loved coming to Lotus Bay and had spent many happy summers swimming off the tiny marina's dock, catching minnows that Josie let her sell in the shop, and capturing fireflies in glass jars along with the children of those who'd stayed in the seven rooms they rented to vacationers who weren't afraid to rough it. That Tori spent so much time there had suited her career-minded mother. When she'd taken a job in Columbus, Ohio, those lazy summer days became a distant memory.

Tori had come back to the area for college, and upon graduation had sent resumes far and wide, including Rochester, NY, which was just an hour away from Lotus Bay, so named for the protected water lilies that clustered around the south end of the bay. They certainly had proliferated around Cannon's Bait & Tackle shop in the intervening years to the point of being a nuisance to navigation.

"As I said," Herb continued, "I don't need a keeper."

"But you *will* need help."

"How long were you planning to stay?"

Tori shrugged. "Maybe a week or two. I hadn't planned on doing much of anything else this summer." No, especially since Billy Fortner was no longer a factor. Their parting had been acrimonious. After living together for more than three years, Billy had decided he felt stifled, used, and had found himself a bleached blonde Chippy who was at least five years younger than Tori—not that she felt old and used up at the tender age of twenty-nine. She was glad they hadn't found the house of their dreams the summer before. It would have made the breakup even messier. As it was, Billy had moved out taking far more than his fair-share of their collected belongings. After two months, Tori was getting used to living sparsely, which was why her grandparents' kitchen, crowded with boxes, a fridge covered in magnets, and a cluttered table and counter, made her feel claustrophobic.

"Have you thought about what you want to do with the business?" Tori asked.

Herb's eyes narrowed. "Don't you start on me about selling it. I've heard just about enough of that from your parents and aunt and uncle."

Tori raised her hands in surrender. "I wasn't going to suggest that at all. In fact, I thought it might be good for you to spend your days in the shop talking to people. Maybe you'll see a rebound in business."

Herb looked chagrined. "It would take more than chatting up customers to get back in the black."

"Well, that's why I'm here. We can work on the house and the shop. I think it would be fun."

A sly grin tugged at Herb's lips. "Would a grown up

girl like you want to touch worms, and spikes, and other slimy stuff?"

"Not really. But isn't that why God invented plastic gloves?"

Herb nodded. "He did, indeed." He took a sip of his coffee, found it unpalatable, and tossed it into the sink. "When was the last time you were in the shop?"

"Last summer. Remember? I came down for the day."

"You and that fella of yours."

"He's not mine anymore," Tori grated.

"So you said." Herb grabbed his jacket. "Let's go outside."

Tori got up from her seat, tossed her coffee down the sink, and then put both their cups in the aged dishwasher. She had never taken her jacket off upon leaving from the graveside service, and followed her grandfather out into the overgrown yard. She looked around the unkempt space.

"I've been meaning to cut the grass," Herb said in his own defense, kicking at a clod of dirt—probably a mole hole.

Tori wasn't about to comment. Instead, she gazed at the ramshackle building that housed the bait shop. It was made of cinder blocks, but the roof was in bad shape. It hadn't been painted in probably twenty years and wasn't exactly inviting. Did fishermen care if a bait shop had curb—or rather shore—appeal? Maybe not. But if they were fishing with their wives—and lot of women enjoyed fishing—a pleasant looking building might give them the edge over their competition across the bridge that spanned the marshy end of the bay.

Herb cut across the grass to the worn path that led to the bait shop, fumbling in his pocket for the keys. He opened the door and switched on the lights.

Tori followed him inside. As always, it smelled rather earthy. Rows of cinder block tanks held minnows and other small fish, night crawlers, and sometimes even a couple of snapping turtles. As a child, they had all fascinated her. She'd been especially fond of all those friendly little minnows swimming around. She hadn't quite grasped the concept that they were meant to lure other fish to their deaths. Not that she was against fishing. Most of the anglers around the area fished for sport, turning their catches loose. The truth was, thanks to pollution, the sunfish, bass, perch, salmon, and pike weren't really good to eat, although some people did take the risk.

A placard attached to the front of each tank warned customers to keep their hands out of the water. Another placard listed the price and merchandise on offer. It hadn't been updated in years, and Tori wondered what the competition was charging. She might have to make a clandestine visit to find out.

"I guess I should turn the CLOSED sign to OPEN," Herb said, and did just that.

"Are you sure you want to do that today of all days?"

He shrugged. "Sitting around the house moping isn't going to bring your grandma back."

Tori sighed. "I suppose you're right." She walked to the cash register and opened it. It had a few dollar bills and some loose change. "How much have you been averaging a day?"

"Twenty ... maybe thirty bucks," Herb admitted sheepishly.

"Aw, Gramps, that's not enough to pay the electric bill."

"I know, I know. Thank goodness for Social Security and my pension."

"Do you have any savings?"

Herb's gaze dipped even lower. "Not anymore."

"It's all gone?" Tori asked, horrified.

"I had to dip into it to keep us afloat. Course, we paid some pretty tough penalties. The damn taxman always has it in for the little guy, while big corporations get bailed out all the time. Life just ain't fair." His voice broke. "Your grandma dying like she did is just another example."

Tori closed the cash drawer and hurried over to give the old man a hug. She didn't know what to say. When she finally pulled away, Herb reached into his coat pocket and pulled out a well-used handkerchief, blew his nose, and cleared his throat.

"Why don't we take a walk around the yard?" Tori suggested.

Herb shrugged. "Got no customers. May as well, I guess."

They left the shop lights on and the door open and left the building. Tori noticed the ice machine wasn't plugged in. "What's going on with the ice machine?"

Again Herb looked embarrassed. "Haven't had enough sales to warrant filling it."

"But, Gramps, fishermen need ice for their catches— and happy hour."

Again he shrugged. "I got a call in to the dealer. I might get a load for Fourth of July weekend. Doesn't seem much call for it until then."

They strolled around the front of the breakwall and paused to look out over the bay. A pair of swans and their four cygnets paddled around. The water was a little choppy, and the babies bobbed up and down looking like toys in a bathtub. "I love looking at the swans."

"So did your grandma. The nest was over there by the bridge. The DEC came out and tried to tamper with it, but your grandma wouldn't let them." He shook his head wryly. "They backed off, deciding she was more dangerous than the mama swan."

Tori felt a smile tug at her lips. And then she made the mistake of looking down at all the empty slips in the dock. By this time of the season, there should have been ten or more.

"People are putting their boats in late this year," she commented.

"No, they ain't. They just aren't docking with me. The lights need fixing and I haven't had the time or the energy to do it. Those that like to take an evening run get pissed if they can't find the dock in the dark."

And Tori couldn't blame them.

She glanced to the north side of the yard where the boarded up guest rooms stood. The NO VACANCY sign had stood guard over the empty unit for years. There were seven rooms in all, and for a while there, the Lotus Lodge had done good business. But then grandma had gotten sicker and couldn't keep up with cleaning all the rooms. They'd gone down to six, then three, and then closed it down for good. The building didn't look as shabby as the bait shop, but after being abandoned for nearly a decade, it would need substantial work to bring it back to a habitable condition.

"I know you don't want to sell the business, Gramps, but can you run it alone?" Tori asked.

"I'm seventy two—not dead. Of course I can run it myself."

"I didn't mean to suggest that at all. I simply meant ... is there any way you could afford to hire someone to come in and help you during high season?"

"No!" he said emphatically. "Besides, I thought you were going to stay for a couple of weeks. If you could get me through Fourth of July, I can handle the rest of the summer myself."

"I will. I've got my duffle in the car. I can go back to Rochester tomorrow and pick up Daisy before lunch, and then we could get started on the house."

"If I ain't too busy in the shop," Herb said. "Weather's supposed to be better tomorrow. I might have a load of customers."

And he might not, either.

Tori looked from the dock's non-functioning lamp-post to the empty guest rooms. If she paid an electrician to come fix the lights, maybe over the summer she could also work on getting at least one of the guest rooms open again. The big Rochester brewery sponsored a fishing derby in August, which was a boon for those who could put up a couple of guests. If she worked really hard, maybe she could get two of them back up to speed by then. After all, now that Billy was gone she had nothing else planned for the summer. Well, she'd send out some resumes and if nothing else, do substitute teaching once the school year started in September.

Tori stared at the shabby Lotus Lodge. She knew she'd have to bide her time about presenting her ideas for refurbishing the rooms to Herb. He was a proud man. If he decided to sell after the season, anything she could do to increase the value of the property would bring him more cash, and that was what he was going to need no matter what he decided. Now that her plans for a grand vacation were gone, she had a few bucks put aside that she could contribute to the project.

Perhaps she needed to nudge him toward accepting the idea of improving the look of the place before she told him all that was on her mind. She liked to take on pet projects such as this. She'd done a number of DIY projects in her own home, as Billy didn't like to dirty his soft hands or risk his back swinging a hammer. When she thought about it, what had she ever seen in the guy in the first place?

She took a couple of steps toward the guest rooms and bent to pull some weeds from the grass.

"Don't bother with that," Herb said. "I'll get it with the lawnmower tomorrow."

Tori straightened. "I thought you were going to be busy with the shop tomorrow?"

"The way things are, I might have an hour or two I can devote to the lawn. If it doesn't rain."

"You said the weather was going to clear."

He scowled. "Do you remember everything everybody tells you?"

"Just you," she said. "I've always paid attention to everything you've ever told me."

It was the old man's turn to smile. "Yeah, well, you're the only one who did. Even your grandma listened to only half of what I ever said."

"She heard the words 'I love you.' And so did I."

"Don't you get mushy on me. I've shed too many tears the last few days. My sinuses are all clogged up and it ain't 'cuz of the pollen count."

Tori tossed the weeds aside and moved closer to the first guest unit. "I wonder what it would take to get just one of these rooms back in shape for the derby."

"Now don't you go getting a lot of grand ideas about reopening the Lodge. It'll be all I can handle to keep the shop in business."

"I was just playing with the idea. I guess I watch too many of those renovation shows like *This Old House* and the stuff on HGTV."

"Your grandma's been using the Lodge as her personal storage unit—and God knows what the hell is in there. A dead body, for all I know."

"That isn't funny, Gramps," Tori chided.

"I've been thinking about what you said. It's gonna take a really big Dumpster to clean out this place. But maybe we could go through all the stuff and hold a sale or something. Some of your grandma's junk has got to be worth something. Then maybe we could afford to get the lights fixed and maybe paint the bait shop."

So, he had been thinking along the same lines as she had.

"Sounds like a great idea."

"It might take more than just a couple of weeks. I don't know as I could do it all myself."

"I told you—I've got the whole summer free. Daisy and I can clear a space in the guest room and make ourselves comfortable. I'll bring her toys and her litter box tomorrow."

"Litter box? Why can't she just go outside like every other cat on the planet?"

Tori shook her head. "She's an indoor cat, and that's the way she's going to stay. It's a deal breaker, Gramps."

Herb scowled. "Oh, all right then. But I ain't gonna empty no cat box."

"I wouldn't expect you to."

"And I ain't gonna feed her. She's your problem."

More like pride and joy.

"I understand." Daisy would win him over in a day or so. Herb really was just an old softie.

Tori took in the doors on all the guest units. They seemed in good shape. Nothing a coat or two of paint couldn't spruce up. But the end unit's door didn't seem to be quite closed. "Gramps, what did Grandma stuff into these units?"

"I don't know. I was happy all the time she was getting it out of the house."

Tori grabbed the door handle, turned it, and found it wasn't locked, but the door wouldn't open. Something appeared to be stuck under it. Fabric, maybe? She yanked on it several times and the door burst open, the momentum tossing her onto the damp grass.

Herb hurried to help her up. "Are you okay?"

"Just a little damp," Tori said and got up, brushing at her rear end, which had taken the brunt of the fall. The door had swung back and she pulled it open, gasping at the sight of an older black man stuffed into the small cavity that wasn't crammed with boxes."

"Gramps!"

Herb stepped up behind her. "Holy smoke. It's Michael Jackson!"

A Ward County Sheriff's Department cruiser's lights bounced off the low buildings that made up the Cannon compound. Tori had always liked that term—compound. It made it sound like her grandparents were rich, like the Kennedys. Of course, to a child's eyes, the compound had been a wonderful playground—a place to play hide and seek, or to fish off the dock, or feed stale bread to the ducks. But now, everything was just shabby, and worse ... they'd found a body at the Lotus Lodge.

"There was no identification on the body. You're sure the deceased's name is Jackson?" the lead detective, a man named Osborn, asked. He wasn't all that tall, about forty, with slicked back dark hair and a paunch that suggested a sedentary lifestyle.

"As well as I know my own."

"How long have you known the deceased man?" They'd been over this ground with at least four deputies, and now they'd have to do it yet again.

"Twenty years at least," Herb said and sighed. "He's been buying bait off me for that long. He lost his dock in a storm last year and kept a little rowboat here. Lived up on Resort Road in a crappy little bungalow."

The deputy scribbled in a small notebook. "And you, ma'am?"

"I only knew him by name—just to say hello. I don't think I've even seen him for at least ten years," Tori said and shivered. She hugged herself, hoping to generate some warmth. They'd been standing out in the chilled air for hours. "Any chance we can go inside and sit down? It's been a long day."

The detective shrugged and held out a hand, suggesting they move to the bait shop, which wasn't going to be much warmer than the great outdoors, but at least the cement floor would be dry. The medical examiner and her team were still clustered around the motel's last unit, working. Tori was glad that once inside the shop, they wouldn't be visible to her.

The lights inside the shop were still on, and from the scores of damp footprints, it looked like the entire Sheriff's Department had trudged through there during the preceding hours, but Tori, Herb, and the detective were the only ones there now. "So you came back from the cemetery and found Mr. Jackson," he muttered.

"No, we didn't," Herb said. "We had coffee, then came out to open the shop. Then we took a walk around the yard before Tori found him. He don't smell, so he can't have been there long."

The detective scowled. "What do you know about the decay of flesh?"

"Look around you, man. This is a bait shop. I've been around dead fish my whole life. If they aren't iced down, it don't take long before they start to stink."

Tori stifled a smile. The detective didn't look happy, but didn't dispute her grandfather's logic.

"When was the last time you talked to Mr. Jackson?"

Herb thought about it. "Last weekend. He bought some night crawlers from me and went fishing."

"Did he say anything pertinent at the time?"

"Yeah. He said he hoped he'd catch something worth eating."

"I mean that might be pertinent to our investigation."

"What do you mean?" Herb asked, and Tori wondered if he was just being obstinate.

"The man didn't stuff himself into that unit. Somebody put him there," the detective said, losing his patience.

"Well, we certainly didn't do it. Kill a paying customer? Do you think I'm out of my mind?"

"Gramps, Gramps!" Tori pleaded. She turned to the detective. "I'm sorry. This has not been a good day."

The detective sighed. "I understand that, ma'am." He took another breath and tried again. "When was the last time you saw Jackson?" he asked Herb.

"Last night. He walked down here to use his boat."

"What time was that?"

"After supper. Maybe seven o'clock."

"Is his boat tied up nearby?"

Herb walked over to the door and looked out at the slips, which were mostly empty. "Yeah, it's there."

Osborn frowned. "Did Mr. Jackson have any enemies?"

Herb shrugged. "Not that I know of. Seems to me he got along with everybody around here. 'Cept maybe Lucinda Bloomfield."

Tori looked up sharply at the name. Lucinda Bloomfield had been a pain in more than just Mr. Jackson's side. For generations the Bloomfield's had owned most of the property at the top of Resort Road. They'd put up PRIVATE PROPERTY signs and Lucinda's elderly father would patrol the perimeter of their estate from a little white golf cart, hollering and shaking his wooden cane at anyone who dared set foot on their sacred land. Though Lucinda was probably only in her mid-forties, she'd inherited the moniker of 'Old Lady Bloomfield' after her mother's death and, like her parents, apparently ruled the end of Resort Road with the same iron fist.

The Bloomfield's had money. Mega bucks. Word was that pictures of the big, meticulously restored and expanded farmhouse and the lush and carefully maintained landscaping had appeared in more than one home decorating magazine.

"Why would this Bloomfield person have a problem with Mr. Jackson?" Osborn asked.

"Because the family has been trying to rid his house

from Resort Road for as long as I can remember," Herb said.

"Why's that?"

"They called it a pocket of Dogpatch. You have to pass by it before you enter their *compound*."

His contempt of the word made Tori wince. They didn't share the same opinion on its definition.

"No one's mentioned the word murder, detective. Isn't it possible Mr. Jackson was ill and simply crawled into our unit and just ... died?" Tori asked.

The man positively glowered. "No."

Tori's heart sank. If that was true, then it was even more imperative that she move in with her grandfather. She knew for a fact that he rarely locked the door to the house. The bait shop was another matter. What it housed was of value to fishermen, and she also knew that just because a man enjoyed the sport didn't make him trustworthy. She'd heard too many tales about the fish that got away.

"Detective?" The lady medical examiner stood at the shop's open doorway. "We're about to move the body. I thought you'd want to know."

"Thanks." Osborn closed his notebook and glanced at Herb. "I think that's all for now. But I may have more questions as our investigation continues."

"I'd be surprised if you didn't," Herb said.

Osborn turned and followed the ME.

"I don't know about you, but I'm hungry," Herb said. "We've got nothing in the house except cookies. Let's head over to The Bay Bar and get us some supper."

The Bay Bar was exactly what the name implied—a bar that was almost directly across from Cannon's Bait & Tackle. They served—what else?—bar food. Greasy burgers and fries, and right about then Tori was more interested in imbibing a margarita than a cheeseburger, but then, maybe she'd go for both.

She headed for the yard and then turned and watched as her grandfather switched off the lights and locked up the bait shop for the night.

They didn't bother going back in the house, but crossed the lawn and then the road to get to the bar. It wasn't exactly swinging on that Tuesday evening, but there were five motorcycles parked outside, and four of the tattooed bikers sat nursing beers on the deck as they burned through a cigarette or two. They nodded to Tori and Herb as they mounted the steps and entered the bar.

It was the typical redneck bar, with three flat-screened TVs mounted on the walls, a generous supply of blue-and-white neon signs courtesy of the Rochester brewery, a Quick Pick game flashing in the corner, and lots of knotty pine. Tori had only been inside once or twice. When she wanted to party, she drove up to Lotus Point. The bars there played her kind of music and made her kind of drinks.

"Well, look who's here," said the guy behind the bar. He was balding, maybe fifty, and sporting a Harley Davison T-shirt. The nametag pinned to his shirt said Paul. "Haven't seen you since the last time you had a fight with your old lady, Herb."

"Yeah, well, I won't be doing that anymore," Herb said as he commandeered a bar stool. "I buried Josie just this afternoon."

Paul looked stricken. "Jeeze, Herb. Nobody told me. I'm awful sorry."

"No sorrier than me," he said. "How about a couple of beers?"

Tori took the seat next to him. "I'd rather have a margarita."

"It comes out of a bottle," Paul warned.

"A beer's fine," she said.

"And you are?" Paul inquired.

"That's my granddaughter, Tori," Herb said.

"Hey, you were just a little squirt the last time I saw you."

"She's a school teacher," Herb said proudly.

"What do you teach?" Paul asked as he grabbed a couple of glasses from under the bar and drew the beers.

"High school English."

"You have my sympathies," Paul said and set a couple of napkins before them before delivering the drinks. "Lots of excitement over at your place this afternoon. Word is you found Michael Jackson dead in one of your rental rooms."

"I don't know how he got there, poor sod. Did the cops come and talk to you yet?"

"Oh, yeah. And I'm sure someone will go up to talk to Lucinda about it pretty damn quick, too."

"You think she killed Jackson?" Herb asked, taking a sip of his beer.

"And dirty her lily white hands? No way. Have him killed; now that's another subject."

"Grandpa said we could get some burgers and fries," Tori said. She didn't want to hear about poor Jackson's death for the rest of the night.

"Sure thing," Paul said. "How do you want them cooked?"

"Rare," Herb said.

"Well done," Tori countered.

"Noreen!" he yelled. "Two burgers—one red, one black—and fries."

"Coming up," came a muffled female voice from the behind a pair of swinging doors to her left.

Tori sipped her beer. She didn't really like beer, and probably should have asked for a Coke. Now to figure out how to get Herb to let her pay for the meal. Then again, she was out of a job. She needed to look for ways to conserve whatever money she had. *You could move out here, get rid of the apartment, and work for the Erie school system as a substitute teacher, then you could help Gramps and save a pile of cash for … what?* She thought about it for a long moment. Something else.

The thought of teaching another class of kids who'd rather be anywhere else had lost its appeal. Maybe she'd just take a year off and help Herb rebuild his business and then decide what to do with the rest of her life. She wasn't about to bring up the subject with her grandfather that night, though. He'd already been through far too much that day.

"You okay, Tori? You look like you're far away," he said.

"I was." She reached over to touch his hand. "But I'm back now."

"I guess I keep forgetting that I'm not the only one who loved your grandma. I'm sure as hell gonna miss that old woman."

Tori fought tears. A couple of the bikers chose that moment to reenter the bar. She wiped her eyes and took another sip of her beer. One of them walked up to the jukebox and fed in a couple of quarters

"Hey, I heard that Michael Jackson died across the street today," he called out and laughed. "Hail to the King of Pop." He pressed a button and suddenly Thriller blared out of the record-machine's speakers.

The idea of zombies, ghosts, and ghouls that the song suggested left a bitter tang in Tori's brain. They'd buried her beloved grandmother just that morning. But instead of ripping the jukebox's plug from the wall, she took a deep gulp of beer and hoped it might soften the raw edge of grief that had encased her heart.

TWO

Tori and Herb left the bar together, but before he would enter the house, Herb took down the flag that had waved that day over the Cannon compound. Tori watched, huddled in her jacket, as he unhooked the flag and reverently folded it. When she'd been a little girl, he used to hum Taps during this solitary ceremony. That night, he looked too beaten for even that extra show of respect.

It was after ten, and Tori made sure all the doors were locked before she sought out her grandfather. After what had happened earlier in the day, she wasn't going to take any chances when it came to their safety. Then again, the old window screens could probably be wrenched off by an angry squirrel.

Herb was comfortably ensconced in his ratty-looking recliner watching TV when Tori kissed him goodnight and retired to the guest room. She'd managed to extricate the bed from the piles of junk her grandmother had accumulated, and as she went through some of the stuff, she wondered about the best way to get rid of it. Tomorrow, when she went to retrieve Daisy, she'd bring back her little digital camera and her laptop. She could take pictures of the articles and upload them to Craigslist. Hopefully they could get rid of a lot of the stuff in a short time. If she rented a tent, they could set it up next to the bait shop and customers who came in by land or water might want to look at their yard-sale offerings. She'd sleep on the idea.

The quiet was broken by her phone jangling in her purse. She dug through the contents, glanced at the number and smiled. It was Kathy Grant—her best friend forever, and one-time college roommate. She stabbed the call icon. "What's up, Kath?"

"Sorry to call so late, my desk clerk called in sick and this was the first chance I got to slip away from reception. I was just calling to see if you and your Gramps are all right."

"That's so sweet of you, thanks. We're doing okay, and thanks so much for coming to the service today. It felt good to have someone in my corner for once."

"Now, now, I'm sure your folks are in your corner."

"Cornered me, maybe."

"Oh, come on. You're sounding like a victim, and that's not you."

"You're right. I'm depressed. My grandma's gone, I've lost my job, the bait shop isn't pulling its weight and Gramps is broke. I'm trying to figure out ways to make this place pay for itself. I was even playing with the idea of resurrecting the Lotus Lodge."

"Really?" Kathy asked, intrigued. "Tell all."

"There's not much to tell. If we can get at least one room going before the fishing derby in August, he could make a couple hundred bucks."

"Why not get all of them ready and your grandfather could make a lot more?"

"Getting him to agree to one will be hard enough."

"What if you had help?" Kathy asked.

A ghost of a smile tugged at Tori's lips. "What are you saying?"

"I've got the next two days off. What if I came out there on my days off for the next few weeks and helped you get the place in shape?"

"Are you crazy?"

"No, you know I've always wanted to run a bed and breakfast."

"The Lotus Lodge is not a B and B."

"But it's in the hospitality business. I'd love to get my hands dirty on a project like that."

Tori sighed. "There's no money to fix it up."

"What about selling some of your grandma's treasures?" Kathy suggested.

"They're more trash than treasure, but yes, I did think about putting a load of them on Craigslist, and having other stuff under a tent by the bait shop."

"Sounds like you've been thinking about this pretty hard."

"Yes, but talking Gramps into reopening the Lodge wouldn't be easy. I mean, it's not just a case of cleaning and painting. There's maintenance, cleaning the rooms after each guest leaves, and all that laundry. Grandma used to do all that way back when."

"He could hire someone to do it."

"At his age, he probably won't want to bother."

"If nothing else, I could at least help you tidy up the place. From what you've said, it sure could use it."

"You've got that right."

"Then why don't I come out tomorrow and plan to spend a couple of days?"

"The house has two tiny guest rooms that once belonged to my dad and aunt. They're both stuffed full of junk and have lumpy old single beds that aren't all that comfortable."

"Didn't you once tell me that the bar across the street rents rooms to fishermen?"

"You'd be roughing it."

"All the more incentive to get the job done fast," Kathy said optimistically.

"Can you afford even their cheap rates right now?"

"I'm saving my money for the future, but I've got enough for a working mini vacation. And my landlady won't mind looking after my cats for a few days."

"I'm going to come into town tomorrow to pick up Daisy and bring back a few of my things. It'll take me a few hours."

"Then why don't I plan to come down in the afternoon?"

"It sure would be good to hang out with you for more than just a couple of hours."

"Then say no more. I'll see you tomorrow."

"Great." Then Tori remembered Michael Jackson. "Um, there's just one tiny problem."

"Oh?"

"Yeah. Gramps and I were doing a little tour around the grounds when we kind of found a dead body."

Silence greeted that remark.

"It was one of Gramps's long-time customers. He might have just crawled into one of Lotus Lodge's unlocked units and ... died."

Again, a long period of silence followed.

"I totally understand if you want to forget the whole idea of coming down," Tori said, her heart sinking.

"Well..." Kathy began, and for a long terrible moment Tori felt all alone and vulnerable. "These things happen."

Tori let out the pent-up breath she'd been holding. She had no clue how Michael Jackson had died. And despite what the deputy had said, she chose to believe that Jackson's death could have been totally innocent.

Or not.

"So, I'll see you tomorrow afternoon," Kathy said at last.

"Okay. 'Til then. And thanks." Tori hit the 'End Call' icon, feeling an overwhelming sense of relief. Kathy was the most organized—and possibly smartest—person Tori had ever met. They'd hit it off from day one at SUNY

Brockport where Kathy pursued a business degree and Tori a teaching degree. Graduation day was one of the saddest days of Tori's life, because it meant the end of their lives as roommates. Kathy had stayed in the area while Tori had returned to Ohio. She hadn't stayed there long. She'd sent resumes to all the school districts in and around Lotus Bay and had hit pay dirt, first with the Rochester City School District, and then with its largest suburb. And now they'd let her go.

If there was one place in this world where Tori felt happiest and unconditionally loved, it was on Lotus Bay. Suddenly the thought of ever going back to that sterile apartment made her spirits plummet. There were too many memories of Billy there. Still, she wasn't sure having Gramps as a roommate was the answer, either.

Luckily, her lease came up for renewal in August. She'd give notice long before that and plan to make a new home somewhere in Ward County, so she'd be near Gramps and available to help him if necessary. Life was a lot less complicated out here in the boonies. At least that's what Tori chose to believe.

She pulled back the spread and climbed into bed, wishing she'd thought to bring her e-reader or a favorite book. She'd bring both, as well as her clock radio, laptop, router, and chargers. Gramps had no Wi-Fi. She'd have to remedy that PDQ if she was to survive in the interim. A call to the cable company was in order.

She punched up the lumpy pillow before turning out the light. She lay down, wrinkling her nose at the pillow's musty scent. Her own pillow was another thing she could bring from home—that, and maybe she'd stop somewhere to buy some Egyptian cotton sheets for the single bed.

A wave of sadness flowed through her. It was at night that she missed Billy the most. That was the best thing about being with someone—a cuddle before drifting off to dreamland. Was Billy spooning with his new love at that very moment? The bastard.

Chaotic thoughts filled Tori's mind, and she was sure there was no way she'd ever get any rest. And yet, her last thought before sleep's oblivion claimed her was the poignant memory of Michael Jackson's worn heels just visible from Lotus Lodge room number three. She dreaded hearing the cause of death, because despite hoping otherwise, she felt sure it wasn't going to be from natural causes.

THREE

Daisy was not a good traveler. Buckled into the back seat of Tori's car, the tabby howled from inside her carrier from the time they'd left the apartment's parking lot until Tori pulled into the Cannon compound at Lotus Bay an hour later. Her carrier had been the last item squeezed into Tori's compact car. Tori had tossed a load of her clothes into large plastic trash bags, filled boxes with staples from her cupboard, and grabbed as many of her creature comforts as she could cram into the hatchback, back seat and passenger side seat. The hamlet outside of the town of Erie had a storage facility. She'd make sure to inquire about their rates at the earliest opportunity, for until she could purge Gramps' house of Grandma's clutter, there'd be little or no room for her own stuff.

The day was sunny with little puffy clouds scudding across the sky. Tori had just about emptied the contents of her car and had settled Daisy with litterbox, food, and water in the cramped guest room when Kathy's white Focus pulled into the Cannon compound's weedy parking area.

"Howdy, stranger," Kathy called as she got out of her car. It had been a mere twenty-four hours since they'd last seen one another. She was dressed for work in a faded pair of jeans and an old t-shirt.

Tori crossed the distance between them and gave her friend a hug. She held on for a long moment and Kathy obliged. "Thanks for coming," she said as she pulled back.

"What're friends for?"

Tori waved a hand to take in the entire Cannon compound. "Well, what do you think?"

Kathy's expression darkened. "It's fallen on even harder times since the last time I was out here."

Tori's eyes filled with tears as she looked at the various buildings that made up the compound through someone else's eyes. The place was a dump.

"Hey," Kathy said with compassion, and gathered Tori into another embrace. "Don't worry. You and I are going to fix this. I'm sure a lot of it is just cosmetic." She pulled back.

Tori forced herself to look her friend in the eye. "Ya think so?"

"I know so. Is your grandfather around? I want to say hello and then we can get started."

"Where do we start?"

"A lawn mower and a weed whacker will make an instant improvement."

"Then what?"

Kathy turned to face the bait shop. The concrete-block building hadn't been painted in decades. "We'll spruce up the shop and give it a little personality, then we'll turn our attention to the Lotus Lodge."

"I haven't yet mentioned that part of the plan to Gramps."

Kathy faced the shabby little motel. "Can we look inside?"

"I'd have to get the keys from Gramps. He says the rooms are crammed full from floor to ceiling, without even a trail leading to the small bathrooms."

"You're going to order a Dumpster, right? Do it today and you might even get it delivered by tomorrow. But I figured we'd paint the shop, first."

"Keep talking. You're giving me hope with every

word."

Kathy smiled. "Is your grandfather in the shop?"

Tori nodded.

Kathy's eyes narrowed. "Has he got any snapping turtles for sale?"

Tori shook her head. "Not right now."

"Good. Then I can't get in trouble for releasing them."

"They're not pets," Tori reminded her. "They're food."

"I only eat mock turtle soup."

"Honey, you're not in the city anymore, and that's the first thing you need to learn. People around here don't see things the same way you and I do."

Kathy nodded. "I'll try to keep that in mind. Come on. We've got work to do."

Kathy wasn't afraid of hard work, and she'd been right; the mowed lawn made a huge difference to improve the compound's curb appeal. Afterward, they sat in the kitchen with sweating glasses of iced tea and a pen and pad making lists of what needed to be done to turn the Cannon's businesses around. Tori ordered the Dumpster and then they'd set off for the hardware store, heading straight for the paint section.

"What color should we buy?" Kathy asked.

"White."

"Oh, no!" Kathy said vehemently.

"I don't think Gramps would go for any other color."

"Isn't his competitor's place a dull and boring brown?"

"You mean Bayside Live Bait & Marina? Yeah."

"Then Cannon's should be on the opposite side of the color wheel."

"What did you have in mind?"

"Caribbean blue—or something teal."

"Oh, no."

"Oh, yes. What's a bait shop represent?"

"Worms."

"No, recreation," Kathy admonished. "Mark my words. Make it colorful and it will stand out all year—especially in winter."

Tori wasn't enthusiastic, but she let Kathy talk her into a special mix that was close to teal. If nothing else, it would be more cheerful than stark white would. But what was her Gramps going to say?

They also bought a quart each of red, white, and black paint to spruce up the signs that had faded so badly that they were barely legible. And they bought a couple of flats of petunias and a dozen geraniums to plant around the house and shop to make the place a little more welcoming. All well and good, but Tori didn't have an income. She hoped there was something worth selling among her grandmother's treasures to pay for these much-needed splurges. They would start the sorting process later that night.

The locally owned grocery store couldn't hold a candle to the big chains in Rochester when it came to prepared foods, but they bought a large sub and some potato salad for their supper. Kathy had baked that morning and brought a big plastic container of Tori's favorite chocolate chip-oatmeal cookies, which didn't have long for this world. They also picked up a large box of heavy-duty trash bags. They were going to need them.

Herb had closed the shop and was waiting for them in the kitchen when they returned from their errands. "I'm hungry as a bear," he said as Tori collected plates, passing them to Kathy, who set the table while Tori retrieved mayo, pickles, and a big pitcher of iced tea from the fridge.

"Did you get me some scratch offs?" Herb asked.

"Gramps, you may as well flush your money down

the toilet as buy lottery tickets," Tori said with disdain.

"One of these days I'm gonna win big and then you'll have to eat your words."

"I'd rather eat this sandwich," she said, taking her seat at the table.

Kathy unwrapped the sub and passed parts of it around. "What will you do if you win?" she asked the old man.

"Move to Florida."

"Florida?" Tori asked, aghast. "What for?"

"It don't snow there."

"Would you be a snowbird?" Kathy asked, and used her fork to spear a couple of gherkins.

"Hell, no. If I move there, I wouldn't come back here."

"Don't you love Lotus Bay?" Tori asked, feeling crushed.

"Not really. The Lodge and the bait shop were your grandma's pet projects, not mine. I never wanted to go into business. There're too many ways to fail."

"It's hard work," Kathy agreed, "but I'd much rather work for myself than someone else."

"Tori tells me you work in a hotel," Herb said, spooning an enormous helping of potato salad onto his plate.

"I do," Kathy said sadly. "But one day I'm going to own a bed and breakfast."

"Good luck with that," Herb muttered with what sounded like disapproval.

"It's what I've always wanted to do. Now I just have to find the perfect property. That is, once my inheritance comes through."

"When's that going to happen?" Herb asked.

"In four months, when I hit thirty," Kathy said and picked up her sandwich, taking a bite.

Herb looked askance at Tori before he spoke again. "So, why did you come here today?"

Kathy swallowed. "To help you and Tori."

"If you're worried about me, don't. I've got everything under control."

"Great," she said, picked up her fork and scooped up some potato salad.

"You girls don't need to hang around here. I took care of Josie and this place for a lot of years. I can take care of myself."

"I know that, Gramps," Tori said, remembering that he hadn't been quite that confident the evening before.

"If you're determined to paint the shop, I'd be grateful, but after that ...." He let the sentence dangle with words unsaid.

Daisy wandered into the kitchen and sat in front of Herb, looking hopeful.

"You know, Mr. Cannon," Kathy began, "you're not the only family member here who needs a lifeline."

"Kathy, don't," Tori warned, but her words had no effect.

Daisy cried, and Herb pulled a piece of ham from his sub, offering it to the cat, who swallowed it whole.

"Tori hasn't been exactly honest with you," Kathy told Herb.

He turned his gaze toward his granddaughter.

"Please!" Tori implored.

"Tori lost her job," Kathy began. "Right now the two of you need each other to survive."

Herb's gaze intensified. "Is that true?"

Tori took a deep breath. "I wasn't going to say anything, but yes. When my lease runs out, I'm not sure where I'll end up. I was sort of thinking it might be here with you. Not forever," she hastened to explain. "Just until I find another job. I thought maybe we could work together over the summer to get the shop back in the black and then...." She didn't finish the sentence.

"If you need money," the old man said, but Tori

shook her head.

"My bet is you've got less than me, but at least you have assets here with the shop—and the Lodge. I was hoping if we could make the most if it this summer, it might carry you through the lean winter months."

"You lost your job?" Herb repeated. "What did you do wrong?"

"Nothing. They cut teachers, not sports programs."

"But you had to do *something* wrong," the old man accused, looking at her with disappointment. "Bosses don't let good people go unless they do something wrong."

"That's not true, Mr. Cannon," Kathy said. "I've been following the school board decisions in the paper. The voters are the ones to blame, not those now out of work."

Tori swallowed, wounded by her grandfather's condemnation. She watched him give the cat another piece of meat. "I'm going to send resumes to every school district in a three-county radius. If nothing else, I can probably substitute-teach and I might pick up some tutoring jobs, too."

"That don't pay much," Herb said sourly and took a bite of his sandwich.

"It's better than starving," Tori muttered. They definitely needed a change of subject. "We won't have Kathy for more than a day or so. I thought maybe tonight we could go through some of the stuff here in the house to see if there's anything worth saving. "Do you want to help us, or do you trust us to decide whether to keep or toss stuff?"

Herb reached for the salt and liberally shook it over his potato salad. "As far as I'm concerned you can toss it all."

She should have expected that reaction. "I thought I'd rent a tent so we could set it up next to the shop and let your customers look at the stuff."

"Renting tents costs money," Herb grumbled. "Money we don't have."

"Actually, I borrowed an E-Z Up canopy from my landlady and brought it with me," Kathy said. "She used to sell jewelry at craft shows. She said you could borrow it for a few weeks. She'll need it back before Labor Day, though. That's when she throws her annual family picnic."

"She'll have it back long before then. I'll make sure of it, and please thank her for us," Tori said.

"Sure thing."

They ate for a few minutes in awkward silence, with only the sound of cutlery on plates breaking the quiet. Daisy rounded the table, but got no scraps from her owner or her best friend. Eventually, she sauntered out of the kitchen.

Kathy finally broke the quiet. "Did the police come back today?"

"No," Tori said

"Yes," Herb answered.

"They did? You didn't tell me."

"Didn't have time," the old man answered.

"What did they say?"

"Not so much said as asked. They wanted to know if the shop was missing any bait."

"Why was that?"

"'Cuz it seems that not only did someone kill Michael Jackson, but they stuffed his mouth full of spikes."

Tori set down her fork and pushed her plate away. "I'm done."

Kathy looked confused. "What are spikes?"

Herb scooped up the last of his potato salad and shoved it into his mouth. He quickly chewed and swallowed before answering. "Maggots."

"Oh!" Kathy pushed her plate away, too. "Why would anyone do that?"

Herb took a bite of his sandwich and shrugged. "Why would anyone *kill* the man?"

"Was the shop missing any bait?" Tori asked.

"I wasn't sure. But you were with me when we came back from the funeral. The door to the shop was locked. I didn't see any signs of a break-in, and with all that's happened in the past week, I couldn't tell if anything had been taken."

"Did they believe you?"

"Probably not."

"What else did they want to know?" Tori asked.

"They just kept asking the same questions over and over until I got mad."

"Oh, Gramps. If you changed your version of the events in any way, shape, or form, they might think you had something to do with Mr. Jackson's death."

"There are plenty of witnesses who can say I was at your grandma's funeral when Jackson died," Herb said flatly.

"Was *killed*," Tori emphasized.

"How did he die?" Kathy asked.

"Strangled," Herb said. "They want to talk to you again, too, Tori."

"I suppose that means they'll be back again tomorrow."

"We'd better start work on the bait shop early," Kathy suggested.

"You're gonna have to wash the walls before you can paint," Herb advised.

"Do you have a power washer?" Tori asked, predicting the answer.

"Nope."

"We'll just have to use scrub brushes and soapy water, then," Kathy said. "What time does the shop open?"

"Six," Herb said.

"We don't have to start that early," Tori hurriedly said.

"I'll set my phone alarm for seven. Can I bum break-fast off of you?" Kathy asked.

"Of course," Tori said, and wondered what she could offer her friend besides toast.

"Great."

Herb ate the last of his sandwich before he, too, pushed his plate away. "I'm gonna watch me some news," he announced and got up, heading for the living room and leaving the supper dishes for Tori. She didn't mind, got up, and started clearing things away.

Kathy watched. "Where do you want to start? In the kitchen, the living room, or your bedroom?"

"My bedroom?" Tori let out a ragged breath and re-turned the pickle jar to the door of the fridge. "That's going to take some getting used to. But once I clear some space, I think I could get a double bed in there. Sleeping in a twin makes me feel like a ten year old." She shook her head ruefully. "I guess we may as well start in here."

Kathy helped her finish clearing the table. Tori rinsed the dishes and Kathy loaded them into the dishwasher.

Tori stood in the middle of the kitchen. "Well, where do we start?"

"How about the magnets on the fridge?" Kathy sug-gested. You could barely see the refrigerator door for all the magnets. Many of them were from tourist spots, with another bunch from local businesses. Five silent minutes later, the fridge was revealed to be white, matching the stove and dishwasher. "I'll wipe it down while you start on one of the counters," Kathy said.

Tori opened the box of garbage bags, taking one out and shaking it open. "I wish you hadn't told Gramps about my job situation," she said tersely.

"It's better to get everything out into the open. Now he knows you don't have some kind of ulterior motive for helping him spruce up the place."

"Except now he thinks I'm here to sponge off of him."

"I don't believe that for a minute," Kathy said, "and neither does he."

Tori looked at the counter. Most of what cluttered it was paper—in the form of old magazines. "We can recycle all this. I'm going out to the lodge to get a box."

"I'll come with you. It's still light. We should take a look at it to see what kind of shape it's really in before you can make a decision about investing in it."

Tori nodded and grabbed a set of keys from a little teapot-shaped rack on the wall and grabbed a heavy-duty flashlight from the counter, checking it first to make sure it worked, then led the way.

The northern sky over Lake Ontario was beginning to glow pink as they walked across the lawn toward the shuttered motel. "I know the bottom units are stuffed full of boxes, but I have no idea about the second floor," Tori said. They looked up. Closed curtains blocked the windows. Tori started for the stairs, but Kathy hung back. "Where did they find the dead man?"

Tori paused and pointed. "This unit." The crime tape was gone. Perhaps Gramps had torn it off to avoid awkward questions from customers. "Do you want to look?"

"Is there anything to see?" Kathy asked.

Tori shook her head.

"What was he like?"

"Mr. Jackson?" Tori shrugged. "A quiet man. I don't remember him ever saying very much."

"I assume he lived alone."

"Years ago he had a family; a wife and two kids. I used to play with the daughter, Anissa. One summer I came back to the bay and she and her mom and brother were gone. I never heard why."

They headed up the stairs. Once on the balcony, Tori sorted through the keys until she came to one marked #7. She inserted it in the lock and turned the handle. The door opened inward. The air was hot and smelled musty, and except for several pieces of furniture, the unit was empty.

"Wow. It looks like it's frozen in time," Kathy said, taking in a dresser, a double bed stripped of sheets, two nightstands, and an old TV on a rolling stand. "But if the other three units up here are like this, it won't take much to get them up and running again."

"I don't know," Tori said doubtfully. "Right off the bat we'd have to get new mattresses, carpets, sheets, curtains, and towels, not to mention check the plumbing and the heater and AC units."

"You've been thinking about this—a lot," Kathy commented.

"Yeah," Tori admitted.

Kathy entered the unit and crossed the shag carpet to the bathroom. It was not a thing of beauty. Pale green tile ran half way up three of the walls and enclosed the tub. The fixtures were plain white. The bathtub's bottom housed a collection of dead flies and spiders.

"Any ideas on how to make a nightmare from the 1970s look like a dream?" Tori asked.

Kathy sighed. "New mirrors, or at least dressing these up, a coat of paint, a piece of art, and a shelf for guests to put their toiletries."

"And in the rooms?"

"New curtains, bedspreads, paint, and a few pictures. You'll also need new TVs and Wi-Fi."

"*I* don't even have Wi-Fi. I've been checking my email on my phone, and it's a royal pain. I meant to call the cable company today. Something else to do tomorrow." She shook her head, her mouth drooping. "It all seems insurmountable."

"It's a challenge," Kathy admitted, "but, man, would I love to get my hands dirty working on it."

"You must be out of your mind."

"It would be great practice for when I buy my own

place."

"I wish I could afford to hire you to run it."

Kathy's eyes widened. "You're tempting me."

"Even with seven units, Gramps and Grandma could never make the place pay for itself. The season is just too short."

"Fish bite in the spring and fall, too, don't they?"

"Technically, they also bite in winter. Once the bay ices over, there are fishing shacks all along the shore."

"Are they just locals, or do people come in from out of town and need lodging?"

Tori shrugged. "Gramps might know." She made a mental note to ask him.

"Did your grandparents ever advertise the lodge?"

"I don't know. They used to have business cards and matchbooks, but that may have been the extent of their promo. They used to be listed in the Triple A guide, but I don't think they ever got more than two diamonds."

"Did the other units have more than one bed?"

"They must have. I remember lots of families staying here. Maybe they had rollaway cots. We'd have to ask Gramps."

"What's the audience you want to attract?" Fishermen and families, too?" Kathy asked.

"Anybody with a credit card. Oh, damn," Tori said. "I don't even know if Gramps takes credit cards in the shop. What if he only does cash?"

"There are lots of options. Don't talk yourself out of all this before you even start," Kathy warned.

"Can I hope to attract any customers when there's been a murder on the premises?" Tori asked.

"Who's going to tell them upfront?"

"Nobody, I guess, but what about after they get here?"

"Establish a cancellation policy. Every other motel chain in the world has one."

"And won't we need a software program to go with

that? And to be tied to a bigger reservations network?"

"You're talking yourself out of it again. Why don't you just start by thinking big-picture before you get to the nitty-gritty?"

"It's the nitty-gritty that scares the hell out of me," Tori said. Her eyes filled with tears. "How did Grandma handle all this?"

"Oh, Tor, don't cry," Kathy said, and captured her friend in a hug.

"My Grandma's gone. I loved her so much and she's gone," Tori managed and broke into heaving sobs.

Kathy embraced her, patting her back. "You go ahead and cry," she soothed.

"Nobody in my family seems to care what happens to Gramps. Since he's not sick, they just left the area. They're all selfish and self-absorbed. This is my *family*— Gramps's *children*—and they just left him!"

"*You're* here. *You're* helping him. That's all that matters. Screw the rest of them," Kathy said. "But you know your Gramps is in good health. They probably think he'll last another twenty years. And there's a good possibility he might do just that."

"I hope he does." Tori pulled back and wiped her eyes. "We'd better look at the other units and then get back to clearing out the kitchen."

Kathy gave Tori's back one last pat and turned for the door. Tori looked around the room and gave a heavy sigh, depression weighing on her, and then she, too, left the room, locking it.

Except for the bathroom tile—in blue, yellow, and pink—the other rooms were a mirror of the first they viewed. "This is encouraging," Kathy said, her voice filled with optimism.

"If you say so," Tori muttered. All she saw were problems, knowing only an infusion of cash could solve them.

They went back down the stairs and Tori unlocked the

door to the first unit. She had to shove hard against the boxes that blocked the room; still, they weren't heavy. "I was hoping I'd find an empty one; I didn't realize there were so many of them," she said. "We'll have to collapse a few of them just to get one out of here."

"Why don't we collapse enough of them so that you can get in and out of here without a struggle?" Kathy suggested. Tori agreed, set the lit flashlight on one of the stacks, and the two of them spent the next ten minutes peeling off wide ribbons of sealing tape and setting the cardboard aside.

"Why on earth did your grandmother collect so many empty boxes?" Kathy asked.

"Who knows? But we can use them to pack up stuff to take to the thrift shop. There's one about ten minutes from here in North Erie."

A bed and dresser appeared from under the boxes, and they stacked the cardboard on the bed's damp mattress. Years of lack of air circulation had encouraged mold growth. "Looks like we'll have to strip this room back to the studs to bring it up to an acceptable level," Tori said, what little hope she had plummeting even further. "I don't think there's anyone local who does that kind of work. It'll probably cost more if they have to add in travel time for a contractor to come in from Rochester."

"You're doing it again; looking for ways to fail instead of succeed," Kathy warned.

"It all feels hopeless right now."

"Well, that's because you're in mourning. You are not going to get over your grandmother's death in just a day, a week, a month, or even a year. But from what you've told me, she loved this little motel. What a wonderful tribute it would be for you to get it back on its feet and make a success of it."

Tori nodded. "I'd love to do that."

"Then make that your goal."

The corners of Tori's mouth quirked into a modest smile. "Thanks, Kath. You always know what to say—how to make me look at alternatives."

"And you do the same for me." Kathy squinted in the nearly dark room. "Grab a box and let's get out of here. We have to find treasure in your grandma's collections to pay for this reno."

Tori's smile broadened. "You almost make me believe it can happen."

"That's because I honestly do believe it can happen. Now, come on. We've got a lot to do in the next couple of hours, and even more to do in the next two days." Kathy grabbed a box and strode out the door. Tori followed, a tiny kernel of hope growing within her.

FOUR

The Bay Bar wasn't exactly hopping when Kathy entered its front door later that evening, but for a dive in the middle of nowhere on a Wednesday evening, it seemed to have a fairly decent amount of patrons.

"What can I get you?" asked Paul, the bartender, who had also checked her into her rental room hours earlier.

"A gin and tonic."

"Coming right up."

Kathy watched as he filled a glass with ice, poured a shot into it, and squirted a dose of tonic water in before putting a slice of lime on the rim of the glass as garnish. He set it before her on a thin paper cocktail napkin.

"Thanks," she said.

He told her the cost and she dug into her pocket for the ten she'd put there after settling into her tiny room. If what they had to offer was the best available at this end of Lotus Bay, then Tori would make out like a bandit when she reopened the Lotus Lodge. Kathy's room boasted two single (and very lumpy) beds, an analog TV, and a tiny bathroom with a three-quarter shower. The best thing that could be said about it was that it *was* clean. But welcoming? No. No. NO! Then again, they catered to fishermen. Did their usual clientele get bombed at the bar after a day of fishing and then fall asleep in a drunken stupor before rising at dawn or shortly after to repeat the process?

"Let me know if you need anything," Paul said without real sincerity, giving her the change before moving back down the bar to a group of bikers who were watching a Mets game on one of the three flat-screen TVs bolted to the walls. A guy with a crew-cut sat alone at one of the tables nursing a beer, his lightweight beige jacket a stark contrast to the bikers' black leather.

Kathy took a sip of her drink and let it rest on her tongue for a few long moments before she swallowed. *Ahhhhhh!*

Tori had looked and sounded exhausted half an hour earlier when Kathy had insisted they quit cleaning house for the night. They had made substantial progress. Herb's kitchen was sparkling clean and totally uncluttered. They'd found some interesting items that could be sold, and filled two boxes for the thrift store, as well as four bags for the Dumpster when it arrived. Tori had shed more than a few tears during the process. She'd held onto items she remembered with great fondness from her childhood, items that would have brought her—and her grandfather—real money if sold, but there was no way Kathy was going to even mention that.

Kathy had never seen her friend in such distress, and her admiration for Tori—that had already been high—had soared when she saw her depth of commitment to help her remaining grandparent.

The swinging doors that separated the bar from the kitchen burst open and a lithe, bleached blonde woman of about fifty, with substantial bags under her eyes, clad in a pink tank top with a stained white bib apron over it, entered the area behind the bar. She stopped a foot or so away from Kathy, filled a glass with ice, and squirted what looked like ginger ale from the well trigger, then took a long drag on it before she sagged against the bar.

"Long day?" Kathy asked. She'd dealt with Paul when registering for her room. Was this woman his wife, or just the short-order cook?

"Oh, yeah."

"I'm Kathy Grant. I'm staying here for the next day or two."

"Noreen Darby. Glad to know you. Enjoy your stay."

"I'm taking a short working vacation. My friend, Tori, is staying with her grandfather across the road. We're helping him sort things out."

"Yeah, I heard Herb's wife died. So sad."

"Did you know her?"

Noreen shook her head. "Never met her. But Herb is kind of a regular here. More so in the winter when it gets pretty dead in these parts."

Kathy nodded. "They're kind of reeling since Mrs. Cannon's death and the discovery of that body on their property."

Noreen shook her head. "Poor Michael."

"Did you know him?"

"Oh, sure. He was a gifted carpenter. He did odd jobs for us on a regular basis."

"Was he a customer, too?"

"No," Noreen said succinctly.

Kathy decided to play dumb. "Oh?"

"Michael was a great guy, but...."

And then Kathy understood. Racism was alive and well in rural New York, but she got the idea that Noreen didn't hold such views. She turned to eye the guy with the crew-cut. He looked the kind who might not welcome someone several shades darker.

"Tori—Mr. Cannon's granddaughter—remembers Mr. Jackson's daughter, but not why she was no longer in her father's life."

Noreen shook her head. "Don't look to me for answers. I've only been a part of The Bay Bar for the last five years when I married Paul."

"How did you meet?" Kathy asked.

Noreen sighed wistfully. "I used to ride a Harley and came out here on a poker run."

"Poker run?"

"Yeah, a charity motorcycle ride event. You check in at several destination points, play a round of cards, and end up at a bar for a barbeque. They're loads of fun. I came here, met Paul and—" She looked down the bar at her husband, a quirky smile forming on her lips. "It was love at first sight." She looked back at Kathy. "Of course I didn't know then that I'd be giving up a life in an office to stand behind a stove ten hours a day."

"Would you go back to that life?" Kathy asked.

Noreen positively grinned. "Not on your life. I gripe about the hours, but I love being my own boss. How long does your friend plan to stay with Herb?"

"Indefinitely. She lost her job. She wants to help him get his business back in the black."

"Would she reopen the Lotus Lodge?" Noreen asked.

"It would take some work. How would you feel about having direct competition?"

"Ecstatic. Our rooms have a ninety percent occupancy rate in July and August. It wouldn't hurt our bar business if five or six of the rooms across the way were filled every night, too."

"How do you do during the winter?"

"Ice fishing fills our rooms on weekends, which helps the bottom line. But the real money comes from snow-mobilers. They get hungry—and thirsty—after hours out in the cold."

"That's good to know. I work in the hotel industry, myself. I'm an assistant manager at a motel in Batavia, but my goal is to someday open my own bed and breakfast."

Noreen shook her head. "It's a tough life. Not only do I cook, but I keep the rooms clean, too. And let me tell you, some of our guests are real pigs—and they're not all men."

"I hear you," Kathy said, taking a sip of her neglected drink. The ice had melted, leaving it watery. "We're starting with the bait shop. We'll scrub the outside walls and start painting it tomorrow."

"We've got a power washer. We'd be glad to loan it to you guys."

"That's very generous of you. I'll take you up on it. Thanks."

"Anything to help out Herb," Noreen said. "I'll be back in the kitchen about eight in the morning. Knock on the door and you can pick it up then."

"Great. Thanks."

Noreen downed the last of her ginger ale. "Time for me to call it quits for the day."

"Do you live above the bar?"

She shook her head. "Too noisy. We own the house next door."

"The one that's for sale?" Kathy asked. She'd noticed the wreck of a house that had probably once been a very nice home.

"No!" Noreen declared and laughed. "For years that place was a rental. It was split into a bunch of apartments, but the last tenants moved out in the spring. They really trashed it. I suggested the local fire department burn it down to the ground as a training exercise, but the owner is convinced he can get at least ten grand for it."

"Why so cheap?" Kathy asked.

"As I said, it's been trashed. It needs an electrical upgrade and a new roof, too. Nobody in their right mind would plow that kind of money into that old hulk."

But what if someone was expecting to come into a substantial inheritance in the not-too-distant future? Someone who wanted to convert an old house into a charming, upscale B and B? Kathy had been thinking of converting an old Victorian home. The house next door looked like a plain box with peeling blue paint. There may have been a covered porch on the front, but it was long gone.

Kathy took another sip of her now very watery drink. *I must be out of my mind to even consider it.*

"I'll see you in the morning," Noreen said as she untied her apron, screwed it into a ball, and tossed it under the bar.

"Good night," Kathy called, watching as the short order cook moved to stand with her husband. She spoke to him for a moment before she left the building via the front door.

Kathy turned back to her drink.

She couldn't buy that old wreck of a building. It was positively ludicrous to even think about it.

She shook away the mental cobwebs clouding her thoughts and glanced down at the bar.

"I came down at the weekend to fish. Some old black guy told me strange things were happening around here," one of the bikers told the bartender.

"Nothing strange *ever* happens around here. *Nothing* ever happens around here," said his companion, who laughed.

Kathy toyed with the stir stick that had come with her drink. Strange happenings. Had Mr. Jackson seen a UFO?

"What else did he say?" the bartender asked.

"Just that he wasn't going to take his boat out on the bay at night anymore."

"Makes sense if he docked at Cannon's. They haven't had a light on at night for a couple of years."

Kathy tuned out the conversation and glanced at the neon clock next to a lighted Coors beer sign on the wall. It was always five o'clock in this bar—but the time was actually about nine-forty. Again she wondered about the house next door. The price was right, but if what Noreen said about its shortcomings were true, it would be a money pit to try to restore it. And what would Tori say about the possibility of Kathy opening a B and B directly across the street from the Lotus Lodge? They'd be in direct competition. Well, not really. The Lotus Lodge was a glorified fish camp, and it catered to fishermen. Kathy wanted to attract honeymooning couples, serve afternoon tea, and with a decidedly higher per-night price tag than the Lotus Lodge.

Still, what could it hurt to make a call to the listing real estate agent? A walk-through might be enough to deter her. A discussion with a general contractor was sure to discourage her.

But what if ...?

The weatherman from Channel 10 news in Rochester had promised sunny skies, but the air was cool and damp when Kathy arrived at the Cannon compound the next morning just after 7:30. Of course, she'd gotten up early, dressed in work clothes, and hiked across the way through the knee-high grass to inspect the butt-ugly house that was for sale next to The Bay Bar. As Noreen had said, it was trashed. Kathy could see that just by looking in through the grimy windows that probably hadn't been washed in a decade or more.

From what she could see of the damage near the foundation, there had once been a substantial porch on the front of the house. She wondered if there was a historical society nearby that might have pictures of the house from the previous century. The windows had been replaced, probably in the 1970s or 1980s for what someone had mistakenly thought were more energy efficient models, but they hadn't weathered well and she could see signs that at least the ones in front had leaked at some point. Add all new windows to the restoration, which would be a small fortune in and of itself.

The more she thought about it, the worse the idea of restoring this ugly duckling into a swan became. With a heavy heart, she'd trucked across the road.

Tori opened the door in her PJs, looking sleepy.

"Have you got coffee?" Kathy asked.

"Yes. That—and iced tea—is all Gramps seems to drink."

Kathy entered the neat and now-inviting kitchen. Daisy sat in the corner eating from a pink bowl decorated with paw prints. "Where's your grandfather?"

"In the shop. He was there before I got up."

"How did you sleep?"

"Not good. I had a nightmare about finding Mr. Jackson, and then I didn't get back to sleep until almost six. How about you?"

"I didn't sleep well, either," Kathy admitted, but it was thoughts of the derelict house across the road that had preoccupied her thoughts.

Tori retrieved a bag of bread from the top of the fridge and stuck two pieces in the toaster, then poured a mug of coffee for Kathy. The words LOTUS LODGE were emblazoned in green with a drawing of a white lotus below.

"That's cute," she said, accepting the mug.

"Grandma had a case of them made way back when. I guess she thought people might buy them, but I don't think it worked out too well. There must be ten of them in the cupboard."

"It's a great idea, but she didn't have the address printed on the backside."

"I never even noticed."

"You could do the same thing and add a web URL."

"Gramps doesn't have a website for the bait shop. Hell, he doesn't even own a cell phone."

"You could set up a site cheap."

"That's a good idea," Tori said as the toast popped up. She put each slice on a plate and reloaded the toaster. She handed Kathy a plate.

"Thanks." Kathy took a seat at the table where napkins, knives, butter, and a jar of raspberry jam awaited. "I've got good news."

"I could use some about now," Tori admitted, still standing by the counter.

"Your neighbors at The Bay Bar are loaning us their power washer so we can prep the bait shop."

"Hey, that's great. Have you ever used one?"

"Yep. Once the walls are dry, we can start painting. We might even finish the job today. Then we can start tackling the Lotus Lodge."

"I don't know, Kath. That's a pretty tall order. Even if we get it in shape, we'd have to get a certificate of occupancy and heaven only knows how many other permits to reopen." She nibbled on the corner of her toast. "You didn't tell the people at the bar about possibly reopening the lodge, did you?"

"Noreen asked about it."

"Who's she?"

"One of the owners. She mans the kitchen."

"What did you tell her?"

"I asked how she'd feel about it reopening."

"And?" Tori asked, sounding nervous.

"Happy as a pig rolling in poop. She thinks it would add to their bar trade."

"She might be right."

"She said things are pretty dead in winter, but mentioned the same as you—ice fishermen, and even better, snowmobilers—help the bottom line."

The second batch of toast popped up. Tori placed one slice on her plate and doled the other out to Kathy, then sat down at the table.

Kathy spread jam on the toast and cut it into triangles, all the time wrestling with her conscience. Should she mention that old wreck of a house to Tori? She'd never lied to her friend before—not even a lie of omission. "What do you know about that house across the road that's for sale?"

"It's a real mess."

"Was it ever pretty?"

"Not that I remember, why?"

"Noreen said the asking price was only ten grand."

Tori studied her face. "I hope you're not thinking what I think you're thinking."

"I am," Kathy admitted.

Tori laughed. "Are you out of your mind?"

"I like to think I'm on a quest for knowledge."

"To find out it's a potential money pit and totally unsuitable for a B and B?"

Kathy nodded. "You got it."

"Shouldn't you do a feasibility study to see if the area can handle that kind of traffic?"

"Definitely. To tell you the truth, it's the price that caught my attention. I've seen wrecks like that in Batavia for a heck of a lot more money."

"Yeah, but it would probably take a hundred grand or more to bring it back to a habitable state. It might be better to just find a chunk of land and start building from scratch. And, as much as I'd love it if you were going to be near here, I think you'd do better to find something in Batavia or Rochester."

"Who goes to Batavia? It's just a pee stop on the Thruway."

"The race track is there."

"That's about it." Kathy polished off the last of her toast. "I'm not saying that wreck is the place for me, but I sure wouldn't mind taking a walk through it. Would you come with me?"

"To be the voice of reason? You bet."

Kathy decided to change the subject. "The conversation at The Bay Bar was all about the murder."

"There's probably not much else to talk about around here," Tori said reasonably.

"Did the guy who died keep his boat here?"

Tori nodded. "Gramps said it was tied up to the dock, why?"

"The dead guy told one of the bikers that he wasn't going to take his boat out on the bay at night anymore because strange stuff was happening."

"Like what?"

She shrugged. "I was wondering about UFOs. Have you ever seen one?"

"No, but I've seen shooting stars. Gramps has seen the northern lights, but I never did."

Kathy looked up at the clock. "You'd better get dressed. I can't lug that power washer across the street by myself."

Tori pushed away from the table and got up. "Okay. Thanks for getting them to loan it to us. It's going to save us half a day of scrubbing. I'll be back in a minute," she said and headed out of the kitchen toward the back of the house and her room, with Daisy following close behind.

Kathy kept staring at the hands of the clock. The real estate office probably didn't open for another hour. Once they got started on power washing the bait shop, she'd suggest they take a break halfway through and then she'd call. Was it possible she could see the place today? She found her gut tightening with anticipation. That house wasn't likely to be *the one* she could successfully turn into a gorgeous bed and breakfast, but just what if it was?

FIVE

The power washing went better than Tori had expected. True to her word, Kathy did know how to use it. Unfortunately, it not only removed the dirt from the paint, but it removed most of the paint from the cinder blocks, too. It was going to take more than one coat to cover them and make the place look welcoming...that is if you could use that word to describe a bait shop.

Herb came out several times to criticize the job, but he didn't fool Tori. He'd also been suppressing the beginnings of a smile. Maybe he thought they could bring the business back, too.

They had to wait for the blocks to dry before they could start painting, and thanks to a stiff breeze off the bay, they hoped to start within the hour. They'd already distributed a drop cloth around the north side of the building, and were assembling cans of paint when the Dumpster arrived. They watched it get unloaded, and before the truck had even left the driveway they started heaving the trash bags into it.

A green Honda Civic pulled into the gravel lot and parked. An older woman, probably in her late sixties, got out. She opened the back door to her car and took out a cake carrier with a transparent dome. Inside was a chocolate frosted cake.

Tori recognized the lady as someone who had been at her grandmother's funeral.

"Victoria!" she called.

Tori walked up to meet her. "Tori," she said amiably, taking in the woman's pale blue cotton-knit shirt with pink embroidered flowers around the neck, dark slacks, and black mules. She wore a triple string of pearls and matching earrings. "Hello. What can I do for you?"

"We met at Josie's funeral the other day. I'm Irene Timmons. I heard you were staying with Herb for a few days. That's so thoughtful of you. He must be terribly lonely with Josie gone."

Tori frowned at the woman's simpering tone. "He's doing okay."

"I'm so glad to hear that. Is he around?" she asked, her gaze straying to where Herb's truck was parked near the house.

"He's in the bait shop. It was so thoughtful of you to bring Gramps a cake. Would you like me to take it inside?"

Irene wrinkled her nose, but shook her head. "I think I'll just take it to him, dear."

Tori shrugged. "Be my guest."

Irene headed for the bait shop. Kathy had finished tossing the trash into the Dumpster and was checking her phone for messages. She pocketed it when Tori joined her. "A neighborly visit?" she asked.

Tori nodded. "A friend of Grandma's. She wanted to check up on Gramps."

"I'll bet."

They headed back to the bait shop. Tori glanced inside. The cake sat on the counter, which seemed to be a buffer zone between Herb and his visitor. Irene was leaning against it, but Herb had retreated until he was standing with his back to a fishing lure display.

Tori picked up a screwdriver, intending to open one of the paint cans, when a battered blue pickup truck pulled up in the Cannon compound's parking lot, coming to a halt in front of the Lotus Lodge. A tall and stocky black woman dressed in overalls, with foot-long dreadlocks, got out of it and stood before the building, just staring at it. She wasn't fat; her taut, chiseled arm muscles hinted of hours of weight training and/or heavy physical labor.

"Why don't you go see what she wants," Kathy suggested. "I can get things going here."

"Okay," Tori said, and left her friend, who'd seemed to be getting antsy. She ambled over to the visitor and looked back. Kathy had already whipped out her cell phone. No doubt calling the real estate office about the wreck across the road. She shrugged and started back toward the newcomer. "Can I help you?" she called.

The woman turned to look at her. Her eyes were filled with tears, and she rubbed the back of her hand across the right one. "Just looking," she said, and turned back to look at the motel.

Tori stepped closer. "Anissa?" she called.

The woman turned and nodded.

"It's me, Tori."

"Shut up," the woman said and somehow managed a soggy laugh.

Tori wasn't sure if her childhood friend would be receptive to a hug, but she held out her arms. Anissa practically fell into her embrace and began to weep, great heaving sobs.

"I'm so sorry," Tori whispered into her ear and patted her back.

"My daddy's dead," Anissa managed between ragged breaths.

"I'm so, so sorry," Tori murmured, not knowing what else to say to ease Anissa's sorrow.

Eventually, the sobs grew more quiet, and Anissa pulled away. "Sorry about that," she managed, dug into the big pocket on the left side of her overalls, and came up with a balled-up tissue. She blew her nose—loudly—

and let out a shaky breath. "How long has it been?" she asked Tori.

"More than twenty years."

"You don't look at all like you did as a kid," Anissa said.

"Neither do you," Tori said, and they both laughed.

Anissa's smile was short lived. "The detective I spoke to said that a woman found my daddy. Was that you?"

Tori nodded, finding it hard to meet Anissa's gaze. "Me and my Gramps."

"How could someone kill my daddy and nobody saw it happen?" Anissa demanded.

"We buried my grandma that day. We were gone from nine in the morning until late in the afternoon."

Anissa nodded and turned back for the motel. "What a dump."

Tori let out a breath. "Yeah."

"I mean, it's a terrible place for someone to die."

"Do the police have any clue what happened?"

"Do you think they care about a dead old black dude?" Anissa asked with disdain.

"I sure hope they do. I'm trying to breathe some life into the business."

"Oh, so my daddy being killed here is bad for business?" Anissa asked hotly.

"That's not what I meant," Tori said, defending herself.

Anissa turned away. "I'm sorry. I'm angry and I guess I just want to blame someone for this."

"I can understand that," Tori said with sympathy. "When did you find out?"

"Last night. It took the cops that long to track me down. I guess it didn't occur to them to look in the phone book."

"Do you live in Rochester?" Tori asked.

Anissa nodded, then she shrugged. "Sort of. I've got

an apartment in half a house, but my lease is up and I haven't had a chance to find a new place. I was going to put my stuff in storage and move in with a friend for a while. I'm between jobs and money is kind of tight," she admitted.

"I can relate to that," Tori said, but wasn't about to go into details.

"I was actually thinking I might stay in daddy's house for a while—at least until the cops figure out what happened. He had a will. He left the place to my brother and me."

"How is James?" Tori asked, looking back at the bait shop; Kathy was still on the phone.

"Probably pulling teeth."

"Oh?" Tori asked, confused.

"He's an oral surgeon. I'm my mother's greatest disappointment. I didn't want to go to college. I followed in my daddy's footsteps and found a job in construction, mostly working on houses. Despite my appearance," she said, taking in her battered truck with a wave of her hand, "it can pay quite well. I just have the unfortunate habit of shooting off my big mouth at the wrong moment and screwing myself in the process."

"Been there, done that," Tori admitted.

"My mother expects me to have a debilitating accident just like daddy. So far, I've been lucky. I've stepped on a few rusty nails and nearly crushed a toe or two, but that's about the extent of the accidents I've had. Not like daddy, whose leg was pretty mangled. It put him out of work for a long time and led to my parent's breakup."

Tori nodded. "Do you still have friends in the area?"

Anissa shook her head. "I lost track of all of them years ago. I hadn't even seen daddy in a couple of months, but I talked to him every few days on the phone."

"Did he mention having any trouble?" Tori asked.

"You mean apart from annoying that witch Lucinda Bloomfield up on the hill?"

"Yeah."

Anissa shrugged. "My daddy wasn't one to complain. All he wanted was to do was watch a little TV, fish a little, and live his life in peace. But he didn't sound his usual cheerful self when we last talked. He was distracted—like he had other things on his—mind, and that wasn't like him. He was always happy to hear from me, but that night he ended our conversation pretty quick."

"Did you tell the police this?"

"Yeah, but it doesn't mean anything to them." She shook her head, her eyes filling with tears once again. "How does that get a good man killed?" she asked, her voice breaking.

Again, Tori had no idea what to say, how to comfort the woman. Her grandmother had died unaware, but Michael Jackson's death had been violent—and his body dragged and dumped not ten feet from where she now stood.

Anissa wiped her eyes and blew her nose once more, staring off in the direction of the bait shop. "You doing some fixing up for your grandfather?"

Tori nodded. "Yeah. Trying to see if I can help him get this place back in the black. He took care of my grandma the last couple of years and things kind of got away from him."

Anissa nodded and sniffed. "If you need some odd jobs done, I'm available. I can do demo, drywall, electrical, and plumbing."

"Right now the budget is practically nil, which is why my friend, Kathy, is here to help me paint the bait shop. She's got it in her head that I should try to reopen the Lotus Lodge."

Anissa turned back to look at the motel. "Girl, if that's your plan, you've got your hands full. Still, if you decide you want to do even a little sprucing up so it doesn't look like such an eyesore, you know where to find me—at least for the next week or so."

"I'll keep it in mind," Tori said.

Anissa started back for her truck. She opened the door and climbed inside. "I guess I'll see you around."

"I hope so," Tori said.

Anissa started the engine and backed up, leaving the lot and heading up Resort Road. Tori watched until she was out of sight, then started back for the bait shop. Kathy had finished her call and was already up the stepladder, slapping paint on the now-dried cinder blocks.

"Who was that?" she asked, not bothering to look away from her task.

"Mr. Jackson's daughter, Anissa."

"I had a feeling," Kathy said.

"How did your phone call to the realtor go?"

Kathy kept her gaze fixed on her paintbrush. "Fine."

"When do you get to see the wreck?"

"This afternoon around four. Want to come?"

"Sure. In fact, you might want to invite Anissa to come along with you. She's into fixing up old houses."

Kathy's head turned so fast she was in danger of whiplash. "Really? Is she a contractor?"

"I don't think so. But it sounds like she's worked for a few."

"Do you have her number?"

Tori shook her head. "But she's going to stay at her father's house for the next couple of days. We could drive over there and see if she's interested. Maybe you could offer to pay her a few bucks for an opinion on the place. I think she could use the money."

Kathy nodded and dipped her brush back into the can that sat on the stepladder's little shelf. "Maybe we can head over to her place after lunch. In the meantime, grab a brush and let's get this sucker painted. We've got lots of other stuff to do today."

Tori glanced at her watch before she stooped to grab one of the four-inch brushes that sat on the tarp. It was a little after ten. That didn't give them much time to paint, visit Anissa, and head over to the wreck. Then again, the June days were long and the sun was shining. Perhaps they could finish the first coat today. Perhaps.

*

Irene didn't leave for another twenty minutes. It was ten minutes after that when Herb poked his head out of the bait shop and hollered, "What in God's name have you done?"

"Great color, huh, Mr. Cannon?" Kathy said enthusiastically.

"In the tropics. Girl, don't you know this is Western New York?" His angry glare was aimed straight at Tori.

"Kathy thinks, and I agree, that we need to stand out from our competition."

"We'll sure as hell stand out—and be the laughing stock of the bay."

"I don't think so," Kathy said. "Give it a couple of weeks. If you're not making double your money on sales, I'll come back and paint it white—and all by myself, too."

Herb smiled. He was a gambling man if the stack of losing lottery tickets they'd found while cleaning the night before was any indication. "You're on."

"You want to give us a hand, Gramps?" Tori asked.

Herb reached a hand around to rub his back. "I'd like to, girls, but that old sciatica has set in again."

"Uh-huh," Tori muttered. "How did your visit with Irene go?" Tori asked.

Herb grimaced. "She hinted that we should hook up."

"What?" Tori asked, appalled. "Grandma's only been in the ground a few days."

"Yeah, well, Irene's been a widow for a while. I expect

every widow in the county will be after me now."

"Are you interested in..." she swallowed, "hooking up?"

"Hell, no! Not with what's available locally, anyway. Besides, your grandma seemed to think Irene nagged her last husband to death." He cleared his throat. "I thought I'd make me a sandwich. It's just about lunchtime. Want me to make you something, too?"

"What did you have in mind?" Kathy asked.

"Egg salad."

Tori grinned. "Nobody makes egg salad like my Gramps. He chops up green olives and mixes them in."

"Sounds great to me," Kathy said.

"Watch the store, willya?" Herb asked. It wouldn't be hard to do. He hadn't had a customer the entire time they'd been painting. They'd made good progress. Tori estimated they'd be finished with the first coat by the time the sandwiches were made.

Sure enough, by the time they wrapped the brushes in plastic and batted the lids onto the paint cans, Herb returned. "I already ate. Your lunch is in the fridge."

"Thanks, Gramps."

"Any customers?" he asked, looking out over the bay.

"Not so far," Kathy said. "But soon they'll be coming in droves."

"Hmmm," was Herb's only reply as he went back into the shop.

Tori looked at her hands, which were a mess with splatters. "I wonder if Gramps has a scrub brush handy."

"Totally unnecessary," Kathy said, as she started toward the house. "Got any baby oil?"

"I think there's some in the bathroom, though God only knows how old it is."

"It should work. Come on. I'm starved."

The baby oil worked like magic—once they employed a scrub brush--and soon the women were sitting at the kitchen table eating lunch.

"This is the best egg salad sandwich I've ever had," Kathy said between bites.

"Told you." Tori poured more iced tea from the sweating pitcher. "So you want to run up to Anissa's place after this?"

"Uh-huh. I also want to take a look at the Bloomfield house. Everyone around here talks about it like it's some kind of mansion."

"Not exactly. It's a big house, but they poured a lot of money into it over the years."

"How many bedrooms?"

"Nobody I know has ever been inside, although supposedly it's been featured in a bunch of magazines."

"They don't have help who talk?"

Tori shrugged. "I haven't been a part of the scene around here for years. I wouldn't even know where to hear the latest gossip."

"Perhaps your grandfather's bait shop?" Kathy suggested.

"Well, maybe if we could get a few customers to come in we might hear something."

"Just wait," Kathy said with confidence.

"If the paint's still tacky when we get back From Anissa's, we'll attack the signs. Have you got a steady hand?"

"You mean for outlining the letters?" Kathy shrugged. "I'll give it a try. It can't look much worse than it does now."

They polished off the last of the sandwiches, loaded the dishwasher, and headed out the door. "I'll drive," Kathy said after Tori had told Herb where they were going and why, then they piled into Kathy's car.

It had been at least a decade, maybe more, since Tori had gone up the Resort Road. Back then, it had been populated with summer cottages and a singlewide trailer or two. Now, the cottages were gone, and in their places were an assortment of year-round homes, from log cabins to a McMansion or two. At the top of the hill was the Bloomfield estate.

The big two-story brick home sat at the top of the hill. Thick columns held up the roof of a wide porch that ran across the front of the house. The lawns were as meticulously groomed as the fairways of an exclusive country club. The landscaping around the front of the home was a riot of reds and pinks. Were they Lucinda Bloomfield's favorite colors?

The road's only eyesore was the ramshackle little home of the man who'd been found in in the Lotus Lodge just days before. One might call Mr. Jackson's house a bungalow, but it was hard to see thanks to the knee-high grass and unkempt bushes that nearly hid it from view.

Anissa's truck was parked outside, and they could see she'd attempted to cut the grass with a rusty hand mower, the likes of which Tori hadn't seen since she'd been at least ten. It was totally unsuitable for the task and Anissa had obviously given up after only managing to cut a swath about a foot wide and ten feet long.

"I can see why old Lady Bloomfield doesn't like the view at the bottom of her drive," Tori muttered.

"Nothing a little pruning, paint, and elbow grease couldn't rectify."

Kathy was such an optimist.

As they approached the side door, they saw a rusty power mower sitting under the plastic canopy that covered the cracked concrete patio. "Maybe I could offer to loan her our mower."

"Hey, if she'll come to look at the house with me, I'll offer to cut the grass for her."

Tori knocked on the door. They looked around self-consciously as they waited.

"Knock again," Kathy whispered.

Tori knocked harder this time, and soon the door swung back. "Ready for some company?"

Anissa filled the doorframe. She'd been crying again. She looked over her shoulder. "Not really, but ... Oh, what the hell. Come on in."

She moved aside and Tori stepped in. "Oh, my," she said with awe as she took in the kitchen, which was not what she was expecting.

"It's beautiful," Kathy said as her gaze traveled around the room to the apron sink and granite counters.

"Sorry about the mess. I was having lunch," Anissa apologized. "I found some bread in the freezer. Care for a peanut butter sandwich?"

"No, thanks. We just ate," Tori said, still taking in the details of the kitchen. A small stainless steel dishwasher stood next to a wine fridge. The cabinets were cherry, sporting polished nickel hardware.

"Wow. Noreen over at The Bay Bar said your father was a gifted carpenter. She wasn't kidding," Kathy murmured.

"The place looks a wreck on the outside. I don't suppose Daddy entertained much, but he did like to putter around and fix things up. And you are?"

"Oh, I'm sorry. Anissa Jackson, this is my friend, Kathy Grant," Tori said.

"Nice to meet you," Kathy said and offered her hand. They shook. "I'm so sorry for your loss."

"Yeah, well ... so am I," Anissa said, her voice wavering. "What can I do for you?"

"I told Kathy about your building and construction experience. We were wondering if we might barter for your expertise."

Anissa's eyes widened. "That sounds interesting."

"I'm going to look at a house this afternoon. I'm in the market for a fixer-upper. I'm from Batavia and don't know any contractors in the area. Tori thought you might be able to advise me."

"And in return?" Anissa asked.

"We'd cut your grass and maybe take a whack at some of those bushes out front."

"Sounds like I'd be getting the better end of the bargain, but I'll take you up on it. Where and when?"

"Meet us outside the Lotus Lodge just before four and we'll walk over."

Anissa's eyes narrowed. "Walk?"

"Yeah, there's a house for sale on the other side of The Bay Bar."

"That horrible wreck?" Anissa asked.

"That's the one," Tori said. "It doesn't seem worth looking at, let alone contemplating saving, but Kathy's a sucker for hard-luck cases."

"That's why we've been friends so long," Kathy said with a sidelong glance at Tori.

"When can you cut the grass?" Anissa asked.

"We've got to finish painting the bait shop, but if it's not too damp this evening, we could cut the grass after six. Either that or first thing tomorrow."

"Works for me," Anissa said.

"Great."

"We'd better get going. The bait shop isn't going to paint itself," Kathy said. "See you around four."

"You got it."

Anissa closed the door on them and they walked back to Kathy's car. Mr. Jackson had taken meticulous care of the inside of his home but not the outside. Therefore, Tori could understand why his nearest neighbor wanted to wipe out the blight that was Jackson's lot. The only question was, did Lucinda Bloomfield want to beautify the neighborhood badly enough to kill?

SIX

The paint was dry on the north side of the bait shop when Tori and Kathy arrived back at the Cannon compound. Tori started the second coat while Kathy began work on restoring the aged wooden signs. First she scraped away the old paint, trusting it was oil based—not lead—and painted the background white before starting the red lettering with the black drop shadow. She'd finished the side of the sign facing east while Tori had repainted the north and east sides of the shop. During that time, the shop saw three customers enter its doors. A hopeful sign.

Tori approached. "It's fifteen minutes until we're supposed to meet the real estate agent," she called.

Kathy put her brush down and admired her work.

"Not bad," Tori said. "Looks like a pro did it."

Kathy smiled. "Thanks. After supper I'll tackle the other side. That is if you don't mind doing the other two sides of the shop.

"I do—but it's got to be done. You were right; I'm loving the color. I sure hope you're also right that it will be good for business."

"Trust me." Kathy tamped down the lids on the paint cans. "I need to clean up and change before we head across the street. Is it okay if I leave these here?"

"I'll move them over to the sidewalk outside the Lotus Lodge—just in case any of our boat people show up. It'll look tidier."

"There's a Dumpster in your front yard and you're worried about a couple of paint cans?"

Tori pouted.

"Okay, okay," Kathy said affably. "I'll be back in a few minutes." She looked both ways before crossing the road. The speed limit on the bridge was only thirty miles per hour, but was raised to fifty-five immediately afterward and drivers didn't hesitate a second before putting their pedals to the metal. She had no desire to be road kill.

Only a few motorcycles were parked in The Bay Bar's parking lot, near her own car. Kathy hurried to wash and change. When she emerged from her room, she saw that Anissa had already arrived and she and Tori were leaning against the bar's deck waiting for her. Anissa was wearing a tool belt strapped around her waist.

"You came prepared," Kathy said, delighted.

"The place probably doesn't have electricity. I brought a flashlight, a hammer, screwdrivers, a stud finder, and a couple of other things that might be useful."

"Shall we walk over to the house?" Tori asked.

Together the women crossed the parking lot for the weedy patch of dirt that ran parallel to the road. The hedges at the side of the yard were completely out of control, soaring some fifteen or more feet into the air and adding to the aura of neglect that clung to the house. It looked even worse in the afternoon light than it had in the morning, but Kathy felt a thrill of excitement just looking at it. She'd looked at a lot of houses in Batavia and never had she felt such a sense of welcome as she got from this sadly abused dwelling. It was stupid. It was a ruin, but she *wanted* it as bad as a kid wants her first bike. She knew Tori would try to talk her out of it, which was why she was glad they'd asked Anissa to join them. Kathy had come close to putting an offer on another fixer-upper until she'd found out there were foundation issues. What idiot built a house on dirt? The beams were so far gone it was a miracle they supported the floor above them, let alone the rest of the building's weight. What bad news would Anissa deliver when she looked over the place? The front yard, if that's what it could be called, was little more than a sand lot sprouting a variety of weeds. A couple hundred thousand years earlier where they now stood was once the bottom of Lake Ontario. It would probably need a couple of tons of topsoil before a decent lawn could grow.

"I'm going to walk around the building to see what's up. Anybody want to join me?" Anissa asked.

Kathy looked down at her sandaled feet and bare legs and thought about snakes and ticks that might be lurking in the thigh-high grass and weeds. "Not right now. Besides, I need to wait for the real estate agent."

"I'll come," Tori volunteered. She hadn't changed from her jeans and sweatshirt.

Kathy watched them walk around the corner, and then turned her gaze back to the front of the house. Most of the paint had worn off the clapboards from years of hostile weather, but the naked wood didn't look in too bad of shape. Kathy was about to mount the steps when a black SUV pulled into what was left of a gravel driveway. Kathy's heart started to pound as a man with thick white hair, dressed in khaki's and a green golf shirt, got out of the car, with a clipboard in hand.

"Kathy Grant?" he called.

"Yes. Mr. Peterson?"

"That's me. Call me Jerry."

Kathy met him halfway and they shook hands. "Hi, Jerry. I'm glad you could fit me into your schedule."

"This place has been on the market so long, I didn't want to miss a chance to show it. What kind of business were you thinking of building on the site? Restaurant? Convenience store?"

Kathy frowned. "Nothing of the kind. If I buy this property, I'd restore the house."

Jerry scowled. "Are you sure that's a good idea?"

"Well, my contractor is wandering around in the back. She'll be able to give me a better idea once we've walked through the place."

Jerry dug into his pants pocket and removed a key. He advanced toward the lockbox on the front door. "Let's get to it."

He unlocked the door and held it open for Kathy to go inside. The air was stifling, and smelled of must, stale urine, and dry rot, but Kathy was not deterred. What had once been a large open foyer had been closed in with drywall, delineating what looked to be a couple of small apartments. The drywall to the left looked like someone had taken an ax to it, and faded pink fiberglass insulation seemed to seep from the wounds. The ceiling above sported peeling paint and lath with missing plaster, making Kathy's heart ache to see such neglect.

"As you can see, the place is in major disrepair," Jerry said unnecessarily.

The door to the left hung on unsteady hinges. Kathy pushed it open and stepped inside. The floor was black and badly water damaged.

The filthy empty fish tank that lay on its side explained that story. A stained-and-torn mattress had been shoved against one corner of the room, and the fireplace was filled with paper, cans, bottles, and other trash. It had been boxed in. Could there be treasure—tile, stone, or a lovely old mantle—under the sheetrock? The tangled mess of what had been the framework of a suspended ceiling hung in ruins overhead, but Kathy could see above it cove molding, and again her heart started to beat faster.

A noise behind her made her jump. "Boy, what a dump," Tori said.

Kathy cringed before forcing a smile and making introductions, while Jerry eyed Anissa with consternation. "You're not local," he said, his voice flat.

"Nope. I'm from Rochester. Tori and I are old friends."

"You're a contractor?" he asked skeptically.

Anissa shot a look at Kathy and smiled. "You don't think a woman is up for the job?"

"Oh, no—not at all. It's just—" But he didn't offer a further explanation.

"Is this place safe to walk through?" Tori asked, sounding worried.

"We'll find out," Anissa said, and turned for the hall that led to the back of the house.

They wandered through the rest of the first floor, which had been turned into three apartments. All the rooms seemed to be filled with trash from its former occupants. The apartment in the back had once housed what seemed to be the original dining room and a large kitchen, the latter of which had been divided to include a terrible little bathroom whose tiled surround seemed to now fill the undersized bathtub.

The kitchen cabinets weren't original, the counter was littered with mouse droppings, and the floor was worn with many holes, revealing layers and layers of old linoleum and even the wide planks of the original subfloor. Kathy's heart sank as her logical mind started totaling up the cost of gutting and replacing just about everything on the first floor.

"Shall we go upstairs?" Anissa asked.

"You go, I'll just hang around down here," Jerry said. He looked discouraged, as though he'd already decided that showing the house had been a colossal waste of his time.

Anissa led the way and Kathy and Tori followed after her. The wide stairs must have once looked magnificent, but many of the balusters were missing, as was the finial on top of the newel post.

"Kath, you can't possibly think this place is worth saving," Tori said.

Kathy looked at Anissa, who merely shrugged.

The top floor had been divided into another three apartments, whose conditions mirrored those below.

"If you're thinking of turning this joint into a B and B, the bathrooms they added to the top floor will make it worthwhile. That is if they aren't full of galvanized pipe," Anissa said. "You never know what's there until you start pulling the walls apart. If it's got a decent attic, you might fit in another two guest rooms."

"What's your assessment so far?" Kathy asked, dreading the answer.

Anissa shrugged. "I dunno. The electrical needs a total revamp. There are fifteen amp fuses in the box at the end of the kitchen—and that's just plain dangerous in a house this size. Did you notice that every room only has one electrical outlet? That's got to change. The roof is iffy. There isn't one gutter on the entire place, which is why there's so much wood rot. And I really need to look at the basement and the furnace and water heaters, which could reveal another whole set of problems."

"Kath, you need to walk away from this money pit," Tori said, her brow furrowed with honest concern.

"Not necessarily," Anissa said, and Kathy noted the angry look Tori shot in her childhood friend's direction

"What do you mean?"

"It depends on your goals. How bad do you want a historic property? How much are you willing to spend to bring it back to a habitable state? How much intestinal fortitude do you have to see the whole restoration project through, and how much do you just plain want it?"

"What do you think it would cost to bring a place like this back to life?" Kathy asked, and her gut tightened.

Anissa shrugged. "It depends on your definition of

restoration. Rehab is cheaper. You could do it for maybe fifty or sixty grand if you went on the cheap. Double, triple, or even more if you want historical accuracy."

"Have you ever restored an historical home?" Kathy asked.

"I've worked on a couple of them, but I've never been a general contractor on such a big project."

"Do you think you could you do it?"

Anissa smiled. "I'd sure like to try."

Tori shook her head. "Kath, you can't be serious. This place is a wreck."

Kathy frowned. "I'm not in a hurry. You know I've got another four months before I get my inheritance. Is anyone else likely to try to buy this place in the interim?"

"Anything's possible," Anissa said.

"You don't have to make a decision today, tomorrow, or even next week," Tori said adamantly.

"That's for sure," Kathy admitted.

"Let's try to find that attic access, and then I'll check the basement," Anissa said.

Kathy nodded, trying to avoid Tori's angry glare.

Anissa found a narrow set of stairs that led to the attic, but neither Kathy nor Tori deigned to follow her up, leaving the two friends alone.

"Kath," Tori began.

"Don't," Kathy warned. "May I remind you that you're trying to resurrect your grandfather's failing bait and tackle shop?"

"Yes, but all it's costing me is a few cans of paint, a little elbow grease, and a lot of hope. The work it would take just to revive this old house, let alone make it pay for itself, is tremendous."

"I watch the same home renovation shows you do. I have a pretty good idea of what I'd be in for. And you've got to know that a big part of the appeal in buying this place is that you'd be across the road."

Tori shook her head. "I don't know *where* I'll be in a couple of months."

"I do," Kathy said with conviction.

"You can't stake your future on what I may or may not do."

"But I can stake my future on what I've been planning, saving, and dreaming about since I was seventeen years old."

Tori held up her hands in surrender. "Okay, okay. I won't say another word."

"Thank you." Kathy looked around the ruined, water-damaged wall in the hall. "I want to walk through the whole house at least one more time. I need to make some notes and take some measurements."

"I'll meet you back at the bait shop," Tori said, gave the hall another onceover and shook her head before she started down the stairs. Kathy followed at a slower pace.

The front door was open and Kathy could see Jerry standing by his car talking on his phone. She turned and entered the apartment on the right. The room had originally been a parlor. It was in the same shape as its twin across the hall, but the room seemed to have double the amount of trash piled almost waist high in some spots. Kathy saw nothing worth salvaging and wondered how many Dumpsters it would take to clear out the place.

She followed a narrow path through the clutter, being careful not to let any of the trash touch her bare toes, making her way across the room to the fireplace. This hearth hadn't been boxed in and was framed by a scarred, but still-beautiful wooden mantle and a Victorian tile surround depicting sweet blue flowers that resembled nothing in a real garden. A few tiles were chipped or cracked, but for the most part they were in better shape than the rest of the house. Like the rest of the room, the firebox was full of trash. A part of a curtain rod lay at her feet. Kathy picked it up and poked at the rubbish, trying to dislodge it to get a better view of the back of the fireplace when she spied a worn black leather wallet. It took three tries before she was able to extricate it. The thing was probably rife with germs, but her interest was piqued. She unfolded it, finding it devoid of cash and credit cards, but there was a valid driver's license lodged in the back behind the picture of two young African-American children. She read the name and address as a wave of cold passed through her.

Michael Jackson, who lived on Resort Road.

Anissa had taken one look at the picture in the wallet and burst into tears. She'd recognized the children in the picture: herself and her older brother at ages eight and ten. Jerry had not been pleased when Kathy had called the Wade County Sheriff's Department to report the find. He wanted to lock up, go home, have a beer, and get ready for the baseball game on TV that evening. It took more than an hour before the lead investigator in the case, Detective Osborn, had shown up at the ramshackle old house.

"You say you found it in the fireplace?" Osborn practically growled. Had he, too, been anticipating an evening home in front of tube? He'd donned latex gloves before handling the wallet.

"That's right," Kathy said.

"Did anyone other than you touch it?"

"His daughter, Anissa," Kathy said, pointing to the weepy woman who sat on the wooden step in front of the house.

Osborn frowned. "You probably obliterated any fingerprint evidence."

"How was I to know the wallet belonged to a murder victim?" Kathy said in her own defense.

"Can I close up the house and go home?" Jerry asked

impatiently.

"No. I need to get a lab team out here to search for any other evidence," Osborn said.

Jerry glowered, looked like he wanted to hit something—or someone—and stormed off for his car to once again sit in the driver's seat and fume.

"Let's go over it all again," Osborn said.

Kathy sighed. "We arrived at the house."

"Just the three of you?"

"No, my friend, Tori Cannon, was with us. She went back home—across the street—to start a second coat of paint on the bait shop. Anissa was checking out the attic, and Jerry was standing in the front yard on his cell phone when I found the wallet."

Osborn looked back at the house. "Were there any windows or doors open when you first went into the house?"

"No."

"And the house was locked?"

"Jerry had to get the key from the lock box hanging from the front door to open it."

"Was there a time when any of you were alone in any of the rooms?"

Kathy shrugged. "As I said, Anissa went to the attic. None of us were in this room alone, so you can count us out as suspects, if that's what you're trying to infer."

Osborn's gaze hardened, then he turned back to look at Anissa. "Do you think she's ready to talk?"

"You make it sound like she's a suspect." Kathy was getting a little annoyed at this guy's line of questioning.

"At this point, everybody's a suspect." He headed for the steps outside. Kathy followed.

"Miss Jackson?" Anissa looked up. "Do you feel up to answering some questions?"

Anissa rubbed her bloodshot eyes and nodded.

"Have you ever seen this wallet before today?"

"Of course I have. I *made* it for my Daddy when I was at summer camp about a million years ago, that's why he never replaced it."

"When was the last time you saw it?"

"I don't know. Maybe a year or two ago."

"And to your knowledge he never had a different, newer wallet."

"Not that I know of."

"Do you know if he had any credit cards?"

"I know he had at least one, but I don't know what company it was with."

"Do you know why someone would want to rob and then kill him?"

"You asked me that this morning, and the answer is still the same, no!"

Osborn looked around them at the weedy yard. "What were you doing here with Miss Grant?"

"I'm her general contractor. We were looking at the house to determine if it's worth saving."

Osborn turned to Kathy. "Is that true?"

"Well, if I buy the house she just might be. Tori and I asked her to accompany us to check out the place. Home remodeling is Anissa's business."

"Yes, she mentioned as much to me this morning," Osborn admitted. "You actually want to buy this place?"

"I might," Kathy said defensively. "Anissa and I have to discuss the pros and cons. Now, if you've got all you need, I'd like to take Anissa next door and buy her a drink. She's had a terrible day."

"Go ahead. But how can I get in contact with you?"

"I'll give you my cell phone number. I have to go back to Batavia tomorrow, but you can call me anytime. I always have it with me."

He wrote down the number. "And you?" Osborn asked Anissa.

"I'm staying at my Daddy's house up on Resort Road

for the foreseeable future." She gave him that telephone number, too.

"Come on, Anissa. Let's go next door."

Anissa pulled herself up, and Kathy threw an arm around her shoulder, leading her across the yard toward the bar.

Happy hour had already begun, as evidenced by the three leather-clad bikers sitting on the deck smoking cigarettes while they sipped their beers. They eyed the women as they trudged up the wooden steps, but said nothing.

Inside the bar was cool, and the music wasn't as loud as it had been the previous night. Paul wasn't behind the bar, but Noreen stood at one end talking to a guy in leathers and a blue bandana. Noreen raised a finger to let them know she'd be with them in a moment, and Kathy and Anissa took seats at the bar. The guy with the crew-cut Kathy had seen the night before was again nursing a beer at a nearby table, looking out over the bay. Outside of fishing, there didn't seem to be a lot for visitors to do. That would have to change if Kathy was to be successful at running a bed and breakfast. She'd do some research to see what else was available to do in the area and make sure her customers knew about it.

"You don't have to buy me a drink. I can pay for my own," Anissa said.

"No, I insist," Kathy said. "After all, I caused you an awful lot of heartache by finding that wallet."

"Not if it helps that cop find who killed my daddy."

Kathy doubted that. But it was puzzling. The house had been locked. Did that mean whoever got inside to dump the wallet in a mountain of trash—with the expectation that it would never be found—have the legal right to be there? Then again, what if the killer had been a former tenant with a key and hadn't needed to get into the lock box to gain entry?

She didn't voice the thought.

Anissa was still wiping her teary eyes when Noreen approached. "Hi, Kathy. What can I get you and your friend?"

"I'll have a gin and tonic—and make it a double." She looked at Anissa.

"I'll have the same, thanks."

"Coming right up."

They watched in silence as Noreen made their drinks, placed thin paper napkins on the bar, and set the glasses on them. "I haven't seen you here before," Noreen said to Anissa. She'd hinted the night before that African-Americans weren't her usual clientele.

"It was Anissa's father who was found across the street at Cannon's the other day," Kathy explained.

"Oh, I'm so sorry," Noreen said with genuine sympathy. "I considered your father a friend."

"Thank you."

"We were just next door. I found Mr. Jackson's wallet inside. It had been discarded there."

"What in the world were you doing in that wreck of a house?" Noreen asked.

"She's thinking of buying it," Anissa answered.

"Oh, honey, no," Noreen said.

"It's something to consider," Kathy said and picked up her glass, taking a sip. Mmm. That was one fine G and T.

The door opened and Tori walked in. She was still dressed in her paint-splattered jeans and sweatshirt. "So here's where I find you two. I saw a couple of cop cars roll up next door and went over to investigate. After he grilled me, Detective Osborn said you were over here." She looked at their drinks. "Don't I get one, too?"

"And another," Kathy said, raising her hand in the air.

Noreen smiled and grabbed another glass. Tori sat

down beside Anissa. "Detective Osborn told me about your father's wallet. I hope this means they'll soon figure out what happened."

"Yeah, me, too," Anissa said and sipped her drink.

Kathy decided to lighten the mood. "Tor, you'll be happy to know that Noreen doesn't think it's a good idea for me to buy the house next door, either."

"I didn't say that," Noreen said, setting Tori's drink down. "Well, not exactly. I would love to have decent neighbors; people who didn't throw rocks at the bar, trying to smash the windows; who didn't dump their trash out the kitchen window and hope the wind will somehow get rid of it. People who didn't use our hose to fill their toilet tanks when the town shuts off their water for nonpayment. I'd love it if someone actually fixed the place up. We've put a lot of money into upgrading the bar. It would be nice if the eyesore next door was either fixed up or razed."

"Anissa is a general contractor," Kathy said.

"Oh, yeah?" Noreen asked, raising an eyebrow.

"Not exactly," Anissa said. "But I'm no slouch when it comes to home renovation."

"If you're even half as good as your father, you'd be a tremendous asset. We could certainly use more contractors around here. We used Ed Vines and had to wait months for him to fit us into his schedule for our new deck. Do you have a portfolio of work online?" Noreen asked.

"I'm in the process of putting one together," Anissa said, which was probably stretching the truth more than a little, but Kathy was willing to cut her some slack.

They sipped their drinks.

Noreen pointed to the paint splatters on Tori's shirt. "I saw you two working on the bait shop earlier today. Great color."

"We're hoping it makes the shop stand out from the

water," Kathy said.

"I'm sure it will."

"It seems to be working. Gramps had seven customers so far, today. That's four more than yesterday," Tori said optimistically, "and the day isn't over yet."

Better, but still not nearly enough to make the shop successful. They'd have to work harder on curb appeal. The competition at the other side of the bridge got all the business from fishermen coming east. They had to make sure that Cannon's would get all the business from anglers heading west.

"Hey, Noreen. Can I have another beer?" the biker guy called from the other end of the bar.

"Duty calls," she said, and left them.

Anissa drained her glass. "I think I'm going to go home before I'm tempted to order another drink. And another. And another. Thanks." She got up from the stool.

"We'll either be down to your place later tonight or first thing in the morning to cut the grass."

Anissa shook her head. "You don't have to."

"A bargain's a bargain," Kathy said. She got up and gave Anissa a quick hug. Tori did likewise. "See you later."

Anissa nodded. "Thanks."

They watched as she left the bar before they both turned back to their drinks. "I feel so sorry for her," Tori said.

"Me, too." They stared at their drinks. "Did you get much painting done on the shop?" Kathy asked.

"The second coat went a lot faster than the first. I've only got the bay side to finish and it's done. That means I can get back to tackling the house tomorrow—maybe get some stuff set up for a yard sale on the weekend. It's too late to put an ad in the weekly rag, but if I can get a few signs up along the road and list it on Craigslist, we might get a few people to stop by."

"Then let's cut Anissa's grass tonight. I can finish

painting the sign in the morning before I leave."

Tori's face fell. "I'd put it out of my mind that you were only here until tomorrow. I'm gonna miss you."

"I can come out next week on my days off and we can do more work around the place."

"I wish I could afford to hire Anissa to help," Tori said wistfully.

"Maybe you can barter for her skills. She's going to need her grass cut again next week."

"Doing that one job isn't equal to the work it would take to whip the compound into shape."

"What's your next project?" Kathy asked.

"After clearing the house? Painting it, and then maybe the boathouse—but not the same color as the shop."

"Of course not, you want them to stand out in contrast to the shop. White is probably best for both."

"That's what I was thinking."

"I'd like to take a look at the boathouse," Kathy said. "I saw a wonderful renovation on HGTV and they were able to rent it for top buck."

"Really?" Tori said.

Kathy nodded. "You need to think about doing anything that will bring revenue to your Cannon brand."

"Brand," Tori repeated and laughed. "You make us sound like Nabisco."

"It's a powerful brand. There's no reason you can't have one in this area, either. Why not rent to high- *and* lower-end customers?"

Tori frowned. "I never gave it a thought."

"Well, you should."

They finished their drinks in companionable silence before Kathy called Noreen back and settled her tab.

"Will we see you again later this evening?" she asked.

"Maybe. Maybe not. But I'll be back to stay for a few days—and probably next week, so maybe you could save me a room," Kathy said as she and Tori rose from their seats.

"Sure thing," Noreen said, and waved goodbye as they headed out the door.

"I've been thinking," Tori began as they looked both ways before crossing the road. "That house across the road was locked when we got there. Anissa and I walked the whole perimeter. No windows were broken. Whoever got in there to hide the wallet had to have had a key."

"That occurred to me, too," Kathy said. "But who says the wallet hadn't been there for months? Despite what Anissa said, the cops can't just assume it was Mr. Jackson's current wallet."

They crossed the lawn heading for the house. "It didn't seem like the police had made any headway in solving the case," Kathy said.

"So I noticed."

They stopped in front of the sign Kathy had already finished painting. It pleased her. "You should keep your eyes and ears open."

Tori turned to face her. "What are you saying? That I should snoop around and try to find out who killed Michael Jackson?"

"Not at all. But, presumably, his friends and neighbors also patronize the bait shop. Everybody likes to talk about scandals. Maybe they'll say something to your Gramps that they wouldn't say to the police."

"Good point. Okay, I'll keep my eyes and ears open. But, in the meantime, I feel so bad for Anissa. She'll never feel better about her father's death, but she'll at least get some kind of closure when the police solve this."

"I feel crummy about leaving you guys tomorrow," Kathy said.

"Hey, at least one of us is gainfully employed. I've got a lot to think about during the next couple of weeks. I may bend your ear so much that it'll hurt."

"I'm here for you," Kathy said sincerely.

Herb rounded the corner of the bait shop, looking ornery. "Are we ever going to have supper?"

"Looks like it's gonna be breakfast, instead," Tori called. "I'll get some waffles going and call you when they're ready."

He nodded and headed back for the shop.

"Waffles?" Kathy asked.

"Nobody's shopped since before Grandma died. The truth is, I think they'd been living on scrambled eggs and toast for quite a while. That's all Gramps knows how to cook. I'll have to start introducing some healthy food back into his diet."

Kathy grinned. "Better you than me."

"Tell me about it."

"Oh, damn," Kathy said, looking down at her dress. "I forgot to stop back at my room to change clothes. We have a lot to do this evening."

"Change and come back for waffles. I think there's some bacon in the freezer, too."

"I never say no to bacon. I'll be back in a jiffy to help."

Tori went to the house and Kathy started back across the grass for the highway and her room at The Bay Bar. She hadn't wanted to say anything to Tori, but she'd already decided she wanted that house. It was foolish. It would be a ton of work and cost a boatload of money, but she wanted it more than the racing bike she'd coveted as a tween.

Her family would be unhappy. Tori would be unhappy, and Kathy knew there'd be days when she'd curse the idea of even looking at the place. But at that moment all she could think about was transforming that ugly duckling of a house into a beautiful swan she'd love and treasure.

Now all she had to do was buy the place. There was a

tiny problem with that—how to pay for it. She had to keep her job until her inheritance came through and she hoped it would equal what her brother had received three years before.

She crossed the road and headed toward her tiny rental room. She'd never done anything so impulsive in her life—especially without a feasibility study, but her gut was telling her this was the right decision.

She just hoped she wouldn't regret it.

SEVEN

It had sounded like an easy plan to pop the lawnmower into Tori's hatchback and head up Resort Road to the Jackson bungalow, but it taken Tori, Kathy, and Herb to lift it in, and four bungee cords to secure it—they hoped. Tori drove like a little old lady, very slow and with her hands gripping the steering wheel for dear life, while Kathy twisted like a pretzel in her seat, keeping an eye on the mower.

At last, they pulled the car up to the edge of the lot. If there was ever a gravel driveway, it had long ago been taken over by grass and weeds. They got out of the car. "Think the two of us can get this mower out of the car?" Kathy asked.

"No. We'd better get Anissa." But they didn't have to move a foot, for Anissa was already heading across the weed patch toward them.

"Aw, you girls didn't have to come out here."

"No, but I'll bet you're glad we did," Tori said and laughed. "Can you give us a hand?"

"Sure thing."

They each grabbed a part of the mower, but it was obvious Anissa took most of the weight, and set it gently on the ground. "Who gets to run it?" she asked.

"Me," Tori said.

"We brought along some clippers, the weed whacker, and a couple of rakes. I figured you and I could hack at the landscaping while Tori cuts the grass. We'll have this place looking like a palace within the hour."

"It's going to take a new coat of paint and probably a new roof to do that, but that can happen on another day," Anissa said. She and Kathy gathered the tools while Tori started the engine. She thought Kathy's time estimate was optimistic, considering how high the weeds had grown, but the lot wasn't nearly as big as the Cannon compound. They'd be finished before dark.

Tori had to cover the same ground over and over again to chop down the sturdy weeds, but after a couple of rows the yard began to resemble a lawn instead of a meadow. She looked up as she started another row and saw a woman dressed in white slacks and an orange blouse standing in the driveway of the big house on the hill, watching them work. From that distance, Tori couldn't discern the woman's expression, but with arms crossed over her chest, her body language conveyed impatience—or perhaps it was annoyance. Lucinda Bloomfield had been angling to buy the property and obliterate the bungalow that for years had been a visual blight next to her property.

Kathy and Anissa hacked at the overgrown bushes around the front of the house and in no time had dragged the debris to a pile at the side of the road. The front of the house was in desperate need of paint, but as Anissa had said, it could wait for another day.

Tori was still attacking the grass/weeds when Kathy and Anissa grabbed the rakes and started on the rows that Tori had already finished. She continued to cut the grass and with each new row looked up at the house on the hill where the woman stood watching. Kathy and Anissa had noticed her, too.

Once the lawn was cut, Tori pushed the mower aside and started working the weed whacker. By the time she finished with that, the others had just about finished raking and were only a step or two behind her. She found a stick to clear out the matted grass that clung to the bottom of the whacker.

"What's going to happen to all the brush?" Tori asked.

"I'm gonna burn it," Anissa said. "I'll wait a few days for it to dry out, then I'll plant some grass seed where it scorches the earth."

"Are you allowed to burn brush?" Kathy asked, aghast. It certainly wasn't allowed where she lived.

"Hell, I'm gonna burn my trash, too. It's legal out here in the sticks."

"Yeah, and lots of people do it," Tori agreed. "But Gramps has a garbage pickup."

They stood back to appraise their work.

"I'm astounded," Anissa said. "What a transformation. The house almost looks like how I remember it as a kid." She turned to face her new friends. "I don't know how to thank you."

"You just did,' Tori said and laughed.

"Uh-oh," Kathy muttered. Tori and Anissa turned to follow her gaze. The woman from the house on the hill approached. A rigid smile covered her mouth, and Tori got the impression it was an expression she didn't often sport.

"Hello," the woman called.

"Hi," Tori and Kathy said in unison. Anissa said nothing, but her back had stiffened.

The woman offered her hand. "I'm Lucinda Bloomfield. Nice to meet you."

Tori made the introductions. "And this is Anissa Jackson."

Anissa still said nothing, but her expression in reaction to the woman's greeting said *'I'll bet.'*

"You ladies have been working hard. Going to put the house up for sale?" Lucinda asked hopefully.

"No," Anissa answered. She offered no other explanation, so Tori jumped in.

"Anissa and I have similar plans to do a cosmetic refresh."

"Cannon," Lucinda said thoughtfully. "You're related to the people who own the Lotus Lodge?" She said the words with a hint of disapproval. No doubt, she considered the shabby and shuttered motel to be yet another eyesore at the foot of the road that led to her elegant mansion.

"Yes."

"Will you be reopening the motel or demolishing it?" Lucinda asked. It sounded as though she'd prefer the latter.

"I'd like to reopen it," Tori bluffed. She'd actually talked herself out of the notion, but her seldom-seen ire had been tweaked.

"The brewery fishing derby is just six weeks away. Surely you can't get it ready for occupancy by then."

Tori shrugged. "I'm going to try. Anissa is a contractor. She's going to help me."

Anissa cocked her head to one side but said nothing. This time her expression said, *I am?*

"A contractor?" Lucinda repeated, as though in disbelief. She eyed Anissa critically.

"Anything a man can do, I can do better," Anissa said finally.

Lucinda took in Anissa's chiseled muscles. "I don't doubt it."

"Why did you want to know if I was going to sell my father's house?" Anissa asked, her voice sharp.

Lucinda shrugged. "It's in need of a lot of repair. I just thought..."

"Wrong," Anissa asserted. "My daddy said you badgered him to sell. Why?"

"Badgered?" Lucinda repeated. "That's an antagonistic word."

"That's what he said. Why would you want this house?" Anissa repeated.

"Not the house, the property. My grandparents bought the land where my home resides over seventy-five years ago. They weren't interested in water access. I am."

"You gonna buy a party barge or something?" Anissa asked, her words sounding like a taunt.

"I have a sailboat. It's currently berthed at Parkland Marina. I'd rather not have to travel that distance when I want to sail her."

"Gee, that's too bad," Anissa said, not sounding a bit sorry.

"Cannon's is a lot closer," Tori suggested, knowing full well that it was far too shabby, and with no amenities, for an expensive sailboat to be moored. Kathy gave her a stern glare.

"You have a beautiful home," Kathy said, sounding desperate to steer the conversation in another direction.

"Thank you. It's been featured in Architectural Digest, Home Beautiful, and Country Living magazines."

"I'm sorry I missed it," Kathy said with sincerity. It was Tori's turn to glare at her friend.

"Well, I'd better get back home. It's time to feed my dogs," Lucinda said.

"Dobermans?" Anissa asked.

"No, Yorkies." If Lucinda was offended by Anissa's suggestion, she didn't show it. She smiled, and this time it seemed a little more genuine. "Welcome to the neighborhood." She turned and started back toward her driveway.

"Thank you," Kathy called after her.

Tori and Anissa turned their gazes on Kathy. "You don't live here," Tori reminded her.

"And technically you don't, either."

"You haven't decided to buy that crappy old house,

have you?" Tori accused.

"Of course not, I mean, not just after one viewing."

"Kathy," Tori admonished.

"We'd better finish up here. We can still get a few hours of work in on your grandpa's house tonight." She looked toward the bungalow. "I'll collect the rakes."

Tori waited until she was out of earshot. "Can't you convince her that buying that house would be a huge mistake?"

Anissa shrugged. "I'm not convinced it would be. If you're gonna stay with your Gramps, why wouldn't you want your best friend nearby?"

"I would love it, but I don't want to see her go broke trying to resurrect that wreck."

"I never got a chance to check out the basement for her. I can't give her a yay or a nay until I do."

"Thank goodness for that."

"Shhh—here she comes," Anissa warned.

Kathy struggled to hold onto the rakes and the weed whacker. "Grab the loppers and we can load up the mower."

Tori did so and joined the two women by the car. Kathy looked disappointed. No doubt, Anissa had told her she couldn't comment on the house. Good.

Tori placed the loppers in the back of the car with the other tools and the three women hefted the mower into the back once more. They secured it with the bungee cords and then turned back to examine their work one last time.

"What color are you going to paint it?" Tori asked, hoping it wouldn't be the same mustard yellow."

"I don't know. Maybe hot pink. That might annoy old Lucinda," Anissa said with a smirk

"You're bad," Kathy scolded.

"Maybe—maybe not," Anissa admitted. She let out a long breath. "I can't thank you guys enough, and not just for helping me with the yard. I feel like I've made a couple of new friends today."

"One new friend," Tori said indicating Kathy, "and got reacquainted with an old one."

Anissa laughed. "Yeah."

"If you get lonely, I'm going to be staying with Gramps through at least the weekend. Then I need to go back to Rochester to start shutting down my apartment."

"So, you weren't shitting old lady Bloomfield. You really *are* going to reopen the Lotus Lodge?" Anissa asked.

Tori shrugged. "I don't know. It was terrible of me, but I just felt the urge to bug her by telling her yes."

"You bad girl, you," Anissa said and laughed.

"Yes, you're very bad," Kathy said with disapproval.

"Don't tell me you like that old bat," Anissa accused.

"I don't know her well enough to make that kind of judgment," Kathy said.

Instant shame gushed through Tori, making her blush. One of the things she admired most about her best friend was her honesty and sense of fairness. "We'd better get going," she said to hide her embarrassment.

"Yeah," Kathy agreed. She turned to Anissa. "Any chance you can come with me to look at the basement of that house tomorrow morning? That is, if I can get Jerry to come back and show it."

"Sure thing."

"Great." They exchanged phone numbers. "I won't be leaving until lunchtime, so I'll call you later tonight or tomorrow morning."

"Okay."

Kathy followed Tori and got in the car.

"See you," Tori said, and started the engine. Kathy waved as they pulled away.

They drove in silence back to the Cannon compound. Tori finally broke the quiet. "So, you're serious about that house?"

"I won't know until Anissa tells me about the basement. There could be all kinds of problems that would be deal breakers; from dry rot, to termites, to foundation issues. Seeing the condition of the rest of the house, I'm pretty sure all the mechanicals are shot and in need of replacement. It might be that the place is only fit for demolition."

"But you hope not," Tori stated.

Kathy shrugged. She opened the passenger door. "Come on. We've got a lot to accomplish tonight."

"Including your call to that real estate agent," Tori said with disapproval.

"Yeah," Kathy agreed. She got out of the car and shut the door, then headed for the house.

Tori got out of the car, but instead of following her friend, she walked up to the road and then along the shoulder until she could see the front yard of what she was already beginning to think of as Kathy's Folly. The police had departed, but there was no sign of crime tape. They must have either determined that finding the wallet was a fluke or a plant, or that there was no reason to believe it was a crime scene.

If she ended up living with Herb, and *if* Kathy bought the house across the street, life could be pretty damn nice. So why was she against the idea of Kathy buying the place?

She needed to think long and hard about that—including questioning her own motives, because just when life had handed her a giant stinking turd with the loss of Billy and her job, Kathy might be on the cusp of fulfilling a long-held dream. Was a green-eyed monster lurking deep within her?

Yeah, she had a lot to think about.

It seemed like Tori wasn't the only one who had ideas about reopening the Lotus Lodge. When she and Kathy started going through the contents of the packed guest room, they found a gross each of white towels in two sizes, matching washcloths, sixteen new bedspreads, and an assortment of Egyptian cotton linens. Most had been purchased on eBay. The fact that her grandparents had never even owned a computer made it a bit of a mystery until Tori grilled Herb.

"Your grandma's friend, Irene, has a computer. That damn woman thought it was a mistake for us to close the Lodge and she never let us forget it. Sure, but it wasn't her who was going to do all the work."

"What would it take for you to reopen?" Kathy asked.

"Hell freezing over," Herb said and laughed.

Tori didn't join in. But after seeing what her grandmother had accumulated—and it was all quality goods—she had a better understanding of what Kathy must have been feeling about that wreck of a house across the road.

Tori got little sleep that night, and it wasn't just the uncomfortable bed. Could she really reopen the Lodge and make a go of it?

Once she decided to broach the subject with her grandfather, she fell into a deep sleep. Still, she was up in time to catch Herb making breakfast for himself.

"Want some scrambled eggs?" he asked, whisking a couple he'd already cracked into a bowl. "They're my specialty."

"No, thanks, Gramps. I'll just pour myself a cup of coffee once it finishes brewing."

"Pour me one, too, will you?"

Tori set out mugs, got out the milk, and poured the coffee. She sat down at the table and waited until the toast popped up and Herb joined her before she spoke. "Gramps," she began.

Herb shoveled a forkful of eggs into his mouth. "Hmm?" he grunted.

"I was thinking...."

Herb swallowed and took a sip of his coffee. "I've been doing a lot of thinking these past few days, too. Maybe your Aunt Janet and Uncle Dave are right. Maybe it is time for me to sell the business."

"What?" Tori asked, horrified.

"I can't believe what a difference sprucing up the shop and the yard has done for business. I've had more customers in the last two days than I've had all month."

"Doesn't that prove that the business can turn around?" Tori asked.

"It sure does. I know it won't sell right away—maybe it'll take a year to find a buyer—but now's the time for me to start thinking about what I want to do for the rest of my life, and it sure as hell ain't selling bait."

Tori's cheeks felt hot, and she fought the urge to cry.

"Don't worry, girl, you can stay here until I sell the place. I'd be glad of your company until you get back on your feet."

"Thanks, Gramps," Tori found herself saying.

"And don't think I haven't noticed how hard you and your friend, Kathy, have been working on clearing out the house. It's beginning to feel more like a home than a warehouse. I never understood why your grandma needed to have so much junk piled around her."

Tori stared at the Lotus Lodge mug in her hand.

"That Dumpster is already half full. By the time you clear out the Lodge it'll be full, eh?" Herb asked.

"Yeah," Tori said quietly.

Herb finished his eggs and sipped his coffee before speaking once more. "Your friend did a nice job repainting the sign for the Lodge, but I wish she hadn't."

Tori said nothing.

"I asked her if she'd do the sign over the shop before she goes. That ought to bring in even more customers, eh?"

"Yeah."

He frowned. "Is that all you can say, girl?"

Tori shrugged.

Daisy wandered into the kitchen. She stopped in front of Tori, then jumped onto her lap. She stood there, rubbed her head against Tori's chin and purred loudly. Tori wrapped her arms around the cat and kissed the top of her head, grateful for her company at a moment when she felt bereft.

Herb got up and took his dishes to the sink. He didn't rinse them or put them in the dishwasher. "Are you going to put stuff outside the shop for sale today?"

"I can," Tori said. She set Daisy down on the floor and got up to take care of the dishes.

Her grandpa nodded and headed for the door. "I'll be in the shop."

The door closed behind him as silent tears flowed from Tori's eyes. It had been a stupid idea to even consider reopening the Lodge. If Herb left Lotus Bay, there'd be nothing left for her to do but try to find another full-time teaching job. She might have to find a roommate—not what she wanted at this stage of life but, with her finances in shambles, she wouldn't have much choice.

Tori wiped her eyes and closed the dishwasher, wondering what she should do first. She needed to wait for Kathy to show up before she could assemble the tent. One problem was a lack of stickers for marking prices on the items, and she wished she'd brought her printer with her two days before. Still, she could group items of like value on separate tables and just put a sign up with the price—if she could find some paper. She might have to take a trip into town.

Odds were she'd make enough money from the sale to pay for the Dumpster, which was rented by the week, and nothing more. She'd need to clear out the Lotus Lodge during the next five days, and without help, too.

Tori had been looking forward to finding more treasures among her grandmother's trash, but now the idea of all that work for no gain made her feel depressed. It looked like all too soon she'd be alone and destitute.

Her heart ached with sorrow—mostly for herself—and she wished for just one more loving hug from her grandmother, who'd always had the power to make her feel safe and secure. Worse was the knowledge it would never happen again.

EIGHT

Kathy had been awake long before sunup but didn't want to disturb Tori if she was sleeping in. She'd packed her bags in anticipation of leaving by noon, but by seven, she couldn't stand another minute of the bad reception on the little TV in her tiny rental room and sent Tori a text.

I've been up for hours, was the reply. *Coffee's hot. Come on over.*

Kathy locked up and was knocking on the door to the small house across the way, just a minute later. As soon as she saw her friend, she knew something was wrong. "Spill it," she said as Tori handed her a mug.

"Gramps is so happy with the work we've done and that we've added so much value to the property that he's going to put it up for sale!"

"Oh, no!"

"Oh, yes," Tori said, close to tears.

"Now don't panic. Do you think there's a chance you could talk him out of it?"

"Probably not. He figures he's got a few good years left and doesn't want to spend them tied to a dying business. And at his age, who could blame him?"

"What if you could manage it? It would be income for him," Kathy suggested.

"I'm not sure I could support both of us on it—especially during the winter, even if I do manage to get hired for substitute teaching."

"Oh, Tor, I'm so sorry." Kathy set her mug on the counter and gave her friend a hug. She pulled back. "But you're not done yet."

"How can you say that?"

"Because I'm sure that not only can you turn this place around, but you can make it profitable. *We* will figure out a way. But first, we've got to finish our curb appeal project. As soon as I finish this coffee, I'm going out there. I will paint the sign over the shop while you set up for your yard sale. You guys need money coming in."

"That's for sure."

"And I'll see what I can do to make your Gramps see things a different way."

"But don't you have to go see the house across the way this morning?"

"Yes, but not until eleven. Anissa is going to join me there, then I'll have to hop in my car and head for home. I have things I need to do before I go into work. I'll be cutting it pretty close as it is."

Tori nodded. "I can't tell you how much I appreciate all that you've done for us."

"You can thank me after we figure out how to keep the Cannon compound in the family's hands—and not be put on sale to the public."

Kathy picked up her mug and chugged the contents, then set it back on the counter. "I'm outta here." She retrieved the paint brushes still wrapped in plastic from the fridge, and headed outside.

The sky to the south was pale blue and cloudless as she walked from the house to the bait shop. The paint cans were where they'd left them the night before. The door to the bait shop was open, and Herb sat on a stool behind the counter, tying flies. "Hey, Mr. Cannon," she called brightly.

"Hi, Kathy. Come to paint the sign?"

"Yes. I thought I might add a hook on the upper right corner. Would that be all right?"

"Honey, whatever you do to spruce up that sign is fine with me."

Tori showed up carrying a stepladder. "Thought you might need this."

"Thanks." Kathy opened the ladder and the paint cans, setting them on the shelf before she climbed. She was already at work painting the white background when a tubby middle-aged man in jeans and a faded Buffalo Bills sweatshirt came up from the dock. He said nothing to her, and entered the shop.

"Hey, Herb, how's it going?"

"Pretty good."

"I'll say. The shop looks great. I see you've got a couple of pretty girls working their tails off for you."

"Watch what you say," Herb warned. "One of them's my granddaughter. What can I do for you, Larry?"

"Glad to see you're fixing up the place. When're the lights on the dock gonna be turned on again?"

"Any day now. I just need a few more customers like you to actually drop some cash so I can pay the electrician."

"I'm done fishing for the day, but I'll buy a bag of chips off of you." Kathy bent down to see the guy grab a package of barbeque potato chips. Herb rang up the sale, and Kathy went back to work, idly listening to their conversation.

"Any word on who killed Jackson?" Larry asked.

"Nope. You got any ideas?"

"Me?"

"You brought it up," Herb pointed out.

"Yeah, as a matter of fact, I do."

Kathy's ears pricked up.

"Who?"

"Don Newton."

Herb laughed. "Why Don?"

"He's your competition, isn't he? Wouldn't he like to see you go out of business and have it all for himself?"

"He's been watching my business die a slow death for years," Herb said acidly.

"Yeah, but now you're sprucing the place up."

"That started *after* Jackson was dead," Herb pointed out.

"Oh."

"Got any other bright ideas?"

"What about Biggie Taylor? Everybody knows he and Jackson didn't get along."

"Biggie don't get along with anyone," Herb said.

"I heard 'em going at it last week out on the bridge. Jackson accused Biggie of stealing his bait."

"He probably did. But how would that get Jackson killed?"

Larry said nothing.

Kathy wondered if she should wait half an hour before she started working on the sign's red lettering. Maybe they should have bought some blue paint instead; or maybe that wouldn't stand out against the shop's new coat of turquoise.

"Have you shared what you saw with the cops?" Herb asked.

"Hell, no. I don't want to get involved."

"Then maybe you shouldn't talk about it at all," Herb advised.

Kathy winced. Mr. Cannon didn't seem to have a clue about giving good customer service. Tori had said Mrs. Cannon had been the force behind the business. Could it have been Herb who'd run it into the ground?

Larry said nothing more. He nearly ran into the ladder as he exited the shop and then marched toward the few cars parked in the lot. He was one unhappy customer. Kathy made a mental note to speak to Tori about that.

Tori approached, laden with a large cardboard box. "The first of many," she said wearily. "Can you give me a hand to set up the tent?"

"Of course." Kathy stepped down from the ladder.

Herb poked his head around the door. "Tori, I'm heading into Worton to get some groceries. Can you watch the shop for a while?"

"Sure, Gramps."

"Good girl," he said and headed for his truck.

"Good girl?" Kathy asked.

"Yeah. I'm afraid Gramps still thinks of me as a ten year old."

They watched the truck pull out onto the highway. "What do you think he'll buy?" Kathy asked.

"Eggs, bread, and junk food. When I get a chance, I'll go into town and get some decent food."

Kathy retrieved the canopy and its poles and they began to set it up. During the exercise, she told Tori about Herb's conversation with Larry.

"Oh, dear," Tori said.

"Of course, maybe he had some beef against the guy. Maybe he doesn't treat all his customers that way."

"Maybe," Tori said half-heartedly. "But why would Gramps want to discourage a potential witness to keep quiet?"

"I guess I hadn't thought about it. I'm more focused on how to improve the shop's bottom line. Do you know Biggie Taylor?"

Tori shook her head. "People come and go around here. You might have a great customer who visits every week all season, and then never see them again. Sounds like this guy is well known, so I could probably find out something about him."

"Do you think we should mention it to Anissa?"

Tori shrugged. "Maybe."

Kathy unfolded the canvas cover and it took them

several minutes to attach it to the frame. Next, they entered the web-filled boathouse, where Herb had said they would find a folding table. It weighed a ton, and they struggled to haul it over to the bait shop. It was filthy, and Tori hosed it down before they set it up under the canopy.

"It should dry off fast in this stiff breeze," Kathy said. "I'll bet the sign I was working on is ready for the next paint color. I'd better get to it."

Tori nodded, and then set off for the house, no doubt to get more boxes of yard-sale treasures.

Kathy opened the can of black paint and began working on the drop shadow around the red lettering. After that, she added the hook in the corner that she'd mentioned to Herb. By the time she finished with that, Tori had covered the folding table with a white sheet and had distributed the contests of the boxes of junk from the house.

"The cable company won't come out until Monday to hook us up to the Internet. Do you think Noreen over at the bar would let me log on?" Tori asked Kathy. "I want to list our sale on Craigslist."

"Buy a drink—or a burger—and I'm sure she'd have no problem."

"Meanwhile, I'd better make some signs to put up along the road using some of the cardboard cartons we collapsed in the Lotus Lodge."

"Good idea." Kathy looked at her watch. The morning had flown by. "I'd better get cleaned up, check out of my room, and pack my car. Jerry from Lotus Realty will be by in less than half an hour."

"I'm surprised Gramps hasn't returned. Sorry, but I can't go over with you until he comes back."

"Don't worry about it. Do what you have to do here, that's your first priority. I'll either call or text you later to let you know how things went."

"Okay," Tori said. Together, they stood back to take in the sign Kathy had finished repainting. "It looks fabulous," Tori said.

Kathy grinned. "Not bad. Now to hope the customers come streaming in."

"I'll let you know—whether they do or not."

A car pulled into the parking lot. They watched as a middle-aged man and a woman got out of the car and then unloaded tackle boxes, fishing rods, and a small cooler from the trunk. They were smiling as they approached the bait shop.

"Hi. Welcome to Cannon's," Tori called.

"Can we get some night crawlers?" the man asked.

"Sure thing. Come into the shop."

"Oh, Terry, you go ahead. I want to look at all the great stuff here on this table," the woman said.

Kathy set the cans of paint under the table, noting that the woman was already setting aside some mismatched plates and glasses. At this rate, Tori might have to restock her table a couple of times during the day.

"Do I pay you?" she asked.

"Tori, in the shop, can help you. I'm just here to do some painting."

The woman nodded.

Kathy headed back to the bar and her tiny room. Once packed, she paid the bill and moved her car to the messy yard next door and waited for Jerry and Anissa to arrive. She got out and stared at the sad state of what once must have been a lovely home. "If it's at all feasible, I'm going to bring you back to life," she promised.

Anissa was the first to arrive. She parked her truck next to Kathy's car and got out. "Good morning."

"I hope it continues to be good, but that all depends on what we find in the basement."

"What's your budget?"

"I'm not sure what my inheritance will be." She told

Anissa what her brother received.

"Wow. Well, you could bank half of it and then borrow against it."

"The way interest rates are these days, I'm not sure it's worth it."

Anissa shrugged.

Jerry arrived and parked next to the truck. He cut the engine and got out. His smile seemed forced. "Good morning."

"Hi," Kathy said. Anissa merely nodded. "Thanks for coming back today. I'm sorry about what happened yester—"

But Jerry held up a hand to save off her apology. "Let's get to it."

They followed him up the stairs to the house and waited while he retrieved the key from the lock box. He ushered them in. "I have another appointment in half an hour, so I'd appreciate it if you could hurry your inspection."

"Of course," Kathy said.

Anissa had thoughtfully brought a powerful flashlight, and Kathy showed her to the door to the basement. Anissa went first, lighting the way. "That was kinda rude of that guy to ask you to hurry up," she groused.

"He probably thinks showing the house is a waste of time."

Reaching the bottom of the steps, they paused. A couple of small windows had been set into the foundation at some point in time, but the light they let in was mostly blocked by the tall grass and weeds around the outside of the house. Anissa ran the light around the rubble foundation. "Looks in pretty good shape."

Kathy was surprised to find that, unlike the upstairs, the basement hadn't been used as another dumping ground by the former tenants. It was a surprise to find that the ceiling height was almost eight feet, which was unusual for a house of this age. A rusty washer and dryer sat defiantly against the back wall next to a long, bulky sink.

Anissa walked along the length of the foundation. She ran the light up and down and then started walking toward the southern-most corner of the room. Kathy followed her to the eastern wall where Anissa touched the stone. "There's some water seepage here, but nothing too bad. Adding gutters and having them drain away from the house would probably take care of that."

A spurt of hope coursed through her, and Kathy was afraid to say anything lest she jinx herself.

They wandered around the rest of the basement and found a pile of old wood and a stack of dirt-and-cobweb covered wooden doors. "This is a find," Anissa said. "These look like the original interior doors. The ones upstairs are crap—hollow core and not up to code. This is a real bonus."

Nearby sat a hulking furnace and one large hot water heater. "Despite the size of that water heater, it's not sufficient for the three bathrooms that are already here. You'd want to add more. You're going to need a whole new HVAC system, and it probably means all new ductwork, too."

"Expensive?"

Anissa nodded.

They walked around the rest of the basement until they came back to the stairs. "Well, what do you think?"

"I think you should tell Jerry he can go, and we'll talk about this outside—and then you have to leave."

"Yeah."

They headed back up the stairs.

Jerry was back outside and on his cell phone once again. They had to wait for him to finish his call. "Sorry. I've got a couple who are moving to this area and want to see at least three houses this afternoon."

"I understand," Kathy said. "I'm going to discuss the scope of possible repairs with my contractor and then I'll get back to you—probably tomorrow."

Jerry reached into the breast pocket of his shirt, withdrawing a business card. "I'll be waiting for your call," he said. He locked up the house and they watched him climb back into his car and take off.

"I don't like that guy," Anissa said unnecessarily.

"I can't say I'm a fan either, but I'd much rather talk about the house. What do you think?"

Anissa actually smiled. "It sounds like a hell of a lot of money, but if you're willing to put a hundred grand into this place, you might just have a palace on your hands."

Kathy couldn't help herself and jumped, then sprang forward to hug Anissa.

"Hold it, hold it!" Anissa cried and pushed back. "Depending on what you want to do, you're looking at a renovation that could take up to a year to finish."

"I understand that, but I'm so relieved to hear you say you think it's a good idea."

"I didn't say that—I said it's worth doing. But I can tell by looking at you that you've already fallen hard for this place and would have bought it whether I said it was fixable or not."

Kathy bowed her head. "You're right. But I'm so relieved you don't think it's a total waste." She looked back at the house. In her mind's eye, she saw it as it could be, not as it currently was.

"Now all you have to do is hope it'll still be on the market when your inheritance comes through."

Kathy sighed, her spirits falling. "Yeah." She did have some money saved—what she'd been putting aside to one day furnish the bed and breakfast of her dreams—but it wasn't enough. Of course, she could probably put ten percent down and get a mortgage, making payments until her inheritance came through. She could come out on her days off to start cleaning up the house and the yard, and maybe even starting some of the demo.

"I think I can pull it off," she said at last. "I'm calling Jerry as soon as I get home and—"

"No," Anissa advised. "You need to think this through. You need to sit down and make a list of pros and cons about this project. First of all, you don't even know if a high-end B and B will draw customers to the area. You've got a redneck bar next-door, and a fish camp across the street. From what I can see, your water access amounts to a swamp out back, and the DEC probably wouldn't even let you put a dock out there."

Kathy frowned. She hadn't thought about that. "But I want it," she said, sounding to herself like a spoiled brat.

"This is a big decision. You don't want to be here a year from now cursing yourself for being an impulsive fool," Anissa warned.

"You're right. I wish you weren't, but you are," Kathy grudgingly admitted. "If I do decide to go ahead and do this, would you consider being my contractor?"

Anissa shook her head. "Honey, you don't even know if I'm any good."

"I trust you."

"You haven't even known me a whole day," Anissa reminded her.

"I'm a good judge of character."

Anissa frowned and shook her head. "If you buy this place, you will talk to at least one other contractor before you hire me or anybody else."

"But would you like the job?"

Anissa shrugged. "You're not going to be ready to start work for another four, five months, maybe longer. I don't know where I'll be or what I'll be doing."

Kathy nodded. The idea of working with Anissa had appealed to her. She liked the idea of women working together toward a shared goal.

Anissa glanced at her watch. "You better get going."

"What are you going to do today?"

"I thought I might visit with Tori. Lord knows I don't know anybody else around here."

"There's always Lucinda Bloomfield."

Anissa pointed a menacing finger at Kathy. "Don't go there."

Kathy smiled. "Okay, I'm leaving. Tell Tori I'll call her later."

"Will do," Anissa said.

Kathy got back in her car and started the engine. She backed into the road, pausing to wave before she headed for the bridge and the road leading home. It was then she thought about what Herb's customer had said about Biggie Taylor and Anissa's father. Should she have said something to her friend? Maybe, maybe not. When she talked to Tori later, she'd encourage her to share what they knew about the situation. If nothing else, she wanted to do something to help Anissa get over the loss of her father. Finding his killer would certainly be a giant step in that direction.

NINE

Tori rearranged the junk—or rather valuable merchandise—on the sale table, wondering when Herb would
get back from the store so she could leave the bait shop
to restock. She'd already had a couple of customers who'd
walked over the bridge to check out the refreshed bait
shop. They'd bought bait or chips. Not huge purchases,
but there was money in the till. They'd also pursued some
yard sale items and bought nearly ten bucks worth of
stuff. Again, not astounding, but it was money coming
in.

Tori looked up at the sound of tires on the gravel parking area, but instead of Herb's truck, it was Anissa's. Tori
smiled and waved. Anissa got out of the truck and walked
over to meet her.

"Well, is she going to buy the place?"

Anissa nodded. "I made her promise she would think
it over for at least a day, but Kathy's a woman with a mission; she wants that house."

Tori sighed. "I was afraid of that. Will she lose her
shirt?"

"If she can see through the whole renovation process,
then find some paying customers, she might just break
even the first couple of years."

"That's not very encouraging," Tori said sourly.

"It's realistic."

"Will you help her fix it up?"

"I don't know where I'll be by the time she closes on the house. As it's empty, it'll be faster than some, but it still takes half of forever for these things to happen. I can't sit around for months at a time on the promise of one job."

Tori nodded.

Anissa looked down at the yard sale items on display. "Hey, you've got some good stuff here."

"Just what my grandma collected over the years. She was a bit of a packrat, I'm afraid. I'm helping Gramps empty out the house."

"Yeah, that Dumpster is already looking pretty full. What did you toss?"

"Papers, plastic containers, broken appliances—junk. Thank goodness the waste company goes through everything for recycling."

Anissa picked up a vegetable peeler. "I could use one of these." She dug into her pocket and pulled out a quarter.

"Oh, you don't have to pay for that."

"Hey, the reason you're selling this stuff is because you need the money, remember?"

"A quarter isn't going to break me."

"Well, I'm not one for accepting charity, either, and I already did that by letting you guys cut my grass and shape up the yard last night."

"Kathy bartered for your services," Tori reminded her.

"Yeah, and I got the better part of the deal. What would I have been doing yesterday afternoon and this morning if I hadn't gone over to the house with her?"

Tori nodded and considered mentioning what Kathy had said about the altercation between her father and Biggie Taylor the week before. Before she could say a word, Herb's truck pulled into the drive and he parked beside the Dumpster.

"Yee-ha!" he called as he got out of the truck. He

grabbed a couple of plastic grocery bags from the back of the pickup and hurried over to join the women. "I won! I won!"

"Won what?" Anissa asked.

"Scratch off."

"How much?" Tori asked, hoping with all her heart it was enough to pay an electrician.

"Ten bucks."

"Is that all?" she nearly wailed. "How much did you spend on tickets?"

"Ten bucks."

"Then you didn't win. You broke even," Tori said with exasperation.

"It's better than nothing," he said, perturbed.

"Congratulations," Anissa said, stifling a laugh.

"At least somebody's happy," he said and glared at Tori. Then his gaze shifted to Anissa. "We're having egg salad for lunch. You want to stay?"

Anissa shook her head. "Oh, no. I just stopped by to say hi to Tori."

Herb shrugged. "If you change your mind, there'll be plenty. I always make enough for at least five sandwiches." He turned for the house.

"He's right. He doesn't know how to make a small batch of egg salad, and it's really good."

"Thanks, anyway."

"Well, would you consider another barter?"

"What do you mean?"

Tori glanced over to the tall lamppost that stood at the head of the dock. "I need an electrician. You said you could do electrical work."

"The lights?" she asked.

Tori nodded.

Anissa walked over the pole and looked up. "Burned out bulbs or do you need new wiring?"

"I don't know what it needs. It hasn't worked for a while and we've lost customers because of it."

"You got a ladder?"

"In the boathouse."

"Let's go get it."

Tori looked from the bait shop to the house. There were no customers in sight, so she went inside, hung the sign Herb used when he needed a bathroom break that said *Back in 5 minutes*, and locked the door. Anissa followed her to the boathouse.

Like the table she and Kathy had retrieved earlier, the wooden ladder was covered in decades worth of dirt and spider webs. "Ick!" Tori complained.

Anissa shrugged. "When you work in construction, you get used to stuff like this." She grabbed the ladder without help, and headed for the door. Tori doubted she could have carried it, but Anissa made the task look easy.

A minute later, Anissa had set the ladder up against the pole. "You steady it from the bottom. I don't trust this old thing."

"Of course," Tori said.

If Anissa was afraid of anything, it didn't show. She practically scampered up the ladder. She took her time examining the lamp, before she started back down the ladder. "The fixture's shot."

"What would it cost to get a new one?"

"A really good one? Six or seven hundred bucks."

"You've got to be kidding!" Tori cried. Anissa shook her head. No wonder Herb hadn't replaced the thing. "We haven't got that kind of money."

"You can get a cheapy for a couple hundred," Anissa said.

Tori let out a shaky breath. "Where?"

"Might have to go to Rochester for one. Why don't you google it?"

Tori nodded, feeling defeated. "Well, we have to have

one. I'll be going back to the city to get more of my stuff on Monday. If I can find something, I'll buy it."

"Why don't I drive you to Rochester? We'll buy a replacement lamp, and then go to your place. You can put your stuff in the back of my truck. You'd get more in it than that tiny clown car you drive."

"Clown car?"

"It is a compact," Anissa pointed out.

"It gets good mileage."

"It's a death trap," Anissa said.

Tori sighed. Maybe it was. She looked at the canopy. Maybe they'd pull in some money with the yar.d sale, but she'd have to raise her prices and list the better stuff on Craigslist. She could use her credit card to buy the light fixture and figure out how to pay Anissa for her labor— as well as pay for her gas to and from Rochester.

"Okay. We'll go Monday."

"Fine."

Tori nodded. Now she really felt she owed Anissa. "Did Kathy mention Biggie Taylor?"

Anissa laughed. "Sounds like a rapper."

"I don't know who he is, but one of Gramps' customers said this guy Biggie Taylor and your father had an argument last weekend over on the bridge. Something about Biggie stealing your father's bait."

Anissa's eyes narrowed. "No, she didn't say anything."

Tori let out a breath. "Kathy overheard the customer talking." She was about to say with Gramps, but thought better of it, especially as he'd warned the guy not to say anything.

"Does your grandfather know this guy?"

"I don't think so. But our competition across the bridge might. When Gramps comes back out, why don't we take a walk over there? That way I can scope the place out, too."

Anissa nodded, her expression somber. "All right."

Tori dug into her pants pocket for the keys to the bait shop and unlocked the door. She took down the sign and came back outside just as a small fishing boat with a man and a woman onboard tied up to the dock.

"Looks like you might have some customers," Anissa said.

"Hey, guys. Can I help you?" Tori called.

"Need to buy some spikes. You got any?" the guy asked, his gaze straying to Anissa.

"Sure. Come on into the shop."

The man followed her into the shop, while the woman perused the yard sale items.

"Heard there was a murder here earlier this week," the man said eagerly.

Tori frowned. "I'm afraid so. The police have asked us not to talk about it," she fibbed. She had no desire to feed his curiosity.

"It was that black guy, Jackson, wasn't it?"

Anissa suddenly appeared in the doorway, alerted by the man using her surname.

Tori nodded, and rang up the sale, but the man didn't seem in a hurry to pay.

"I guess I've known the old guy about ten years."

"Is that so?" Tori said neutrally.

"Poor guy was crazy."

"Oh?"

He nodded, leaning against the counter, like he was getting ready to launch into a long story. "Everybody on the bay has been talking about it."

"To the police?" Tori asked.

"Are you kidding? I told you the guy was crazy, and we'd be crazy to talk to the cops."

"Why was he crazy?" Tori asked.

"He kept on and on about lights on the bay at night. Of course there are lights on the bay. It's the law. Your boat has to have lights on it for safety, but he kept insisting it was something different, but he couldn't say what."

"You really should tell the police. I'd be glad to give you the lead detective's name."

The man shook his head, finally fishing for his wallet. "Nah, I don't want to get involved."

"If nobody gets involved, they'll never find out who killed Mr. Jackson. That person might kill again."

"I'm not worried. I live over in Salmon Creek."

"How do you know the killer lives around here?" Anissa asked.

The guy's head turned so fast he was in danger of whiplash. He eyed Anissa, his bravado dissipating He shrugged, then turned back and handed Tori a ten. She made change.

"Honey," the woman called from outside. "Come look at this."

The man picked up his foam container of bait and sidled past Anissa. She stepped inside. "Lights on the bay at night?" she repeated.

"He's right. A boat is supposed to have a green light in the bow and a red one in the stern."

"You sound like a regular sailor," she commented.

"I took a boating safety course when I was ten and passed with flying colors," Tori bragged.

Anissa merely scowled.

"Hello!" the woman outside called. "I'd like to buy some of your stuff."

Tori walked around the counter and went outside to take care of her new customer.

The woman ended up dropping almost eighteen dollars, buying salt shakers, mixing bowls, a kitchen scale, crocheted potholders, an assortment of cooking utensils, and a number of mismatched bowls and plates. Tori was only too happy to pack the stuff into boxes and carry it to the boat where the woman's impatient husband waited. As they were casting off—and starting what sounded like it might be a good argument—Tori rejoined Anissa.

"Now we have two unsubstantiated facts to check concerning my daddy's death," Anissa said.

"We?" Tori asked.

"Well, you did say you'd walk over the bridge with me."

"I did. But I think we should also call Detective Osborn."

Anissa glowered. "I don't think that man gives a rat's ass about finding my daddy's killer."

"It's only been a couple of days," Tori said reasonably.

"You might not be so patient if it was somebody you loved who'd been found dead," Anissa said coldly.

Shame rushed through her, and Tori frowned. "I'm sorry, Anissa. I did lose someone this week, it wasn't quite as sudden as your loss, but I have an inkling of what you're going through. Maybe we can help each other get through our grief."

Anissa nodded and sighed. "I've got a couple of bottles of wine back at my place. If you've got nothing better to do tonight, why don't you come by and we'll commiserate."

"Sounds great."

They heard the screen door to the house slam, and Herb came back out. He held half a sandwich in one hand and a coffee mug in the other. He joined them in front of the sale table. "Hey, looks like you sold a lot of stuff."

"Yeah, and we're going to need to sell a whole lot more to pay for a new light fixture for the dock," Tori said. "Anissa had a look. We're going to pick one up on Monday when we go into Rochester to get more of my stuff."

"I'm glad your grandma's junk can help pay for it.

Goodness knows it wasn't doing us any good." He took a big bite of his sandwich, chewed, and swallowed. "I made a bunch of sandwiches and left them in the fridge for you girls."

Anissa frowned at the word 'girls.'

"Thanks, Gramps. We'll have them in a while. We're going to put the ladder away and then take a walk across the bridge to check out the competition," Tori said.

Herb raised an eyebrow, stared at her for a moment, then shook his head. "Don't let Don tell you any fish tales about me," he warned.

"I hadn't planned on bringing up your name," Tori said. "We'll be back in a while."

Herb polished off the last bite of his sandwich and entered the bait shop.

Tori helped Anissa carry the ladder back to the boathouse, then they crossed the parking area and headed for the road. "Remember when we used to go fishing on the bridge when we were kids?"

Anissa managed a smile. "As I recall, I was afraid of worms, and you had to bait my hook."

"And now you're braver than me by doing scary things like climbing ladders and doing electrical work."

"Working construction, I've dealt with all kinds of nasty stuff. Petrified mice and rats; active wasp nests when ripping out drywall; black mold, termites, cockroaches. You name it, I've had to deal with it. But I still wouldn't want to pick up a worm."

Tori laughed.

They paused at the center of the bridge, where it had been bumped out to accommodate people fishing so that they wouldn't block the wooden deck that acted as a sidewalk. In the water were the dinner-plate sized lotus leaves. Any time now, the water would be filled with the delicate white flowers. Some people who'd bought bait didn't heed the no-littering signs and foam containers floated among the leaves as well. *Slobs*, Tori thought.

They rested their arms on the railing and looked out over the bay. "I love it here," Tori said. "I want to live here forever."

Anissa laughed. "Now you sound like Kathy."

"Yeah, but she's loved it here for two days. I've loved it here all my life. How about you?"

Anissa's gaze was focused on the water below them. "I guess I love it here, too. I was happy when I lived here. I can't say I've felt that way for most of the rest of my life."

"My Gramps wants to sell the place. He says I can stay here until he sells it, but I guess I'll eventually have to go back to Rochester. But not until I find another job and put some money in the bank. My boyfriend left and I just can't hack the rent in my place by myself right now."

"I'll bet it'll be hard to sell a bait-and-tackle shop. Your grandpa's place could be on the market for years," Anissa said. "That would give you some time to regroup."

Tori managed a wry laugh. "I can but hope." She pushed away from the railing and they began walking once again.

Like Cannon's Bait & Tackle, the Bayside Live Bait & Marina was a squat building, but its façade was clad in vertical wood siding that was painted a drab brown. A hulking ice machine sat outside, filled with cubes and blocks, and signs tacked on the front of the building promised bait, boats for rent, dock space, accommodations, a gas pump, and a launch, where boats came and went all day.

"You don't have a launch, do you?" Anissa asked.

"No, Gramps never had the money to invest in one. Everybody has to use this one—or the ones up at the point—to get their boats in the water, which is too bad. A lot of guys with boats don't want to pay for a slip. They might only launch their boats a couple of times a year. This guy makes money every time they use his launch.

Sometimes there're as many as twenty pickups and trailers lining the hill. My Gramps doesn't charge as much as he does for a slip. I'll bet he hasn't changed his prices in years."

"Then shouldn't all his slips be spoken for?" Anissa asked.

"You'd think." Tori took a deep breath to gather her courage and entered the bait shop. It was well lit with walls painted a light yellow. The entire back wall was filled with fishing lures and other tackle—far more than Cannon's had to offer. Two older good old boys dressed in jeans, flannel shirts, and orange life vests stood at the counter. Was the man behind it the owner or an employee? Of course, their conversation had stopped in mid-sentence when the women arrived.

"Can I help you girls?" the counterman said.

"Why do men insist on calling me a *girl*? I haven't been a girl in almost twenty years," Anissa bristled.

The guy ignored her mild rebuke, turning his gaze to Tori.

"We were wondering if you'd seen Biggie Taylor around?" she asked.

The counterman frowned. "Now what would a couple of nice girls like you want with a thug like that?"

"Don't let Biggie hear you call him that," said one of the customers. "He'll cold cock you."

The counterman shrugged. "Not if he ever wants to rent a boat off me again."

"He's a thug?" Anissa asked. "Does he go around threatening people? Maybe steal their bait? Maybe *kills* them."

"Whoa—whoa!" said the same customer, "I'm getting out of here."

"I'll join you," said his friend, and the two of them hurried out the door.

"Tell me more about this thug," Anissa insisted.

"Why do you want to know?" The counterman asked.

"Because word is he wasn't very nice to my daddy last week. Now my daddy's dead."

"I'm real sorry about that, ma'am. Jackson was a good customer of mine."

Tori frowned. She'd thought he'd been Gramps's good customer.

"What can you tell me about Mr. Taylor?" Anissa asked.

Counterman shrugged. "He comes to fish on the bridge just about every Saturday during the summer. Sometimes he rents a boat, but only when he's flush—which isn't often."

"I'm sorry; what's your name?" Tori asked.

"Don Newton. And you are?"

"Tori," she said succinctly, unwilling to give her surname. So, he was Bayside's owner. "We heard that last weekend Mr. Taylor stole Mr. Johnson's bait, or at least that they had words about it."

"I wouldn't be surprised. As I said, he's little more than a thug. Not at all like the rest of my customers," he hurriedly explained.

"Do you think he could have killed my daddy?" Anissa asked.

Newton shrugged. "I don't know. There's a big difference between being a bully and being a killer. I admit I don't like Biggie, but he's always paid his way with me."

"So, you're not afraid of this guy—like your customers are."

"I've got a semi-automatic sitting under the counter. Anybody messes with me and I'll have no problem exercising my second amendment rights." His expression was as hard as his voice.

"What do you know about Lucinda Bloomfield?" Anissa asked.

"That bitch? She'd like to see all of us around here go

out of business. She doesn't like trade." He said the word as though it was offensive.

"Why do you say that?" Tori asked.

"She's as hard-assed as her old man ever was."

"And just what has she done to give her this reputation?"

"It's her attitude."

"Have you ever spoken with her?" Tori pressed.

"No. She wouldn't lower herself to speak to the likes of me—or you."

"Why wouldn't she talk to me?"

"You are Herb Cannon's granddaughter."

Word did indeed get around.

"As a matter of fact, I have spoken to her. She didn't seem that bad to me."

"Watch out for her property manager."

"She has a property manager?" Anissa asked.

"She owns more than just the big house on the hill, you know."

They didn't.

"In the city, the Bloomfields would be called slum lords. Here they're just redneck landlords. Lucinda's property manager, Avery Simon, is just as mean a bully as Biggie Taylor when it comes to collecting Lucinda's rents. Don't pay and she starts eviction, then goes to court to make sure she's paid what's owed her."

"Surely she doesn't go to court herself."

"She keeps an attorney on retainer. He more than earns his keep," Dan said.

A car pulled up outside, and a man and woman got out. He opened the back door and pulled out a couple of fishing rods, then they headed for the door to the shop.

"Thanks for talking to us," Tori said, and she and Anissa started for the door.

"How can I help you folks?" Don asked the customers.

Tori walked over to the boat concrete boat launch

that sloped into the water. "Man, if we had one of these, we'd make out like a bandit. What do you think it would cost to pour all that cement?"

"A lot more than a new light for your dock, that's for sure," Anissa said. "Hey, it sounded to me like you were actually defending Lucinda Bloomfield to that guy. Why?"

Tori shrugged. "I get annoyed when people badmouth women for no reason. She's not my enemy."

"No, but you weren't above having a little fun with her last night."

Tori nodded and felt ashamed. Still, what was Lucinda's beef against trade when she apparently was a hardened businesswoman herself?

"Come on. Let's go get a few of those egg salad sandwiches. I'm starved."

They walked back across the bridge in silence. Tori wondered if Anissa was thinking about Avery Simon, wondering if he was bully enough to strangle someone who annoyed his employer one time too many. But what about the spikes that had filled Jackson's mouth? That seemed like a punishment—or maybe a warning to others: *don't talk, or this could happen to you, too.*

What was it that someone didn't want Jackson to talk about?

TEN

Kathy was late for work. She'd hit some construction on Route 19 that had traffic backed up a good five miles. She'd intended to go home before heading to the hotel, but nixed that idea when the dashboard clock gave her the bad news.

"Don't look now, but we're in trouble," said Dana, her evening desk clerk.

"Why?"

"We're over capacity."

"How the heck did that happen?"

"That tour bus that came in at three. They booked fifteen rooms, but needed nineteen. And we had an influx of gamblers come in. The day shift gave away our remaining four rooms."

"Oh, no," Kathy groaned. It was up to her to find rooms at their competition to accommodate the overflow. Guests usually were not happy to find that once they arrived at their destination that they would have to get back in the car and go to another hotel—and sometimes another exit down the New York State Thruway.

"Besides that," Dana said, as though relishing the delivery of bad news. "The pool pump died this morning, too."

Kathy groaned. "What else can go wrong?"

"Bonita quit this morning, so they're still working on getting the rooms up on the third floor ready for guests."

"But it's already almost four thirty."

"I know it," Dana said.

"Worst of all, Anderson, from headquarters, is in the office waiting for you."

"He's already here?" Kathy asked with dread.

Dana nodded. "He's been here since three."

"Oh, crap. Did you at least give him a cup of coffee or something? What's he been doing all this time?"

"Checking the computer and digging through our paper files."

The daytime manager wasn't all that efficient when it came to filing, and Kathy had devised a new system. Anderson was known for leaving the place a wreck after one of his inspection tours.

"Well, I guess I'd better go face him."

"Better you than me," Dana said smirking.

Rodney Anderson was a formidable man. In his early fifties, he defied the limitations of that age by being fit, good looking, with a full head of salt-and-pepper hair and the reputation of being a hard-nosed bastard. They hadn't clashed during their first meeting some two months before, but they hadn't exactly gotten along well, either. Anderson seemed to find fault with just about everything at this particular hotel, even though it had one of the best reputations in the area. He was determined standards should be higher, no matter what mechanicals failed and the employee situation was on any given day.

The door to her office was ajar, but Kathy knocked just the same.

"Come in."

Kathy poked her head inside. "Hey, Rod. What are you doing here today? Did we have an appointment?"

"Obviously not, otherwise I might have found you at your post. You are getting paid to be here for an eight-hour shift."

Oh, dear. It was going to be one of *those* kinds of conversations.

"I was out of town for a couple of days, and the traffic on Route 19 was—"

"Yeah; handy excuse." He gestured for her to sit in her own guest chair. She sat. He tapped at a piece of paper on the desk before him. "You were a day late filing the M-36 report last month."

Oh, crap, which report was that? She had to file about forty of them a month.

"I'm sorry. It won't happen again."

"It better not."

"The rooms on the third floor still haven't been serviced."

"Yes, Dana at the desk said one of our maids quit this morning."

"Why didn't you go up and help them?"

"It isn't exactly in my job description," she began.

"A manager can and should be able and willing to do any job that needs to be done," he said tersely, his brown eyes cold and narrowed.

"Except that she quit on Martin's watch, not mine. I've only been here for about five minutes, and—"

"I don't want to hear excuses."

Kathy frowned. "Rod, is something wrong?"

"Wrong? What could possibly be wrong?"

"Nothing. I thought perhaps—"

"You're paid for *work*, not opinions."

Kathy took a breath, fuming in silence.

Anderson got up from the desk, towering over her. "I've walked through every inch of this hotel during the past hour and I've got a list as long as my arm of what could be done better, what could be cleaner, and what could lose you your job."

"Excuse me," Kathy said, "But I wasn't scheduled to work for the past two days. I don't see how everything could have fallen apart in so short a time. What did Martin have to say?"

"He's on report, and so are you!"

"For what?"

"A burned out light bulb on the third floor hallway. Scuff marks on the floor of the elevator. Vending machines with empty slots."

"Oh, come on, Rod. You know that we don't service those machines."

"Then you should be hounding the vendor to keep them full. Our patrons expect it."

Less than a block away was a strip mall with a grocery store, a big box store, and a pharmacy that sold everything under the sun, including junk food, pop, and candy. Since the items he described could be found there for much less, it was rare that the vending machines on site went empty of anything.

Kathy's mind was awhirl. "Just what does being on report mean?"

"If you incur any more infractions, you'll be up for disciplinary action."

"For a burned out light bulb and some scuffs on the elevator floor?"

"We may not be the highest-end hotel in the area, but we strive to give our customers the best experience they can possibly have. And we expect all our employees to give one-hundred-and-ten percent effort. You're lacking."

"I don't think so."

"I beg your pardon?" Anderson practically bellowed.

"I said, I don't think so. I've worked my tail off since I came onboard three months ago. Since then, our customer satisfaction surveys have shown a ten-percent improvement."

"Not good enough."

"They mentioned customer service above and beyond expectations, and cleanliness as being exceptional."

"We can do much better than that—*if* you're willing

to show some initiative and work your employees harder."

"I haven't seen anyone shirk their duties."

"Except for yourself—how often do you arrive late for your shift?"

"Virtually never," she said, her simmering anger rising to a near boil.

"That's what you say."

"Why don't you ask my employees?"

"Whose employees?" Anderson demanded. They glared at one another for long moments before Anderson spoke again. "Now, get up to the third floor and get those rooms cleaned. The clerk said we were overbooked and we need to be ready for the patrons."

"Who's going to call to find rooms for those we can't accommodate?"

"You can do that after you've cleaned a few toilets."

Kathy stood. "No."

"I gave you an order."

"And I'm telling you no. And if you can't accept that, then you're free to go clean those toilets yourself, because I'm out of here."

"You can't quit."

"Watch me," she said.

She strode over to the desk, pulled out a few personal items she'd accumulated during the past few months, shoved them into an empty paper box and headed for the door.

"Don't expect a reference," Anderson called after her.

Kathy didn't look back.

"Kathy—hey, Kath, where are you going?" a panicked Dana called after her, but Kathy strode through the hotel's front entrance and headed straight for her car. She unlocked the back, shoved the box inside, slammed the hatchback and got in the car. She pulled out her cell phone and punched in the number on the card sitting on the beverage restraint device next to her right knee. The phone rang four times before an answering machine kicked in. She waited for the beep.

"Jerry? This is Kathy Grant. I want to put in a full-price offer for the house near the Lotus Bay bridge. And I want the earliest closing date you can arrange. Please call me back any time tonight or tomorrow morning. Thanks."

She left her number.

She'd probably just made two very stupid decisions, one she might regret within the hour, and yet ... she couldn't stop grinning.

"My daddy didn't love me enough," Anissa said, topping off her glass once more. Her words were beginning to slur and Tori wondered if a guest could cut off a host when inebriation threatened.

Tori reached for another fig bar. Boy, they sure tasted good with a glass of wine. She sat back on the couch in the bungalow's cozy living room. "Why do you say that?"

"Because he didn't fight for me. He let my mama take me and James away and he never came after us."

"But surely you saw him over the years."

"Not very often. He didn't even send us Christmas cards."

"But you said you talked to him a lot lately."

"Yeah, but that's only because I called him." Anissa leaned back in the creased leather recliner in the bungalow's tiny living room and wiped at her teary eyes. "And now it's too late for us to ever be close."

"Yeah, but didn't you say your mother kept you from seeing him?"

"Are you trying to make her the villain?" Anissa accused.

"No!" *Note to self. Never drink with Anissa again. At least not without feeding her first,* Tori thought. "What else have you got to eat around here?"

"Nothing. I haven't been to the store yet."

Neither had Tori, but now wasn't the time. Besides, she was pretty sure Tom's Market closed at eight, and it was nearly nine. Anissa hadn't waited for Tori to arrive before she'd poured herself a couple of glasses of wine. That was the danger of being alone with one's grief. Her grandfather wasn't much of a drinker, but he'd bought himself a six-pack when he'd gone to the store earlier that day, and when she left he was halfway through it.

Oh, what the hell, she thought, and topped up her own glass from the bottle on the coffee table. If she polished off the last of the wine, Anissa couldn't.

"Why don't you tell me about your daddy?"

Anissa's eyes began to leak again. "I loved him. I wanted to be just like him, that's why I took shop in high school. I had to really work at math. You know—measure twice, cut once and all that."

"What do you mean? With saws and stuff?" Tori asked.

Anissa nodded. "Daddy made most of the furniture in this place; like that coffee table. It's cherry. Look at that finish. I'm pretty good with polyurethane, but not as good as daddy was. It just takes patience, he used to tell me."

"What else did he make?"

"The dining room furniture. Did you see the spindles on those chairs?"

"I must have missed them," Tori admitted. "What was he like? Did he have any other hobbies?"

"He read a lot. He said he'd read just about everything in the Worton Library. He didn't have the money to buy many books. I gave him a subscription to *Fine Home-building* and *Handy* magazines for Christmas last year."

Tori looked across the room to a small bookshelf that

housed the collection. "He must have cooked for himself. Was he any good at it?"

"No. That was one task he never mastered. Eggs were about all he ever cooked. Everything else came out of a can."

"Sounds like my Gramps," Tori said with a laugh.

"When he was a young man, he used to write poetry. It wasn't very good. Mostly rhymey stuff." Anissa gazed at the ceiling and began to recite, "You are my little girl; my precious little pearl. You fill my heart with joy; I'm glad you're not a boy." She giggled. "That was my favorite one. He used to tell me that every night when he tucked me in."

"Did he have a poem for your brother?"

"Not that I remember. After the accident, he kept a journal. Some shrink at the hospital told him he might be able to accept his limitations better if he wrote about them."

"Did he keep it up?"

"Yeah. I asked him what I could get him for his birthday last year and he said he'd be happy with a journal from the dollar store." She shook her head. "I got him a couple of really nice leather-bound ones and he chewed me out for spending so much money."

"I'm sure he was just concerned about your spending too much of your money on him. My grandparents were the same way. It's funny, my brother and I were taught just to say thank you—no matter what we got. I guess our elders were of the 'do as I say, not as I do' point of view."

Anissa drained her glass. "Damn. Now the wine's all gone. The liquor store in Worton will be closed by now, too."

It's just as well; you've had enough, Tori thought. "So where are all these journals your daddy wrote in?"

Anissa frowned and looked around the room to the bookcase that housed the magazines. "There."

"Do you think he wrote anything recently? Maybe he wrote about his encounter with Biggie Taylor."

Anissa got up from her chair and weaved toward the bookshelf. Holding on to the shelf, she knelt down in front of it. Tori joined her as Anissa started pulling out the bound volumes and tossing them on the floor.

"Hey, stop—stop!" Tori said. She opened one at random. It was dated ten years before. "You might want to read these one day. But for now, let's just look for the latest one." She handed the book back to Anissa. Tori grabbed five or six and looked at the dates. None of them were recent. She shelved them and reached for another one. Anissa hadn't put any back on the shelves, she was too busy reading.

Tori went through all the books and—wouldn't you know it—it was the last one that had the most recent entries. Most of them appeared to be about fishing, the weather, and what book Mr. Jackson had finished and returned to the library. But most interesting was the fact that the last couple of entries had been ripped from the journal.

"Anissa, look at this." She handed Anissa the book.

"Who could have done this?"

"Your daddy's killer?"

"Or the police," she accused.

"What do you mean?"

"They were here after he died. They left the place in a terrible mess, too. I'll bet they took the pages. Why would they want to find my daddy's killer? He was just some old black man—not worth their time."

"Oh, don't say that. But I do think it's worth asking Detective Osborn about it. I mean, shouldn't they at least have given you a receipt or something?"

"I will call that man first thing in the morning. I'd do it now, but I know for sure he wouldn't answer after hours."

"You're probably right."

Anissa looked to be on the verge of tears once more. She was angry with her father for abandoning her as a child, and she was angry with him for being killed, never to give her the close relationship she had so craved. Comparing their losses didn't make Tori's easier to bear, but it did put it into better perspective. She'd known without a doubt that she was loved unconditionally by her grandmother. And even if her grandfather's mindset was still in the previous century, she had no doubt that he loved her, too.

"It's getting late," Tori said. "I'd better get going."

Anissa looked at the clock on the mantle. "What are you talking about? It's not even ten."

"But when you've been up since first light, it seems like a very long day."

Anissa shrugged. "Maybe you're right. I haven't gone to bed before midnight since I lost my job. Do you think there's anybody in this redneck county that would hire a black woman to do odd jobs, let alone act as a general contractor?"

"You won't know until you look for work."

"I don't have a computer out here. How would I find potential customers?"

"No cell phone?" Tori asked.

"It was the first thing I had to give up. Thank goodness my contract was over."

"I've got my laptop, but no Wi-Fi. Kathy said they have it over at the bar. Why don't you come down to our house tomorrow and we'll go over to the bar to see if they'll let us get online. If nothing else, you can keep me company while I deal with the yard sale customers."

"It beats sitting here all alone. You've got a deal."

"Maybe we can even go fishing for a while."

"Now you're talking," Anissa said. "Apparently, I've got a boat tied up at your dock—unless my daddy owed your grandpa a slip fee. Then I might have to sell it."

"You keep looking at worst-case scenarios. Give yourself a break," Tori admonished, sounding an awful lot like Kathy.

"Leaping to conclusions is the only exercise I get," Anissa admitted with a soggy laugh.

The two women got up from the floor and walked toward the bungalow's back door.

"Thanks for coming over tonight, Tori. I know I wasn't good company, but I promise to make it up to you next time."

"Hey, what are friends for?"

"I sure could use a friend right now."

Tory embraced her old-yet-new friend. "Me, too." She pulled back. "Good night."

Anissa walked out with her. The lights were on at the big house up the hill. Tori could see the silhouette of a woman—no doubt Lucinda Bloomfield—gazing out over her domain from a large window in the center of her home. Was she just as lonely as Tori felt at that moment? She got in her car, started the engine, and gave Anissa a wave before she drove down the long dark road toward the Cannon compound. Most of the houses were virtually invisible. Her headlights cut a swath through the darkness between the near-million-dollar homes that lined the road on either side.

What if someone wanted to buy the Cannon compound only to tear down the house, the shop, the boathouse, the docks, and the old Lotus Lodge to build yet another McMansion? The view was lovely. It might be worth it for someone to get rid of what Don Newton had hinted as ugly trade just to start fresh. That's what someone ought to do with the house Kathy considered buying.

The wine in her stomach had turned as sour as vinegar and Tori felt sick at heart. It wasn't just grief at the loss of her grandmother that tore at her soul. It was the real possibility that she would lose her connection to Lotus Bay. Despite all the setbacks in her life, the one constant was coming back to the Cannon compound and the unconditional love it represented.

Kathy was right. If her grandfather wanted to shed the responsibility, she would have to find a way to pay for and make the place her own.

Just how that feat was to be accomplished was a complete mystery to her.

ELEVEN

Salvaged cardboard from the collapsed cartons in the Lotus Lodge and paint left from refurbishing the bait shop and accompanying signs were the tools Tori had to work with late that night to make signs for the yard sale. Thankfully she was able to post the sale particulars to Craigslist via her smart phone. Now all she had to do was cross her fingers that someone (and preferably *many* someones) would see the listing and come to check out her grandmother's treasures.

After a restless night, she was up before Herb, pricing some of the things she and Kathy had found in the spare bedroom. When had her grandmother started collecting porcelain dolls? Most of them weren't worth much, but a few would need to go on eBay. There were china flowerpots, brown transferware, bone china teacups (although Kathy had had her eye on them, and Tori had decided to gift them to her for all her help), plus books, and knick-knacks, and … it was overwhelming.

Herb made an appearance, poured himself a cup of coffee, and made yet more scrambled eggs.

"Wouldn't you like something else to eat for breakfast?" Tori asked.

"No time to hard boil them, but I might do that later for lunch."

"Don't you worry about cholesterol?"

"Nope."

Tori desperately needed to make a run to the grocery store to buy some *real* food.

By the time they'd both eaten, Tori was ready to put out her signs in case any early birds wanted to check out their sale items.

She'd just come back from staking the signs on either side of the bridge and up the road to Worton when a familiar car pulled into the Cannon's gravel parking lot. With hands firmly planted on hips, she waited for the car's occupant to get out.

"Hi!" Kathy called. "I saw your yard sale sign at the other end of the bridge."

"What are you doing here?"

"I came to help."

"What about work tonight?" Tori asked.

Kathy waved a hand and pulled a face. "Not a problem anymore. I quit."

"You what?" Tori called.

"Let's talk about this later," Kathy said. "Got any coffee?"

"Just the dregs."

"I'll make a fresh pot," Kathy said, and headed for the house.

Tori followed. Sure enough, Kathy went straight for the pot, rinsed it out, and took the canister from the cupboard, obviously feeling quite at home.

"I think we should talk about your job situation now. Or should I say your *lack* of a job situation?"

"If you insist," Kathy said, looking like she wanted to roll her eyes.

"I do. We can't both be out of work."

"Who says we're out of work? We have *tons* of work to do … that is if you're going to reopen the Lotus Lodge and I'm going to open my B and B. Isn't it great? We're going to live across the road from each other—maybe for the rest of our lives."

"I don't know where I'm going to be six months from now, let alone the rest of my life."

"Well, I know where *I'm* going to be."

Tori's eyes narrowed. "Tell me you didn't."

"Didn't what?" Kathy said, turning back to check on the coffee's progress.

"Didn't buy that wreck of a house."

"I didn't. I put an offer on it. I won't know if they accepted it until I hear back from Jerry, and hopefully that will be this morning. I had hoped to hear last night, but I suppose it was short notice."

Tori practically collapsed into a chair at the table. "How could you quit your job? You've only been there three months."

"Let's just say upper management and I had a teensy disagreement over my role at the hotel. The guy wasn't very nice, and I thought to myself, 'you know, I don't have to take this kind of crap.' In four months I'll get my inheritance, and then I can make my dream a reality."

"You don't know how much you're getting."

"I have a pretty good idea."

"How are you going to live in the meantime?"

Kathy's gaze strayed to the back of the house and the nearly cleared out guest bedroom.

"Oh, Kath, you know I'd love to be roommates again, but this isn't my house. I'm only a squatter here, myself."

"Well, I've still got a month left on my lease in Batavia, anyway. But I will be looking to move here as soon as I can. I was up half of the night writing down plans for the house. I can't wait to talk to Anissa later today to get her ideas. But I figured I could at least help you out with your sale this morning and we could make other plans. And maybe I'd start making some lists for the Lotus Lodge, too."

"You and your lists," Tori said, shaking her head.

"It beats sitting around and wondering why we're not

married."

"You know perfectly well why we're not married."

"No one asked," Kathy said.

Tori scowled. "We weren't willing to just settle for anyone."

"Did Billy ever ask you?"

"No, and right about I'm really happy he didn't. I always knew he wasn't *the* one, and you knew that about Peter, too."

"I sure did. I wanted my B and B and he knew I wasn't going to wait until retirement time for it to happen. Why would anyone in their right mind want all the backbreaking work to running a B and B after they retire, when they should start to slow down and enjoy life?"

"How about this one: because they couldn't afford to do it when they were young?" Tori suggested.

"Well, I can. Or I will be able to, once my inheritance comes in."

"You've staked your whole future on that inheritance. What if—just what if—it isn't as much as your brother got?"

"Then I will have to jump off the bay bridge and drown among the lotuses." Tori wasn't amused. "I will find a way to make it work."

If anyone could do it, it was Kathy. "Besides," she added. "What if instead of me getting married, my destiny is to give other women the wedding of their dreams at my B and B?"

"You could be right," Tori conceded.

The coffeemaker started making gurgling noises, letting them know the brew cycle was over. "Now, what's on tap for today?"

"Once we finish our coffee, help me get some of those boxes out from the guest room. I assume you'd like to stay the night?"

"I sure would, since I can no longer even afford to stay

in one of those dinky rooms across the street, and it would be nice if the bed was cleared. What are you going to tell your Gramps?"

"That we have a guest. I won't mention that it could be long-term. Let's let him get used to the idea, first."

"Great. Do you have any flour? I'm feeling the urge to bake something decadent for dessert tonight."

"No. In fact, I still haven't gone shopping."

"Then I will. I haven't got much on my credit card this month—yet—and I'm just so excited I could explode with happiness."

"Yeah, well don't explode anywhere around here. It's taken days to tidy this place."

They heard a car drive onto the gravel lot outside. "Hey, this could be your first customer. You'd better get outside. I'll bring you your coffee," Kathy said.

Tori got up and went outside to greet her first customer of the day. While she did so, another car pulled up. And then another.

It looked like it might be a lucrative day after all.

The sale was sensational. Not only had people seen the signs Tori had put up, but they'd seen her ad on Craigslist, too. They came in droves, and they bought items as fast as Tori could price them. She and Kathy took turns going back into the house to bring out more and more boxes of stuff, while Herb gave a sales pitch for the empty boat slips and tried to sell bait and tackle to anybody who'd listen.

Things didn't slow down until almost noon, when Herb came back out to tell them he'd made yet another batch of his famous egg salad and had left sandwiches in the fridge wrapped in plastic for what he now called "my girls."

"We're softening him up," Kathy whispered to Tori,

who looked skeptical.

They were just heading into the house when Anissa's battered truck pulled into the lot. Kathy's phone rang at the very same time. "It's Jerry," she called excitedly, and walked across the lot to stand by the Lotus Lodge to take the call in privacy, but still managed to give a wave to Anissa in passing.

Anissa approached the sale table. "How's it going?"

"We've already made enough to buy a cheap light for the dock, and maybe even pay you to put it up," Tori said and smiled.

"That's great."

"What brings you here so early on this lovely sunny day?"

"My daddy didn't have cable. His VHS collection is kinda heavy on bad B movies, and there's nothing much to read."

"You mean you're bored?"

"You got it."

"Were you able to get hold of Detective Osborn?" Tori asked.

Anissa shook her head. "Someone took a message and said he'd get back to me on Monday. Yeah, right."

Tori didn't know how to reply to that.

"What's Kathy doing here? I thought she wasn't coming back until next week."

Tori frowned. "She quit her job last night and made an offer on that wreck of a house." She jerked her thumb over her shoulder toward the road.

"But she promised me she'd wait at least twenty-four hours before making a decision," Anissa said, sounding just a tad annoyed.

"She's talking to the real estate agent now." They turned to look. Instead of a smile, Kathy looked upset. Though she wasn't shouting, she seemed to be making an emphatic point about something.

"She sure doesn't look happy," Anissa said.

No, she didn't.

A man came up from the dock and stopped before the table, looking over the wares on offer and Tori turned her attention to him. He was interested in a new, still-in-the-box crockpot, but he didn't like the ten-dollar price tag and wanted to haggle. Tori had looked the item up online and found it was worth at least thirty bucks, and she wasn't about to budge on her ten-dollar price. He tried to distract her, he tried to cajole her, but she remained adamant and it was with reluctance that he parted with a ratty-looking ten-dollar bill from his equally ratty-looking wallet. By then Kathy had finished her call.

"I can't believe it—I can't believe it!" she nearly shouted.

"What's wrong?" Tori asked.

"The owners won't entertain my offer until after someone else looks at the house this afternoon."

"Who in their right mind would want that wreck?" Tori asked, and Kathy shot daggers at her. "I mean, who else could possibly want it *right now*? It's been sitting there empty for months."

"Jerry said he got a call yesterday evening after he talked to me from someone else who wants to look at the property, and that they may want to make an offer, too."

"That's too bad," Anissa said.

"Does this kind of thing happen a lot?" Kathy asked.

Anissa looked sheepish, but nodded anyway.

"Why ... why?" Kathy demanded.

"It happens a lot when someone shows interest in an undervalued property. But it could just be a way to start a bidding war. Someone pretends to show interest, makes an offer, and then they push the truly interested buyer into making a higher offer."

"How can you possibly think that place is undervalued?" Tori asked.

"The property is on the water," Anissa said simply.

"A mere technicality. It's a marsh out back," Kathy countered.

"Yeah, but according to the town, it's on water, and they can assign any value they want to the property, no matter what the actual condition of the house may be."

"That's so unfair!" Tori said.

"You might want to see what the value is on this place. Any improvements you make could cause your tax bill to spiral upward. Just painting the bait shop may have raised it ten grand."

Tori's mouth dropped in shock. "But, the paint cost us less than a hundred bucks."

"It's extremely difficult to argue with county tax assessors," Anissa pointed out.

Kathy looked away, her eyes filling with tears. She'd staked her future, even quit her job, at the prospect of getting the house and now....

"They could be bluffing, right?" Tori offered.

"Absolutely," Anissa said.

"And if they're not?"

She shrugged. "It's a risk you'll have to take."

The silence was terribly awkward.

"What time did the real estate agent say they were going to go look at the property?" Tori asked.

"He didn't. Just sometime late this afternoon."

Tori looked over at the boathouse. The upstairs loft was probably filled with junk, but from there they would have an eagle's view of the house across the street. She told Kathy so.

"Great idea."

"The windows are filthy, though."

"Hey, give me a bucket of water and a rag and I'm good to go," Kathy assured her.

"Let's do it," Anissa agreed.

"I need to hang around here in case any more yard

sale customers come," Tori said.

"That's okay."

"There's a ladder in the boathouse," Anissa said. "Tori and I used it yesterday. I'll go get it out while you get the water." She started off.

"Gramps has all kinds of buckets in the shop," Tori said, "but no hot water."

"Heck, if I have to, I'll dip it out of the bay," Kathy said. "Does your Gramps have a pair of binoculars? I want to see who shows up. Maybe I can gauge their interest by the make of their car."

"You hope," Tori said, without conviction. "And, yeah, I'm sure he's got binoculars. I remember using them as a kid."

They started for the bait shop and Herb gave them a bucket. He hinted very strongly that the shop windows could use a good wash, as well as those on the house, but neither Tori nor Kathy committed to cleaning them on that particular day.

As soon as the ladder was out, Anissa hung onto it while Kathy climbed and washed the first of three windows on the boathouse's upper level. She must have felt a little guilty, because she then cleaned those on the ground floor while Anissa collapsed the ladder and took it back inside. Kathy dumped the dirty water and took another bucket full of clean water into the boathouse.

A car pulled up, and Tori made another seven dollars in sales before she heard a loud crack and one of the windows in the boathouse opened. Anissa propped it open with a board and called, "It's hot in here."

A stiff breeze blew over the bay, and Tori felt anything but hot.

"There's loads of good stuff up here. You ought to come up and have a look. Maybe stuff you could sell," Anissa called.

"I'll be there in a while," Tori called. She headed into

the bait shop. Herb was between customers, tying a fly. "Gramps?" He didn't look up. "What's in the boathouse loft?"

"Just a load of junk. A lot of old duck decoys, oars, and water skis without mates."

"Do you mind if I try to sell it?"

"Not a bit. It means I'll have less to do when I get rid of this place ... although maybe I could get more by selling it 'as is.'"

"You know, Gramps, you don't have to sell at all. I'm willing to help you out. I'm willing—"

Herb finally looked up from the fly. "Honey, I've been at this far too long. It about killed your grandmother, and what do we have to show for all that work?"

"A pretty little bait shop," Tori offered.

Herb's smile was short-lived. "Only as of yesterday."

"I was thinking, once we get the new light in, we could clear out the boathouse and—"

"Don't waste your time thinking. I've made up my mind."

Tori sensed that this was not the time to continue this particular conversation. "Can I borrow your binoculars?"

"Gonna do some bird watching?"

"You might say that."

"They're in the closet off the living room."

Tori nodded, and without another word, she turned and headed for the house. A minute later, she was on her way to the boathouse but paused to try out the binoculars. She looked down at the dock, where a couple of men were sitting in the back of their Bayliner drinking beer and casting over the side. She could see a Nitro fishing boat coming out of the water at the Bayside Live Bait & Marina launch. The sound of Kathy and Anissa roaming around the boathouse loft caught her attention, reminding her of her mission.

Inside the boathouse, it was dark and dusty. She

climbed the built-in wooden ladder to the second floor. She hadn't been up there since she was a child, and it was as full of junk as she remembered, most of it dirty and broken. She maneuvered around the piles to join her friends. Kathy had just finished washing the last window on that side of the boathouse.

"Of course, I'd open the front here and put in a deck," Anissa was saying. "What a great view, and the rental potential would be enormous."

"Making plans for the future?" Tori asked sourly.

"Just wishful thinking," Anissa said. "Whoever built this place built solid. It's got great bones."

"I brought the binoculars," Tori called to Kathy.

"Thanks. "

"As we've got time to kill, I was wondering if you ladies would want to join me on the bay bridge to look for Biggie Taylor?" Anissa asked.

"I don't think you should talk to him," Tori advised.

"Why not? I only want to ask him why he was harassing my daddy."

"You heard what they said over at the Bayside shop. He's trouble," Tori said.

"I am not afraid of a bully."

"You haven't seen how big he is," Kathy pointed out.

"Yeah, and with a name like Biggie, he's got to be enormous," Tori said.

"The bigger they are, the more they splash when they're tossed off the bridge," Anissa said. Her gaze was intense. "Well, who's coming with me?"

"I'll go," Kathy volunteered. "I feel bad for not mentioning the guy to you yesterday. I'm just mad enough at whoever wants to look at my house that I may help you toss this Biggie character into the drink."

"I'd go, too, but I've got the yard sale to take care of," Tori said. "Have you got your cell phone Kathy? I want you to be able to call 911 if there's trouble."

"I've got it in my pocket," she said, patting the top of her thigh."

"When you guys get back, we can have a picnic out in front of the Lotus Lodge."

"Sounds good to me," Kathy said. "I baked last night. I've got some cutout cookies in the shape of little houses all nicely decorated in a Tupperware container out in the car."

"I'm all for cookies," Anissa said. "Come on. Let's get this over with."

Tori watched as her friends crossed the parking area and headed west along the side of the road for the bridge.

A blue minivan pulled into the parking and a woman got out, leaving her male companion behind. "Am I too late for all the goodies?" she asked.

"Still plenty of good stuff," Tori assured her, but she stepped back to let the woman examine everything on the table and what she had spread out on the tarp in the grass. Her gaze drifted to the bridge, but she couldn't see Kathy and Anissa. She just hoped they weren't walking into trouble.

Though Kathy had driven over the bridge a number of times, she'd never actually walked across it. It was low to the water, but higher than she'd thought—at least a good six feet or more. She and Anissa didn't speak as they tramped along the heavy wooden decking toward a group of three men who were fishing.

"Think these guys will know who Biggie Taylor is?" Kathy asked.

"All we gotta do is ask," Anissa said.

They walked up to the fishermen, three black men dressed in jeans and sweatshirts, their lines hanging over the side of the bridge, chairs, coolers, and a radio with hip-hop music blasting.

"Hey, guys," Anissa called. "Aren't you afraid the music is going to scare away the fish?"

"Nope," one of them said.

"Then how come we haven't caught one fish yet? We haven't even had a nibble," said his compadre.

"You guys know someone named Biggie Taylor?"

Two of the men shook their heads. The third kept his gaze on his pole."

"Sir?" Anissa prompted.

"I don't know him. I know *of* him," he said, not bothering to meet her gaze. "You want to stay away from that brother."

"Actually, I don't. I want to speak to him. He disrespected my daddy, and now daddy's dead."

The man turned to face her. "Your daddy was Michael?" Anissa nodded. "I'm real sorry, ma'am."

"Thank you. Do you know where I can find Mr. Taylor?"

The man's gaze swiveled to his left. "That be him in the green shirt down a-ways. But don't you tell him I told you so."

"Thank you. I won't."

Anissa strode purposely forward, leaving Kathy the scramble to catch up. "Thanks," she called over her shoulder. She caught up with Anissa, whose legs were easily three or four inches longer than Kathy's, giving her a much longer stride. "What are you going to say to him?"

"I have no idea."

Kathy's heart began to pound, and it wasn't just the aerobic exercise from the brisk walk. Biggie Taylor was a very big man. He was not only tall, but also built like a linebacker. Though it was quite breezy on the water, his dark skin glistened with sweat. Like the other anglers, he had his creature comforts circled around him, but no companions to talk to. He probably scared everybody away. Kathy felt a thrill of fear rush through her, but she wasn't about to abandon her new friend, either.

"Mr. Taylor?" Anissa called.

Taylor turned at the sound of her voice. His shoulders were massive. Did he press weights, too? "Who wants to know?"

"Me," Anissa said, and walked right up to him. Kathy halted a few feet away, snaking her hand into her pocket to clasp her cell phone.

"Who are you?"

"Michael Jackson was my daddy. I understand you and he had words last weekend. He was found dead on Tuesday."

"I didn't have nothing to do with that," Taylor said in adamant defense.

"You had words."

"He said I was trying to steal his bait."

"Were you?"

"Not steal; borrow. What's a couple of worms between friends?"

"Were you my daddy's friend?" she pressed.

"I'm everybody's friend," he bluffed, and turned his gaze back to his pole.

"That's not what I hear. People 'round here are scared of you."

"Aw, I never hurt no one."

"Then why do you want to be perceived as a bully? I'm sure your mama never taught you to be that way."

Taylor's head bowed. "No, ma'am."

"Do I look like a ma'am to you?" Anissa asked.

Taylor turned his massive head in her direction. "No, miss. But you sound like a ma'am."

Kathy found it hard to keep a smile from creeping onto her lips. Anissa actually had this guy cowed.

"I'm going to be living in these parts from here on out and if I hear you've been messing with anyone—especially old people—you will be one unhappy man," she promised.

Taylor's head sank lower. "Yes, miss."

"What's your name?"

He looked up at her. "Biggie; you already knew that."

"That isn't what your mama calls you."

"No, miss. She calls me DeWayne."

Anissa held out her hand. "Hello, DeWayne. I'm Anissa. I'm pleased to meet you."

He looked up and shook her hand.

"This is my friend, Kathy."

Kathy held out her hand to shake. His grasp was surprisingly gentle. "Glad to know you, DeWayne."

"Do you come here to fish every Saturday?" Anissa asked.

"Mostly," he admitted.

"Do you know if anybody else messed with my daddy?"

Taylor frowned. "I don't know for sure, but I know what your daddy said to me."

"And that was?"

"That somebody might come after him for what he saw."

"Did he say who he was afraid of, or just what it was he saw?"

"I'm not sure. He wasn't telling his story to me."

"Who was he talking to?"

"A white guy with a crew-cut. He wasn't fishing; he was just hanging 'round the bridge. It looked like he made a point to track down your daddy."

"But you didn't hear what they said?"

"No, miss."

"Why didn't you tell the police about this?"

"I ain't talking to no po-lice. They wouldn't be interested in anything I got to say—just try to pin something bad on me. That's the way the po-lice work, and you know it."

Anissa said nothing.

"Please, Mr. Taylor, tell us everything you know. Anissa can't find closure until we find out who killed her father," Kathy said.

"Would it be easier for you to talk to them if I was with you? I'd look out for you," Anissa said.

"You'd do that?"

"I'd do anything to catch the bastard who killed my daddy," Anissa said vehemently.

Taylor looked away, but finally shrugged. "Shit, I guess I could do that for you. But I don't live 'round here. I come in from Rochester. Saturdays are the only days I got to fish."

"The detective is off on weekends. But maybe he and I could come visit you at home sometime this week?"

"I guess," he said with a shrug.

"I haven't got a cell phone, but do you mind if Kathy takes your number and address down?"

"Whatever," Taylor said. He gave Kathy the information and she input it into her phone.

"I will call you after I talk to Detective Osborn. Thank you," Anissa said. She offered Taylor her hand once more. They shook on it. "We'll talk soon," she promised and then turned.

"Nice to have met you," Kathy said before she, too, turned to follow Anissa. She didn't speak until they were well out of Taylor's earshot. "Wow, you handled that well."

"I was scared half to death," Anissa admitted.

Kathy laughed. "That wasn't my impression."

"I wasn't in the drama club in high school for nothing," Anissa bragged. "I'm just glad that guy was more bluff than menace. But I don't doubt he took some of my daddy's worms. Now we just have to figure out who this guy with the crew-cut is."

"You know, I saw somebody like that in The Bay Bar the other night. He was a loner—didn't seem to fit in with the usual biker crowd."

"And you did?" Anissa asked wryly.

'Like you, I can hold my own."

Anissa smiled. "I don't doubt it. They approached the fishermen they'd spoken to earlier.

"You girls okay?" one of them asked.

"Of course," Anissa said. "Excuse us. We have a picnic to go to."

They waved good-bye.

"It's egg salad again," Kathy said with a sigh.

"But we didn't have to make it," Anissa pointed out.

"That's true. I promised Tori I'd make something decadent for dessert tonight, but now there won't be time." She slowed her pace. They were now parallel to the weather- and time-worn house. Kathy felt a pout tug at her lips. "What if I don't get this place?"

"If you don't, it wasn't meant to be. There are other houses, Kath. This is a depressed area. I'm sure there are loads of houses in need of some TLC."

"But so close to the water? Right across the street from where Tori will be living?"

"If her grandpa ups and sells, she won't be here. Will you want to live out here in the sticks on your own come winter?"

Kathy sighed. "I think so. And I'm not giving up on Tori. She's as determined as I am. If she really wants to stay here on Lotus Bay, she'll figure out a way."

Anissa nodded. "I don't doubt it. Now come on. Confronting a bully makes me hungry enough to eat my left foot."

"Well, we can't have that. Egg salad, here we come."

Thanks to a lull in yard sale customers, Tori was able to haul out a metal bistro set from the boathouse and wash it off before Kathy and Anissa returned from their trip across the bay bridge. It was drying in the sun outside the Lotus Lodge when they came back. Tori thought it looked cute and decided to leave it in front of the motel. It made the derelict building look a tiny bit more inviting. She really needed to get in those other rooms and decide what to do with the junk that had accumulated. Especially if any of it could be sold to help Gramps's bottom line.

"So, what happened?" Tori asked.

"Let's eat and then talk," Kathy suggested. She and Anissa helped Tori gather the sandwiches, glasses, and iced tea, and carry them outside to the nearly dry table. Tori used an old towel to wipe up the last of the water while Kathy retrieved the container of homemade cookies from her car. They sat down at the table.

"So, sounds like you had Biggie Taylor wrapped around your little finger," Tori said, topping up her glass.

"You should have seen Anissa in action," Kathy said, grinning.

"Big guys don't always have big balls," Anissa explained. "I had a feeling he just needed to be put in his place. He certainly won't give *this* Jackson any trouble in the future."

"But what about the guy with the crew-cut?" Tori asked.

"I've seen him in the bar twice, so I'm sure Noreen will know who he is," Kathy said.

"But will she protect one of her regulars?" Tori asked.

"That we don't know. But it sure can't hurt to ask. Besides, he didn't seem to fit in."

"Did you have any more yard sale customers while we were gone?"

Tori shook her head. "I think I'm going to close up for the day, and I don't think I'll bother to set up for tomorrow. Instead, I want to concentrate on clearing out the rest of the house and then the other three rooms in the Lotus Lodge. Monday, Anissa and I are going to Rochester to get the rest of my stuff."

"Do you think you can cram it all in her truck?"

"If we all three drove in our own vehicles, I'm sure we could move everything at once."

"What are you going to do if you don't get that house?" Anissa asked.

"I guess I'll have to find another job. Just something to hold me until I get my inheritance. But as Anissa pointed out to me, there are lots of houses in the area that might be bed and breakfast material. I might spend a week just looking at everything. Now that I've been bitten by the bug, I'm eager to start planning that part of my future. Still, I'm keeping my eye on the house across the street. But in the meantime, I'm at your service."

"I'm dying to know what's left in the Lotus Lodge," Tori said, then realized just what she'd said and how it might have affected Anissa.

She shook her head and sighed. "Don't worry; I'm not going to jump all over you for saying that. The fact is my daddy didn't die in your lodge. I don't know where he did die, but he was stuffed in that room after someone killed him. I haven't got anything better to do, so I'd be glad to help you clear the place out."

"Thanks. I'll take you up on it."

"You guys get started and I'll take the dishes inside and put them in the dishwasher," Kathy offered.

Tori pulled a set of keys from her jeans pocket. "Ready when you are," she told Anissa.

Tori chose to open unit two, believing it would be better not to push Anissa to confront the place where her father had been found. As she suspected, the room was filled with boxes, but unlike the first unit, in which the boxes were empty, these were filled with more of her grandmother's treasures. Stained embroidered doilies, vintage hand towels, mixed-and-matched bone china plates; tarnished silverware; old vinyl records from the 1950s and 60s. A huge box was filled with old oil paintings in chipped gold frames. It was like pawing through a warehouse.

"Some of this is pretty good stuff," Anissa said as they rummaged through the boxes.

"I wonder if Kathy could use some of it for her B and B."

"Give her first pick and sell the rest."

Kathy stuck her head inside the door. "Find anything good?"

"I think so. Take a look."

Kathy's eyes widened with pleasure as she rummaged through some of the boxes. "I love it."

"I thought you might say that. We're going to have to take some of this into the first unit just so we can sort it."

"I'll give you a hand," Kathy said, but I need to keep watching to see if Jerry shows up at the house."

So they began a kind of bucket brigade of boxes. When they had cleared out about ten boxes, they paused so that they could start sorting. "We'll do four piles," Tori said. "Sell, trash, donate, and Kathy's B and B."

"You can't just give me the stuff," Kathy said. "It belongs to your grandfather."

"As far as he's concerned, we can throw away everything. But don't worry, I'll take care of him. And you don't have to worry about paying us, either. I intend to work your butt off," she said and smiled.

Kathy looked over her shoulder, trying to take in her rear end. "It could stand to lose a few inches."

Soon the piles began to grow. They filled a big box with trash and Anissa hefted it out to the dumpster. The sell and donate piles were about equal, and Kathy's pile was the largest."

"I just hope I get the house so I have somewhere to use all this great stuff," she said wistfully.

Anissa came back to stand in front of the unit's open

doorway. "Hey, Kath, I think your real estate agent just pulled up at the house."

"Oh! Where did I put the binoculars?" Kathy cried, tossing a chenille bedspread into a box and hurrying outside.

"They're on the bistro table."

Kathy grabbed them and ran for the boathouse, with Tori and Anissa right behind her.

The three of them clambered up the ladder and rushed for the windows like something out of an old Keystone Cops movie. Tori and Anissa crowded around Kathy just as another car pulled into the parking lot. "Uh-oh," she murmured.

"What's wrong?" Tori asked, angling to get a better view.

Kathy shoved her head outside the window to get the best view possible. Tori moved to another one of the windows. An overgrown willow partially blocked her view of the house, but she could still see the back end of the second car parked in the yard.

"Oh, no!" Kathy wailed and seemed to tip forward. Thank goodness, Anissa was standing close by and grabbed her by the shirt before she could tumble out the window.

"Kathy!" Tori shouted.

"I'm ruined, I'm ruined!" Kathy wailed.

"You nearly got yourself killed!" Tori managed to say, her heart pounding.

"Look, look!" Kathy implored and handed Tori the binoculars.

Tori looked out the window and her stomach did another flip-flop. Standing beside Jerry, the real estate agent, was none other than Lucinda Bloomfield.

TWELVE

"What is *she* doing at *my* house?" Kathy demanded.

"It's not your house," Anissa said reasonably. Kathy turned a murderous glare on her. "Yet!" Anissa quickly amended.

"I'm sure there's a perfectly good explanation," Tori said.

"Like what?" Kathy demanded.

Tori couldn't immediately come up with an answer.

"That guy at the bait shop across the bridge said Lucinda didn't like trade, and yet she extracts rent from a lot of people. Maybe she decided to make that house one of her crappy rentals," Anissa reminded Tori.

"Do you think she knew I was planning to open a B and B?" Kathy asked.

"Jerry could have told her."

"I don't think so. Not the way he acted on Thursday. When he first showed me the house—he acted like he thought I was wasting his time. Why would he ever contact her about it?" She handed the binoculars back to Tori.

"To get a higher commission? If she owns so much property, she might well be his best customer."

"I'm going over there to find out," Kathy declared.

"Oh, no you're not," Tori said, handing the binoculars to Anissa. "Not when you're so upset. I'll go."

"Tori's right," Anissa chimed in. "She'll get to the bottom of this."

"Oh, all right," Kathy agreed.

"Will you look out for more yard sale customers?" Tori asked.

"Sure thing," Anissa agreed.

"I'm staying up here with the binoculars," Kathy said.

"I'll keep her company until someone shows up to look at your stuff," Anissa said.

Tori nodded and headed for the ladder. What on earth was she going to say to Lucinda? *You can't buy this house; Kathy wants it and she quit her job and staked her future to get it.* That wasn't liable to generate sympathy, either. And she couldn't come across as angry or even annoyed. Curiosity. Yeah, that's how she'd handle it.

Tori looked both ways before crossing the road and walked along the shoulder to the house. At the foot of the driveway, she turned. She couldn't see Kathy in the boathouse window, but she did see a flash of sunlight reflect off the binocular lenses.

Jerry and Lucinda were nowhere to be seen, but the front door to the ramshackle house was wide open. Tori climbed the steps. "Hello! Anybody here?"

"In the kitchen," Jerry called. Tori traveled down the hall, but when Jerry saw her, his smile faded. "Oh, it's you."

Lucinda stood in the center of the room, her arms pinned to her side, clutching her purse as though expecting to be mugged at any moment. Standing nearby was a tall lanky man wearing a Lotus Bay Yacht Club ball cap. Could he be Lucinda's property manager, Avery Simon? Lucinda looked in Tori's direction. "Hello."

"Hi," Tori said.

The four of them looked at each other for long awkward seconds. Tori took in the litter on the counter and floor that Lucinda had carefully avoided. Finally, Jerry spoke. "What do you want?"

"I saw your car in the driveway and decided to come over to see the house again."

"You weren't planning on making an offer, were you?" Jerry asked.

"Well, no, but—"

"Then I'd appreciate it if you'd leave. Ms. Bloomfield has an appointment. You can call my office to make one, too."

"I don't have a problem with her being here," Lucinda said.

"Thank you," Tori said politely, but her mind was racing. Now what was she supposed to say?

Jerry turned his back on Tori. "What did you have in mind for the property?" he asked Lucinda.

"I wanted to see what condition it was in." She looked at the holes in the plaster and the general destruction all around her.

"It would take a huge investment just to make it habitable," Simon said.

"It's a prime location. Since there's already commercial property next door and across the street, I'm sure there'd be no problem with the zoning board should you want to develop it commercially. It's currently zoned as residential if you'd like to go in that direction, too."

"I haven't decided," Lucinda said coolly.

"I'm surprised you'd be interested in it at all," Tori said.

"And why's that?" Lucinda asked rather bluntly.

"You've got the best house in the entire county."

"But no water access as you well know," Lucinda countered.

"It's pretty much a swamp out back. Probably protected. And you'd never get a boat in here. About all you can do is paddle a canoe under the bay bridge."

"There's a rumor that Cannon's might be for sale in the near future," Lucinda said.

Tori felt her stomach tighten. "Who says?"

Lucinda shrugged. "I hear things."

Had her Gramps already been talking to customers about it? Lucinda could buy the compound with the spare change in her purse, knock down the house, boathouse and Lotus Lodge in a day and build another mansion with more than one hundred feet of prime waterfront. But could she stand living across the street from The Bay Bar, and across the way from Bayside Live Bait & Marina and the transients that came to fish on a daily basis during three seasons of the year?

Tori decided to push her. "Like what?"

"That someone is thinking of opening an upscale bed and breakfast in this location."

Tori swallowed. How could she possibly know that? Then again, she, Kathy and Anissa had spoken about it in the bar. Could someone there have told Lucinda about it? The Bay Bar claimed mostly bikers as clientele, and Lucinda certainly didn't fit that demographic. Had Simon been in the bar and they hadn't noticed?

"Would you object to that?" she asked.

"On the contrary, I'd welcome it."

"So, you're not here to put a bid on the property?"

"Not at this time."

"Oh," Jerry said, his voice falling.

"But I also heard that something belonging to the late Mr. Jackson was found on the premises," Lucinda said.

"What's that got to do with why you wanted to see the house?" Jerry asked curtly. By the immediate change in his expression, he seemed to realize he might have just annoyed the richest woman in the county. "I mean, why trouble yourself with such information?"

"Mr. Jackson was my next-door neighbor. I don't like the idea that there's a murderer anywhere near my home."

"It was a wallet," Tori volunteered. "There was a picture of his children in it. His daughter identified it for the police."

"So I understand," Lucinda said. She turned to Jerry. "I think I've seen enough. Thank you for your time, Mr. Peterson. Avery and I can see ourselves out." She gave Tori a nod and hurried out of the house, with Simon following.

"What did you have to show up for?" Jerry accused.

"She said she wasn't interested in buying the place. Why do you think she really came to see the house?"

"I don't care, but my clients sure do."

"Did you present Kathy's offer?"

"I spoke to them on the phone. When they heard Lucinda Bloomfield wanted to see it, they said they wanted to wait and see if she would put in a better offer. They're going to be very disappointed."

"When the police were here the other day, did they find anything else concerning Mr. Jackson's death?"

"If they did, they didn't tell me."

"Did they just take anything they wanted without giving you a receipt?"

"I didn't think the owners would care. They just want to sell. Now, come on. I want to lock up and get out of here." He held out a hand, pointing to the door.

Tori turned and slowly walked through the trash-filled home. As she passed the parlor, she wrinkled her nose at an unpleasant odor, but it wasn't something she'd noticed when in the house two days before."

"Come on, hurry up," Jerry said. Impatiently.

"Are you the only agent showing the house?" she asked Jerry.

"It's a multiple listing, but so far nobody else has asked to show it. It's getting on to my dinner time," he said, becoming more and more annoyed.

"Oh, all right." Tori hurried out the door.

Jerry locked the house and went to his car. Without

saying another word, he got inside, started the engine, and backed out into the highway, nearly clipping a motorcycle that was heading east. The driver threw him a one-finger salute, and slowed even more, before pulling into The Bay Bar's parking lot. Jerry's wheels spun and he took off across the bay bridge.

Tori watched his car until it crossed the bridge and disappeared up the bend on the hill, then she crossed the highway, heading back to the Cannon compound.

Kathy and Anissa were waiting for her.

"Well?" Kathy demanded.

"Lucinda's not interested in buying the house, at least right now. Her property manager said it would be a huge investment, but she didn't seem to have a good reason for being there, either."

"I don't like that woman," Anissa said. "For all I know it was her who had my daddy killed so she could get his property."

"But she hasn't asked you again if you want to sell. You haven't had any trouble, have you?"

Anissa shook her head. "I don't think she'll be so blatant to come after me so soon after daddy's death."

"She said having a murderer in the neighborhood had her worried, but it was odd. She had to be there for a reason. I think my showing up may have scared her off."

"Good," Kathy said.

"But something funny is going on at the house. I asked Jerry if he'd shown it to anyone other than us and Lucinda, and he said no. But I swear there were empty cans and fast-food papers in the kitchen that hadn't been there the other day. And worse, the front parlor smelled like pee. There was a fresh stain on the wall, too."

"Do you think someone's squatting in the house?" Kathy asked.

"If they are, they must only be there at night."

Anissa looked thoughtful. "My daddy said he'd seen

lights out on the bay."

"But what do the two things have in common?" Kathy asked.

"I don't know," Tori said. "But maybe we should try to find out."

"How would we do that?" Kathy asked.

"Hold a stake-out."

"Oh, sure. Who do you think we are? Nancy Drew and Company?" Kathy asked flippantly.

"Hey," Tori continued, "you were the one who told me I should keep an eye out for suspicious stuff. And it worked for us when we caught the person stealing my panties from the laundry room."

"Say what?" Anissa asked.

Kathy sighed. "Yes, I guess I did. But where are we going to hide so that whoever is getting into the house doesn't see us?"

Tori looked in the direction of the boathouse. "We've got the perfect vantage point. Now all we need to do is find a few more pairs of binoculars."

Kathy shook her head. "It'll be too dark. We might see movement, but moonbeams won't give enough light to actually see anything in that yard or close to the house."

"How do you know?"

"I peeked at night."

"Well, where do you suggest we hide? The shrubs are out of control next to The Bay Bar, and the other side of the house is all marsh. And I don't know about you, but I don't want to be hanging around outside in the cold and damp while being eaten alive by mosquitoes."

"Me, either," Anissa said.

"It's okay," Kathy said. "This is my project and I'll figure out how to do this."

"Why can't we just sit in a car like cops do?" Anissa asked.

"We can't park on the highway," Tori said.

"No, but you've got big patch of grass under that big old willow. Why can't you park there?"

"The branches," Kathy said.

"You ever hear of clippers?" Anissa offered.

"The tree does look rather unkempt," Kathy agreed.

"Have you forgotten we're in the middle of the sorting project?" Tori asked.

"We can finish that tomorrow," Kathy said. "Meanwhile, we might be able to figure out who's squatting in my house and why."

"Okay, okay," Tori agreed.

"Come on," Kathy said. Let's get the clippers and the loppers out. We can toss everything into the dumpster." She looked over at Anissa. "Are you game?"

She shrugged. "I may as well be. But there's nothing to eat in my house, so someone is going to have to feed me. Just one request: no more egg salad, please."

The tree pruning was a great success. They cut the branches at about a six foot level, which would make it a lot easier to cut the grass, and it gave them plenty of room to park Kathy's and Tori's cars. They decided parking one would look suspicious, parking two only slightly less so.

Afterward, Tori and Kathy headed into the village to get some groceries. Anissa went home saying she'd return in time for supper and their stake-out duty.

"What are you going to tell your Gramps?" Kathy asked as she pushed the shopping cart beside the market's meat counter.

"Gee, I hadn't thought of that. Slumber party?"

"Did you mention to him that I'm staying for a few days?"

"It may have slipped my mind. But don't worry. He's an easy-going kind of guy."

Kathy picked up a package of chicken breasts and placed it in the cart. "I'll sleep in the boathouse if I have to, but I need to be around my house."

"It's not yours yet."

"But it will be. I have faith."

Lucky you, Tori thought. Her future appeared to be a black hole where hope was in short supply.

Kathy selected a package of pork chops and some burgers. They moved on to the produce department, where they grabbed a couple of bags of salad, a cucumber, radishes, and tomatoes. "If we can get a couple of plants in this week, we should have decent-tasting ones by Labor Day."

"Where are you going to plant them?"

"By the side of the Lotus Lodge, and in my side yard."

Tori was tired of mentioning that Kathy didn't yet own the property.

"Are we done?" Tori asked.

"No. I need to get some flour, brown sugar, eggs, and a few spices. I need to bake, and I don't think your Gramps will mind if I share the bounty. I'll pay for the groceries."

"You will not. You're unemployed," Tori pointed out.

"So are you. And I'll have money coming in when my birthday arrives. We're not so sure about you."

"Thanks for reminding me," Tori said flatly. "Okay, you pay for the stuff; I'll go buy Gramps a couple of lottery tickets. Maybe he'll win the Mega Millions, give me the compound, and move to Florida."

"I'll cross my fingers for him," Kathy said with sarcasm. They gathered up the last of the groceries and Kathy headed for the checkout while Tori went to the service counter where she was fourth in line. By the time she got to the desk, there were three more people behind her. Apparently, Tom's Market was the go-to place to buy lottery tickets. By the time she finished her transaction,

Kathy was waiting. They walked to the car.

"What if we have to pull an all-nighter?" Tori asked.

"We did it in college all the time."

"That was eight years ago. These days, I get crabby if I don't get my full eight hours of sleep."

"You sound like a grandmother," Kathy teased, then grimaced. "I'm sorry. I forgot it's been less than a week since you lost your grandma."

"It's okay. I do pretty well during the day. It's at night when I have time to think that I start to cry."

They loaded the groceries in the back of the car and Kathy returned the cart to the store, then they took off.

"I love that little store. I love this little village," Kathy commented as they passed the self-clean car wash.

"Not many amenities, but Rochester is only an hour away. And you can order just about anything online these days. There's nothing wrong with door-to-door de-livery."

Kathy took in the scenery like a tourist. She seemed to have rose-colored glasses on. Did she even see how many run-down houses and rickety barns lined the highway? Most people thought of poverty as being just an urban problem, but there was plenty of it right there in Ward County, where the summer people in their pretty little cottages on the water bore an unfair portion of the tax burden. Before she got serious about trying to persuade Herb against selling their property, she had better make a point of asking about the county and school taxes.

They arrived back at the house and Kathy insisted on making dinner. Tori didn't object. Her specialty appeared to be making coffee and boiling water for tea. Take-out was always the best option at her house.

Tori went back out to the yard and packed up the un-sold yard sale items. Some of the iffy ones went straight into the Dumpster. Herb closed the door to the bait shop and locked it at precisely six o'clock, just as Tori was closing the door to Lotus Lodge's unit 1.

"What's for supper?" he asked, rubbing hands together.

"Chicken. Kathy's cooking, so at least it'll taste good."

Anissa's blue truck rumbled to a halt in the parking area. She got out, carrying a brown paper bag. "I didn't know what you were serving, so I brought a bottle of red and white."

"Either works for me," Herb said, as they ambled over to the house.

The aroma of Italian spices greeted them as they walked into the kitchen. "Something smells good," Herb said.

Kathy looked up from the salad she was assembling. "It'll be ready in about fifteen minutes."

"Then we've got time for a drink," Anissa said, and set the bag on the counter. "Sorry they're not chilled I know it's gauche, but we can toss a few ice cubes into the glasses."

"I've done it before," Tori admitted.

"I'm going to wash up," Herb said. "Been handling worms half the day," he said and disappeared in the direction of the bathroom.

Tori gestured for Anissa to take a seat at the table and washed her hands at the kitchen sink. By the time she sat down, Kathy had opened the Chardonnay. She set the bottle, glasses, and a bowl of ice and some tongs on the table, then sat down. Herb joined them a minute later.

"Oh, Gramps, I forgot. I got you some lottery tickets," Tori said, and reached for her purse on the counter. She retrieved them and handed them to her grandfather.

"No scratch-offs?" he asked.

"I didn't know which ones to buy."

"You didn't get Powerball."

"The odds are astronomical. I figured you had a better shot at Mega Millions."

"What's the jackpot?"

She shrugged. "I don't know. Twenty million. Something like that."

"It'll have to do," Herb groused, and shoved the tickets into the breast pocket of his flannel shirt. "Thanks."

"Mr. Cannon," Anissa said, her voice subdued. "Have you ever seen strange lights out on the bay?"

"Nope," he said succinctly. "Lights from boats, yes. Strange lights? Nope."

"Why would people be out on the bay late at night?" Kathy asked. "Isn't it dangerous?"

"Only if you don't know what you're doing," Herb said.

"Did you ever do much night fishing?" Tori asked.

Herb shook his head. "I don't really like fishing. I always thought I might like to learn to play golf. Maybe I'll do that when I retire to Florida."

"When are you going to do that, Mr. Cannon?" Anissa asked.

"As soon as I sell this place—or I win the Powerball."

"Never," Tori mouthed.

"You hear anything about that house yet?" Herb asked Kathy.

She shook her head. "No. Tori thinks I made a hasty decision in making an offer."

"I'll say. You don't really know anything about the area, do you?"

She shook her head. "But I like it here."

"It's nice. In the summer," he amended. "Come winter? It's like living on the moon. Dark, cold, and inhospitable."

"I thought I might look up the local historical society to see if I can find some pictures of the house in better days, and to find out the history of the area."

"Nothing much ever happened around here," Herb said. He frowned, as though rethinking that last statement. "Well, not since prohibition, anyway."

"Prohibition?"

"Yeah, smugglers used to sneak beer, gin, and whiskey across the lake from Canada. They say a house up on Willow Point has a really big basement where they used to stash the stuff before they could distribute it."

"Really?" Anissa asked.

"No lie."

"I never heard that before," Tori said.

"There's lots of things you haven't heard," Herb said, pouring himself a glass of wine. He bypassed the ice.

"Why would rum runners want to come to such an out-of-the-way place?" Tori asked.

"I think you just answered your own question," Herb said. "You think this place is dead now, think how it must have been a hundred years ago. There was a bridge, but nothing else."

"How would a boat find its way across the lake in the dark?"

"Where there's a will, there's a way," Herb said, taking a sip of his wine. He grimaced. "We got any beer left?"

Kathy got up to get him a can from the fridge.

"What have you girls got planned for this evening?"

Kathy and Anissa looked to Tori to answer.

"We thought we might just hang out in the boat house."

"What for?"

"Isn't there supposed to be a meteor shower tonight?" Kathy offered.

"Not that I heard," Herb said, cracking the tab on his beer.

"Anissa and I have a lot of years to catch up on," Tori said.

"That boat house is really dirty. Are you sure you want to sit up there with all the spiders and God knows what else?" Herb asked.

"Kathy cleaned the windows," Tori said.

"Anything else?"

"Not yet," Kathy admitted.

They sipped their adult beverages. It was Kathy who broke the quiet. "Tori says you want to sell the business."

Herb's eyes widened and he cocked his head to look at his granddaughter. He did not seem pleased, but he did answer the question. "I'm thinking about it."

"What do you think it's worth?"

"Kath!" Tori implored.

"I need to get a feel for what the business climate is here in this part of Ward County."

A plausible, if dubious explanation.

Herb shrugged. "Half a million."

Tori nearly choked on her wine. "Are you crazy?"

Herb looked at her quizzically. "No. There're houses on the east side of the bay that are going for more than that and on much smaller lots."

"Have you thought about holding the mortgage for a potential buyer?" Kathy pressed.

"No. You got someone in mind?" he asked, looking across the table at Anissa.

"Yes, Tori."

"Kath!" Tori cried again.

"Tori?" Herb asked. "Why would she want to waste her life here?"

"Because she loves this place," Kathy said matter-of-factly.

Herb turned to look at his granddaughter. "And why is that?"

A walloping surge of emotion swelled within her and Tori had to force herself to speak. "Because this is the place where I've felt most loved."

"Your mom and dad love you," Herb said.

"Yeah, but you and Grandma loved me more."

"Oh, Tori, you know that's not true."

"No, Gramps, I don't," she said in all sincerity.

It was a terribly awkward moment that Kathy quickly diffused. "So, what would you let Tori buy the business from you for?"

For a long moment, Herb looked thoughtful, but then he shook his head. "No, I couldn't do it—not in good conscience. Because this place would suck her life away, and in the end she'd just resent it and me."

His words stung like acid on a wound. He had no faith in her or her abilities. Well, what had she expected?

Tori pushed back her chair. "If you'll excuse me," she said, rose, and headed for the back of the house.

The door to what she now thought of as her room was ajar. Daisy was sacked out on the bed. She opened her eyes and blinked as Tori came in and sat down beside her, then rose and stretched before climbing onto Tori's lap.

"I knew you'd be here for me," she whispered into the cat's fur, hugging her tightly. Daisy purred even louder.

Tori sat there, staring at nothing, feeling empty—too empty to even cry. What would she do with the rest of her life? Days ago, she was set to send out resumes to schools in three different counties. Now the thought of going back to the classroom made her feel miserable. Talking with Kathy about the possibilities for the bait shop and reviving the Lotus Lodge had sparked the entrepreneurial spirit within her. The idea of living across the street from Kathy had been another perk she couldn't have anticipated a week before. Despite her grandfather's announcement about selling, until Kathy had actually asked him point blank about the possibility of letting her acquire the business, she'd still held out hope.

Now she felt a grief akin to losing her grandmother. And maybe that was part of the problem. If she could no longer be a part of Lotus Bay, her grandmother would be forever lost to her.

That was stupid. She'd hold her grandmother in her

heart forever, but somehow the idea of losing this little piece of paradise would wound her forever.

Daisy suddenly jumped down to the floor and Tori's head turned at the sound of a knock at the still-open door. Herb stood before her. "Can I come in?"

Tori shrugged, hanging her head once more.

Herb stepped inside the room and sat beside her, resting his hands on his thighs and looking very uncomfortable. "I never knew you loved this place so much."

"I always thought you did."

"I told you; this place was your grandmother's dream, not mine. You never told me you were interested in going into business."

"It's a recent development," Tori admitted.

"What would your mom and dad say if I let you take over the business?"

"Hopefully, 'good luck.'"

"And if they didn't?"

"You may have noticed; we're not all that close."

Herb nodded. "Your grandmother and I were unhappy that our kids grew up and moved away. We figured they would, but not to other states. She was heartbroken."

"And you?"

"I always thought your dad would show an interest in the business. That we could be Cannon and Son."

"But not Cannon and Granddaughter?"

"It never occurred to me," he said. He let out a long breath. "I tried to talk your grandma into leaving this place, but she wouldn't hear of it. The word 'snowbird' became a dirty one around here. But that's what *I* want. You can understand that, can't you?"

"What if I could turn this place around? What if I could make it pay for both of us?"

"Honey, you'd have to be a miracle worker."

"You've got your pension and social security. Could

you live on that in Florida?"

"I sure could, but it's only that money that's kept this place going. I couldn't pay the taxes here *and* live down south."

"I could get a job substitute teaching during the winter and run this place in the summer."

"It wouldn't be enough," Herb said firmly. "I'm sorry, Tori, but you need to face reality."

Tori nodded. "I guess I'll pack up tomorrow and go back to Rochester. Maybe I can find a roommate and get a job at McDonalds."

"Aw, don't be like that. I told you, you can stay here as long as you want. I like having you and your friends around. I don't suppose I'll find a buyer right away. Might be a year or more. That should be long enough for you to get back on your feet."

"I'd like to stay," she said.

"Good." He patted her knee. "Kathy said supper was nearly ready. You coming?"

Tori nodded.

Herb got up and headed out the door. Tori followed, literally dragging her feet.

When she got to the kitchen, the table had been set and Herb had retaken his seat. Tori helped Kathy serve supper before she sat down, too.

Conversation was nil as they passed the salad bowl and helped themselves to it and boiled sweet corn Kathy must have found in the freezer. Herb dug in, but Tori had no appetite.

"Kathy, I knew you could bake cookies, but I had no idea you were such a good cook," Herb said.

"If I intend to serve guests at my bed and breakfast, I had to learn to cook. My mother was terrible at it. She gave me a copy of Mastering the Art of French Cooking when I was in high school. It took me a couple of years, but I made almost every recipe."

"Which ones didn't you make?" Anissa asked.

"Aspic," Kathy said and wrinkled her nose. "I mean, where do you buy leg of cow to make gelatin, anyway?"

Tori managed a week giggle.

"Eat up," Herb advised, and gave her a wink.

Tori picked up her fork and caught sight of Kathy who gave her a comforting smile that seemed to say we'll talk later. If there was a way for Tori to ever own the Cannon compound, it would be Kathy who figured it out.

A little kernel of hope flickered within her once again.

THIRTEEN

Clouds had gathered in the sky to the west, which was stained with Easter egg colors of peachy-pinks and mellow blues. "It sure is pretty here," Anissa said as the three women headed for the boathouse. "I think I'm going to like living here. Now if I can just support myself to afford it."

Tori said nothing, but took the lead. Herb kept an old Chris Craft wooden boat that looked like it had been an extra from the movie *On Golden Pond*. Tori remembered riding in it years ago, but Herb hadn't launched it in at least a decade. It would need a lot of work if some collector wanted to restore it. But it sat in the boat house, taking up valuable space that could have been used by a paying tenant. She'd mention that to Herb. There had to be more ways they could promote what they had and make the business pay for itself. She'd mention it to Kathy first, but not that night. They had other things to contend with.

Tori threw a switch and the dusty light bulb hanging over the boat barely brightened the gloom.

"I think your grandpa's right," Anissa said, looking around at the cobwebs that seemed to fill every corner. "This place is filthy. And I think Kathy's right; we're never going to be able to see what's going on at the house from here."

"I know, but I wanted Gramps to see us come out

here. We'll leave the light on and go sit in Kathy's car
when it's fully dark," Tori said.

"Is there anywhere to sit?" Kathy asked.

"I thought I saw some old folding chairs up in the
loft. We may as well go up there."

Kathy and Anissa followed her up the ladder. Another
dusty light bulb failed to brighten that space, too. Tarps
covered a pile in one corner. Tori pulled one free and
found a load of metal lawn chairs that had once been
painted in primary colors, but were now rusty and dirty
from disuse.

"A wire brush would get rid of most of the rust on
these and we could repaint them to look like new," Kathy
suggested. "They'd look darling out on the lawn. Great
for curb appeal."

"Sounds like you want to help Gramps sell this place."

"Don't be so quick to give up on your dreams. I'm
not."

"You've got an inheritance coming in a few months;
I don't."

"Me, either," Anissa said.

"That talk you had with him didn't go well, did it?"
Kathy asked.

Tori shook her head.

"I wouldn't push the idea now, but we'll figure something out."

"And if he sells it fast?"

"We'll figure something out," Kathy repeated with authority.

Tori would have loved to believe her.

They pulled the chairs out and dusted them off as best
they could before pulling them to the windows on the
south side of the boathouse. "That was really interesting
what your grandpa had to say about rum runners," Anissa
said. "I had no idea that kind of thing happened around
here."

"Did you know there were stops for the underground railroad all along the shore of Lake Ontario." Kathy asked.

"How do you know?" Tori asked.

"I've been Googling like crazy since I first thought of buying that house across the road. I need to find ways to market the whole guest experience, and sell the area to people as well."

"You're going to have to call it something other than the house across the road—if you get it, that is," Anissa warned. "Have you got a name for your B and B?"

"That's one idea I haven't come up with yet. Willow Point is nearby, but not close enough. Still, there is a willow tree on the property, but it doesn't look healthy. I can't use that in the name if the thing is going to fall over in the next big wind storm."

"Good point."

They spent the next half-hour brainstorming names, but Kathy shook her head so often she was in danger of incurring an injury. By then only a whisper of light shone over the hills surrounding the bay.

"We should probably go sit in the car now," Tori advised.

"I'm not sitting in the back," Anissa said firmly. "I get car sick."

"The car won't be moving," Kathy pointed out.

"Are you sure you want to risk it?" Anissa asked.

Tori tried to stifle a smile.

They climbed down the ladder and Tori did a little reconnaissance. The drapes were drawn in the living room, but she could see flickering light from the television. Herb was probably snoring in his recliner. Still, they crept around the darkened Lotus Lodge and walked in the shadows near Resort Road to reach the highway, then tread on the sandy shoulders of the highway so as not to get their shoes wet from the heavy dew. Kathy unlocked the car and they climbed in, with Tori in the back. "We're going to have to share the binoculars," she said.

"Say someone does come along to squat in your house overnight; where do you think they're going to come from? The bar?" Anissa asked.

"I don't think it's one of their customers," Kathy said. "They've got bathrooms for both sexes."

"I want to know how they're getting in without smashing a window or kicking in the door," Tori said.

"A key, of course," Kathy said matter-of-factly.

"Yes, but who's supplying it? Presumably, the owner doesn't want someone messing with his property if he hopes to sell it—especially people who are going to use it as their personal toilet. It's definitely detrimental to making a sale," Tori pointed out.

"What if," Anissa began, "whoever is using the house is also the one riding on the bay in the middle of the night?"

"The lights your daddy saw?" Tori asked.

"Why not?"

"Like the rum runners?" Kathy asked.

"Yeah. Think about it, this is rural New York, hundreds of thousands of acres of nothing but fruit trees to be picked. Some farmers might hire illegal immigrants."

"I haven't seen any Homeland Security vehicles patrolling the area," Tori said.

"But they do around the port of Rochester. I've seen them parked," Kathy said.

"I've seen them, too," Anissa said.

"What if it's worse than illegal aliens?"

"You mean terrorists?" Kathy asked.

Tori shrugged. "We don't have secure borders."

"You think we should be worried about an invasion from Canada? They seem like pretty friendly people to me," Anissa said.

"Could be drug runners," Kathy suggested.

"Maybe," Tori said. "And what about that guy we heard about with the crew-cut? He's been hanging around here lately, but nobody seems to know anything about him."

"He's usually at the bar in the evenings. We could go talk to him."

"And say what? 'Hi, guy, are you smuggling illegal aliens, or dope, or terrorists?' Yeah, I'm sure he'd spill the beans to two little white gals like you," Anissa said.

"Would he spill to you?"

"You think I'm going to walk into that biker bar at night without a bodyguard? No-sir-ee," Anissa declared.

"The bikers aren't that bad," Kathy said.

"Yeah, they're usually old guys reminiscing about their glory days," Tori agreed. "I mean, I hardly ever see a young person on a bike, and when I do, they're stupid not to be wearing leathers."

"I wonder what time your daddy saw those lights on the bay," Kathy said.

"I got the impression it was late," Anissa said.

"How late is late?" Tori asked.

"Middle of the night. I wish those pages hadn't been missing from his diary. I'll bet they would have told us all about his suspicions," Tori said.

"His house wasn't broken into. How would someone know he wrote that down in a diary?" Kathy asked.

"Yeah, how?" Tori agreed. "Those missing pages could just be a coincidence. I mean, were there pages missing from any of the other journals?"

Anissa hesitated. "I couldn't say for sure. I haven't read them yet. It's still too soon after he passed for me to face them."

Tori could understand that. Her grandmother had recorded the message for the business's voice mail greeting. She was sure she'd cry the next time she heard it, but she hoped Herb wouldn't suggest they change it any time soon, either.

"What are we going to do if we catch somebody breaking into the house?" Anissa asked.

"Call 911," Kathy said emphatically. "There's no way we should put ourselves in harm's way."

"And how fast do you think they're going to come out here in the sticks?" Anissa said.

"The State Police have a barracks just outside of Worton. They could probably be here in ten or fifteen minutes," Tori said.

"And if the bad guys saw us watching, they might be long gone before the cops could ever get here," Anissa pointed out.

"Then at least whoever was trespassing would stop peeing in my house," Kathy said.

"It's not your house!" Anissa cried.

"Yet," Kathy remarked.

Tori sighed. "We don't even know if anyone is going to show up at the house tonight—or tomorrow. How long should we keep up a stakeout? Days? A week?"

"Yeah, and why would a bunch of bad guys draw attention to themselves on a weekend?" Anissa asked. "I mean, this place is pretty dead now, but I've got to think there's less risk of being caught on a weeknight."

"So, you think we're wasting our time?" Kathy asked.

"If we'd brought the bottle of wine with us I might have had a different opinion."

"I could go get it," Tori suggested.

Anissa shook her head.

"But think about it. Friday and Saturday are the busiest nights of the week, and yet someone was in that house last night and left their calling card on the wall," Tori pointed out.

"Yeah," Kathy agreed. "They're either very brave or very stupid."

"I'll go with stupid," Anissa said. She sighed. "Do you

guys mind if I bow out of this little stakeout? I don't know if I have a taste for this kind of adventure."

"That's okay," Kathy assured her. "You're probably right about us wasting our time. But I'm willing to sit here for another few hours just to make sure."

"I'll keep you company. It's either that or listen to Gramps snore. He doesn't give up the remote—even when he's fast asleep."

"I'll catch up with you tomorrow and we'll finalize plans about going to Rochester to get more of your stuff," Anissa told Tori.

"Sounds good."

"Good night," Anissa said, and got out of the car.

Tori got out, too, taking her place in the front seat. She and Kathy sat in silence and in less than a minute, they heard the engine on the big blue pickup rumble to life. They listened until it faded into the distance.

"I wish her daddy's diary hadn't been tampered with," Kathy commented. "Maybe he was killed because he figured out whatever was going on around here."

"What if he just pissed someone off?" Tori asked.

"You mean someone like Biggie Taylor?"

"Maybe. What if he just messed up a page or two of his journal by spilling coffee on it and ripped them out? It could be that you and I have just watched too many crime shows during our lives and have vivid imaginations, which is why the worst appeals to us."

"I like to think I have an *active* imagination, especially when it comes to problem solving," Kathy said. "You can't be successful if you don't think outside the box."

Tori retrieved her phone and checked the time. It was only 10:30. Maybe what they should have done was take turns on watch, with one of them spelling the other after three or four hours, but then where was the fun in that? Not that they'd actually had any fun so far—but it was probably good that Anissa had gone home, because now she and Kathy could talk candidly.

"I was angry that you brought up the subject of me running Gramps's business."

"I know," Kathy said, "but I knew you'd forgive me. You know I'd never do anything to hurt you."

"Yeah, I do, and now it's out in the open. But his mind is made up."

"Oh, he says that now, but we will change the way he feels," Kathy said with authority.

"I wish I had your faith. How do you think that will happen?"

"I'll have to think about it." Kathy moved the binoculars up to her eyes and stared at the house bathed in shadow.

"Jerry never called back with an answer about your offer, did he?"

"Technically, it expired about five hours ago."

"Will you submit another one?"

Kathy lowered the binoculars and sighed. "Yes, but I'm annoyed to have to do so."

"You offered full price. Do you think they wanted to jack up the price after Lucinda Bloomfield looked at the house?"

"Maybe. If she said she wasn't interested in buying, I can't see why they'd reject my offer. If I have to, I'll offer a cash deal."

"But isn't that everything you've got in the bank? How will you live until your inheritance comes through?"

Kathy bit her lip. "I'll figure something out."

Tori reached for the binoculars, and looked at the house. "Unless you've got eyes like a cat, you probably can't see much more with these things than I can."

"No," Kathy admitted.

"Let's walk out on the bridge and see if we can see boats on the bay."

"We may as well. We're not accomplishing anything here."

They got out of the car, quietly closing the doors so as not to arouse suspicion from Herb in the house, then they started for the bridge. The sound of music and laughter from the bar across the street drifted over them, along with the smell of cigarette smoke. The sky was completely black with only a few scattered clouds on the horizon. The stars were out in full force, and Tori easily picked out Polaris. They walked to the middle of the bridge and looked out over the water.

"If we were standing on higher ground, we'd be better able to see boats out there," Tori said.

"I wonder if the view would be better from Anissa's place. The house has to be at least ten or fifteen feet higher than here."

"Maybe, but she's facing west. The islands at the north end of the bay might block out some boat activity."

"Should we go back to the boat house?" Kathy asked.

"It faces west, too. We'd only see a small part of the bay. "

"Sounds like we're wasting our time," Kathy said, sounding depressed. "Maybe we should think things through."

"If we were spies, we'd have infrared goggles. Then we could see everything that's going on in the shadows around the house," Tori said.

"And where would we get a pair? Military surplus?"

"I'll bet we could buy a pair online—at Amazon or maybe eBay."

"You think?" Kathy asked.

"You can get just about anything online these days."

"Yeah, but we don't have the money or the time."

"Then we'll just have to go back to the car and hope we see something."

Kathy slapped her cheek. "Good, because I feel like I'm being eaten alive."

They headed back to the car.

Kathy took command of the binoculars once again and trained her eyes on the house across the road.

"Let's think about this logically. If someone was coming across the lake, and then squatting at your house, they'd have to tie their boat up somewhere."

"Yeah," Kathy agreed.

"And the closest place to dock is right in our back yard—or front, depending on your point of view."

"You think someone's using your dock?"

"The lights have been broken for years. It's pitch black out there. Gramps and Grandma slept like logs. I doubt they would have heard anyone cut through the yard. "

"We could go move your car and watch the path from the dock."

"Yeah," Tori agreed. "But whoever is using the dock probably wouldn't sneak around the compound as long as there're lights on in the house."

"What time does your Gramps usually go to bed?"

"Eleven-thirty, after the news."

"So why don't we go inside, make a pot of coffee, eat some cookies, and when he goes to bed, we'll tell him we'll lock up for the night."

"I'll bet nobody will make a move for at least an hour after the lights are out. The guest room window overlooks the yard," Tori said.

"Yeah, but what if they cut through behind the back of the house instead of circling around?"

"Good point."

"I still think sitting in your car would be the best vantage point. We could go back outside once the lights are out."

"Sounds like a plan," Tori said, but didn't make a move.

"What else?" Kathy asked.

"Well, whoever is squatting seems to leave before daylight, right?"

"Yeah."

"So that means someone is picking them up."

"I wonder what the timing is. There has to be a time lag between when they get in and when they're picked up. Otherwise, there'd be no need for anyone to squat in the house. It may be a period of several hours."

"I saw fast food wrappers on the counter that weren't there the other day. I wonder if whoever picks up the squatters also feeds them."

"Where would they get fast food around here?"

"There's a McDonalds at the far side of the village up on the main highway. I'm pretty sure they're open twenty-four/seven."

"What happens when you get your dock light fixed?"

"That's a good question. And it *will* be fixed by Tuesday at the latest."

"But the bad guys don't know that."

"That's right."

Kathy shook her head. "This all sounds like a great movie plot, but it's all supposition on our part."

"Yeah. If nothing else, we've had fun speculating."

"*You've* had fun thinking about it. Someone's peeing in my potential house and I want it to stop. I'm the one who's going to have to clean it!"

Tori allowed herself a smile. "Come on, let's go inside. We might as well be comfortable while we wait."

FOURTEEN

Tori moved her car back to the compound's main parking area. When they reentered the house, they heard a voice coming from the living room, and it wasn't the TV. "Sounds like your Gramps is on the phone," Kathy whispered. "Who could he be talking to at this hour?"

Tori shrugged, and the women crept closer to the arch that separated the rooms for better eavesdropping purposes.

"Yeah, I know," Herb was saying, "she wants to run the place. Have you heard of anything more insane?" He laughed, but then he was quiet for at least a minute.

"I hope you're kidding. You know how hard Josie worked to keep this place afloat—goodness knows, she told you everything."

Must be Irene, Tori mouthed. Kathy nodded.

"Yeah, she and her friend have been working hard to spruce the place up, but—"

They leaned in closer. Too bad he wasn't using a speaker phone; then they could have heard both sides of the conversation.

"No. I'd never hear the end of it from her parents if I let her—"

Tori clenched her hands and shook them, obviously frustrated.

"Yeah, but—" Herb said. He was quiet for a few seconds. "Yeah, but—"

Was Irene on Tori's side?

"Okay, okay. I'll think about it."

Was he being honest or did he just want to shut Irene up?

Tori motioned to Kathy and they tiptoed back to the door. She opened, then slammed it. "Gramps, we're back!" she called. She turned back to Kathy. "Should I make a pot of coffee?"

"May as well," Kathy said. "It could be a long night."

Tori filled the pot, measured the coffee, and hit the switch, then she got out a couple of cups. She looked up to see Herb standing in the doorway from the living room. "Do you want a cup of coffee, Gramps?"

"I'll never get to sleep if I do." He leaned against the wall.

"We're gonna have cookies, too," Kathy said, reaching for the plastic container that sat on the top of the fridge. "We'd love to have you join us."

Herb shook his head. "Nah, I'm going to go to bed early tonight. I have a lot to think about."

Tori pursed her lips to keep a smile from forming. She put her hands behind her back and crossed her fingers, too. "Sleep well, Gramps."

Herb nodded and turned back for the living room.

They waited until they heard his bedroom door close before they spoke.

"Maybe things are going to turn around," Kathy said.

"I'm not counting on anything just yet, but I'm going to allow myself just a teensy bit of hope."

Kathy went into the living room and turned off the lights. By the time she returned, Tori had poured the coffee into a Thermos. She checked the time: just after eleven. Grabbing the mugs by their handles with one hand, she scooped up the thermos with the other. Kathy grabbed the cookie container and the binoculars before they turned off the kitchen lights and snuck out the back door.

They walked through the darkened lot and got into Tori's car, then quietly closed the doors. "Now we wait," Tori said.

"And talk," Kathy said. "I wonder why Irene thinks you should take over the business?"

"I don't care what her motives are as long as she's successful."

Tori pushed her seat back until she had enough room to play waitress and pour the coffee, and Kathy opened the cookie container. It didn't matter what Kathy baked, it all tasted good.

The first hour went by pretty fast. Kathy wanted to brainstorm changes she needed to make to the house across the way to make it habitable. She was already thinking about how she'd decorate it, too, and incorporate what they'd found stored in the Lotus Lodge. Tori restrained herself from yet again pointing out she didn't yet have the house and just listened, while her own mind wandered as to what her first steps might be should she ever be able to refurbish the shabby little motel. And was Anissa right? Could she one day tackle the boathouse and make it into a stunning rental as well? They were pipe dreams, but they appealed to her anyway.

Sitting in the car for two hours, with two cups of coffee pressing on her bladder, made for an uncomfortable situation. "I don't know what to do. What if I go inside and that's the exact moment someone ties up to our dock?"

"Why don't we take turns?" Kathy suggested. "You can go first. You may as well take the cups and Thermos in. Meanwhile, I'll keep watch." To prove it, she picked up the binoculars.

"Okay." Tori gathered up their stuff, quietly opened the car door and went inside. She was back less than five minutes later. "Okay, your turn," she said, but Kathy waved a hand and shushed her.

"I think I see some movement by the dock."

"You're kidding."

Kathy passed the binoculars over to Tori. "No, I'm not."

Tori stared into the darkness beyond the house. At first she was sure Kathy was mistaken, but then she saw silhouettes moving among the shadows. "Oh, good heavens," she whispered as she took in the shapes. Two taller figures herded a number of smaller ones. They cut around the back of the house, heading toward the road.

"What do we do?" Kathy asked.

"We can't call 911 yet. Not until we see them trespassing in the house."

"What do you make of them?"

"They looked like a couple of big guys and a bunch of kids."

"Why would someone smuggle children across the lake from Canada—if that's what they're doing."

Tori's mind shifted into worried overdrive. "I hate to think it, but what if they're trafficking in some kind of slavery?"

"What do you mean?" Kathy asked, aghast.

"Prostitution, sexual slavery—I've heard that people have been abducted to serve as surrogates and even for organ harvesting."

"Oh, come on," Kathy said.

"I'm not kidding. We've got to do something—and fast!" Tori was a teacher. The thought of children being molested in any way by ruthless predators sickened her.

They waited until there was no more movement, and then silently exited the car. Tori led the way up to Resort Road, circling around to the main road. The Bay Bar still had a few patrons, but nobody was out on the deck. They waited and watched as the burly figures herded the silent band of children across the street, running for the shelter

of the unruly hedges that formed an effective barrier between the bar and the empty house. Once the group was
out of sight, Tori and Kathy made their move, jogging
along the shoulder of the road. Coming to the big willow, they darted to the side of Kathy's car and crouched
down.

"I don't think they saw us," Kathy whispered.

"We've got to get closer."

"I wish we'd brought the binoculars."

"Let's cross the road. We can sneak up at the edge of
the hedges to see what they're up to."

"Right."

Tori led the way. They could hear the thumping bass
from the bar's jukebox, which would effectively cover any
noise the squatters made. Tori and Kathy stayed at the far
edge of the hedge. From that vantage point, they could
see only one figure on the steps, standing in front of the
door. He couldn't have had a key, for it took too long for
him to get it open, and Tori wondered if he was picking
the lock. The door finally swung open and the figure ushered the others inside before the door closed again.

"They are now officially trespassing," Kathy said. "I'm
calling the cops. You keep watch." She turned away.

Tori squinted, hoping to better see what was happening. To do that, she really needed to get closer. It was so
dark, she wondered if she could peer into one of the windows without being seen. Chances were the intruders
would stick to the back of the house so any lights they
might be using wouldn't be seen from the road. It was in
the kitchen out back where she'd seen the new batch of
fast food wrappers, and figured that's where they'd be.

Darting around the end of the hedge, she stuck close
to it until she came up to the house. She edged along the
building, wondering what kind of insect life she was
likely to encounter, until she came to the first window.
Standing on tiptoes, Tori peered through the dirt-en-

crusted glass but couldn't see a thing. She moved to the next window, which was just as filthy. Nothing to see there, either.

She sidled along the house until she came to the back. Slowly, she moved until she could see into the kitchen. A flashlight sat on the littered counter, its beam pointing away from where she stood. Six children sat on the filthy floor, their backs to the counters where the rubbish wasn't piled quite as high, eating what looked like slices of white bread with nothing on it. They looked Asian, malnourished, dirty, and scared. The two men, dressed all in black, stood to one side, conversing. The tall one was white, the shorter one could have been Asian, but in the available light, it was hard to tell. If nothing else, their body language made them look menacing.

Tori ducked back down, wondering what she should do. The prudent thing to do was to wait until the police came—but what if they were delayed by an accident or some other petty crime? What if they considered trespassing too minor an infraction to warrant a visit from one of the few cars on patrol? And what if she did nothing and the creeps who were transporting these kids got away with their human contraband? How long had this operation been in effect? How many other children had they kidnapped and what had become of them?

What happened to Kathy? Did 911 have her on hold, or had they told her to keep a low profile and wait until a Sheriff's cruiser could be dispatched?

Muscles rigid with tension, Tori dared to look through the window once again. The children still sat on the floor, but one of the guys had left the room. The shorter man was on the phone, probably calling whoever was supposed to pick them up. He seemed to be angry. She could hear him shouting, but thanks to the booming music coming from the bar, she couldn't make out what he was saying. The children cowered, looking like they expected to be punished, a couple of them were in tears.

Tori ducked down again, her stomach churning. She had to do something to save those kids. But what? Even if she stormed the house, yelling for the children to run, she realized they might not speak English and would have no idea what she was telling them to do. She might frighten them even more. But would waiting doom them to a worse fate? And what might those scary-looking guys do to her?

Tori wondered if she dared look into that kitchen again. It was stupid, reckless, but someone needed to look out for those children, and—

A hand grabbed her arm, pulling her off kilter, the grip crushing. "Ow!" she cried.

"What are you doing here, bitch?" the big guy she'd seen inside demanded.

"Nothing. I was just—" *Hanging around?* That wasn't going to cut it. "I saw you breaking into the house, and...." That wasn't going to help, either. "Let me go!"

But he didn't let go. Instead, he slammed his fist into her left temple. She fell against the house, her head slamming into the clapboards, stars dancing before her eyes, and slumped down into the weeds. Dazed, she was barely aware as he grabbed her by both wrists and started dragging her around to the back of the house. Her shirt rode up and prickly weeds, grass, and stones dug into her skin. "Let me go," she called weakly, her voice sounding wobbly, but the brute ignored her.

When they got to the back door, he stopped and kicked her in the gut. Tori writhed on the ground, curling into a ball of agony, and the guy kicked her again. "Bitch! That'll teach you to stick your nose where it doesn't belong."

Tori couldn't speak—she could barely breathe—as the man grabbed her like a sack of potatoes and tossed her over his shoulder. He stomped up the steps into the kitchen and tossed her on the floor, the piles of rubbish doing little to break her fall.

The children screamed and cried while, towering above her, the second man was hollered at them in a language she couldn't understand.

"Shut up!" the brute hollered, louder than everyone else. The children's cries softened to whimpers.

"What da hell we gonna do with her?" the second man demanded, training the powerful flashlight's beam directly into Tori's eyes.

"Let me think, dammit, let me think!" the brute hollered, and for good measure, kicked Tori one more time, her knee exploding in agony. "Stop, stop!" she begged, knowing it was useless.

Kathy! Where are you?

"I told you we should wait. It to close to you killing that man."

"You killed Michael Jackson?" Tori asked.

"Shut up!"

"He saw your boat on the bay," she guessed. "He followed you here. He knew what you were up to. He was going to report you!"

"Yeah, well, he didn't. And neither will you, bitch. I'll fill your mouth with maggots, too."

Tori stared into the man's dark cold eyes. She didn't doubt him for a moment.

FIFTEEN

Kathy finished speaking with the 911 dispatcher and turned back to the hedge, only to find that Tori had vanished. Knowing how upset her friend was at the thought of children in danger, Kathy had an inkling of where her friend had gone, but decided to take a circuitous route. She stuck to the east side of the hedge, fumbling in the dark. Branches swiped her cheek and tangled in her hair, along with a sticky film that clung to her face. She clawed at the webs, hoping there wasn't a live occupant in the middle of it. She stifled a scream and shuffled along.

"What are you doing here, bitch!" an angry male voice cried.

"Ow!" Tori wailed.

Kathy's heart nearly leapt into her throat at the sound of her friend in pain. She couldn't see what was going on, but heard a dull thud and then scrabbling on the other side of the hedge. Fear closed her throat—she couldn't make a sound as she heard Tori groan and the sound of something heavy being dragged away.

Kathy followed the sound for a terrible few seconds, and then it faded out. Terrified, she put an arm in front of her face and plunged through the hedge. Sharp branches scraped her hand, her head, and tore at her clothes as she clawed her way through the four or five feet full of branches. She broke free in time to see the dark figure kick her best friend in the stomach.

Terrified, Kathy's breath caught at seeing Tori writhe in pain. Then the guy picked her up, tossed her over his shoulder, and headed into the house.

Kathy turned away, fumbling for her phone once more and stabbing the numbers 911.

"Ward County 911. What is your emergency?"

"Help me! My best friend has just been attacked by some big goon!"

"Calm down. Where are you?"

"I'm at 8766 Ridge Road, next door to The Bay Bar. I just got off the phone with another 911 dispatcher about trespassers at the same address. One of them saw my friend and attacked her. I think he's taken her hostage!"

"Are you safe?"

"Yes, but—"

"Stay away from the house. Go to a safe location and wait for the Sheriff's deputy to arrive."

"But my friend—!" Kathy cried.

"Won't be helped if you're in trouble, too," said the calm female voice.

"She's hurt. He kicked her. What if he kills her before the deputy can get here? I've got to get help. I've got to—" Kathy didn't finish the sentence. She shoved her phone back into her pocket and turned for the bar, nearly tripping over her own feet in her haste as she bypassed the hedge and hurried along the side of the house.

She stumble-ran across the grassy area in front of the bar, swung around the side of the deck and barreled up the steps, then threw open the door. "Help!"

Paul looked up from his stance behind the bar, and a couple of the bikers turned to see what the commotion was.

"Tori's in trouble. A guy broke into the house next door and he attacked her."

Except for the pounding music, the bar had gone

silent.

"C'mon, guys," yelled one of the bikers dressed in black leathers, with a blue-and-white bandana covering his head. He slammed his beer bottle onto the top of the bar. "Let's give the little lady a hand."

"Hold it," called a voice from the front corner of the room. The guy with the crew-cut stood. He withdrew a badge from his jacket pocket. "Ronald Field, Homeland Security."

"See, I told you that guy was a fed of some kind," Bandana-Guy said.

"Everyone stay put," Field said with authority. "A federal investigation is in progress. Don't interfere under penalty of prosecution."

"Listen to him, guys," Paul implored. "You know the feds would just love to nail a bunch of bikers."

Kathy glared at Field. "Are you going to save my friend?"

"I don't have authority to move against the people in that house."

"What did you see?" Paul asked.

"A couple of mean guys. They tied up to Cannon's dock and herded a bunch of kids into the house. Tori think's they're traffickers."

"Traffickers!" Bandana-Guy practically exploded.

"Kids?" another one of the guys shouted, furious.

"If there's kids involved, you can't just go bursting in. They might get hurt." Paul pointed out.

"I ain't letting any kids get exploited," yelled Bandana-Guy, and threw an arm into the air, beckoning his comrades to follow.

"You're all under arrest," Field hollered, but the bikers ignored him and moved en masse toward the door, with Kathy leading the way.

Once outside, she paused in the parking lot. "They're at the back of the house, in the kitchen. There's no lights.

How will you see?"

"What's the layout of the house?" Bandana-Guy asked.

"There's a door to the kitchen at the back. The front door is probably unlocked. The hallway goes straight back to the kitchen."

He nodded, then turned to his friends. "Terry, Rick, John—you go through the front door. Give a yell. As soon as we hear you enter, the rest of us will storm the back."

"Give us two minutes to get into position, and then bust in."

"You got it."

"I'll show you how I got there," Kathy said.

They followed her to the hedge where she and Tori had first watched the squatters when they'd arrived. She pointed to the deepening darkness. "This way to the back of the house."

The group split up, with the majority of the bikers following Kathy. She had no idea where she'd first pushed through the hedge, and had to take a good guess. "Cover your faces," she advised, before she plunged in. They followed close behind. Kathy burst through the hedge and nearly stumbled into the yard with the guys right behind her. They sidled up to the back of the house, and waited. Kathy swallowed, listening hard. What if they couldn't hear the diversion from the bikers out front? What if the brute had already killed Tori? What about the children?

Suddenly, they heard a racket, and Bandana-Guy jumped onto the step, threw open the back door and hollered, "Bonzai!"

The others echoed his shout and stormed into the kitchen, with Kathy bringing up the rear.

The room exploded in a cacophony of screams and shouts. A shot rang out and Kathy could just make out Bandana-Guy barreling into the tall brute, knocking him to the floor. Another two bikers joined the melee and the four of them rolled around the garbage-strewn floor, the air blue with curses and shouts.

A flashlight on the counter gave off just enough light so that Kathy could see the children huddled in a corner, screaming and crying, and in the opposite corner lay Tori, curled in a ball with her hands covering her head as though to fend off blows.

Kathy went to her and tried to pull her hands away, but Tori screamed and lashed out.

"Tor, it's me, it's me! Kathy!" she shouted.

Tori froze, staring up at her, and Kathy gathered her suddenly sobbing friend in her arms. "It's okay, it's okay."

"The kids, the kids!" Tori wailed.

"We'll take care of them, I promise," Kathy shouted above the rest of the caterwauling.

The sound of a siren cut the air, and then was suddenly silenced.

Bandana-Guy and the other bikers had finally subdued the brute and yanked him to his feet. "How do we get out of here?" he asked Kathy.

She pointed. "Down the hall to the front door."

"Come on, scum," Bandana-Guy said, and he and the other bikers hauled the dazed and staggering man forward.

Kathy tried to help Tori to her feet, but she fell back in pain as her right knee collapsed under her. "We've got to help those kids," Tori cried.

Now that it was quieter, the children had stopped screaming, but their whimpering was heartbreaking. Kathy again tried to haul Tori to her feet, and this time succeeded. They hobbled across the messy kitchen and paused before a little girl.

"It's okay, it's okay," Kathy said gently. "We're here to help you."

If anything, the children seemed even more frightened and huddled together into a solid mass in the corner.

"Shhh," Tori said. "We won't hurt you, I promise," but her words were of no comfort to the frightened children.

"Maybe we'd better back off," Kathy advised.

"Yeah," Tori agreed. "But I won't leave them. Not until I'm sure they're safe."

"We won't leave them," Kathy assured her. "Are you okay?"

"I've been better," Tori said, her voice strained.

Thundering footsteps preceded the appearance of an armed deputy. "What the hell's going on?" he demanded.

"The bikers—they got the bad guys, and with no help from Homeland Security," Kathy said bitterly. "These kids," she said, sweeping her arm through the air to point to the children, "are their contraband."

"What are you two doing here?" he demanded.

"Saving the day," Tori said wearily.

And so they had.

SIXTEEN

Tori watched as Herb traced the confines of the small ER cubicle for at least the hundredth time. There was no mistaking the depth of his anger.

"How could you do something so stupid?" Herb bellowed for at least the tenth time.

Dressed in only a hospital gown, Tori sat on the edge of the ER bed, swinging her one good leg. The other one was bruised and badly swollen, and the thought of putting weight on her knee filled her with dread. She hadn't caught sight of her face in the mirror yet, but she'd been told she had the beginnings of a spectacular shiner.

Kathy sat in one of the hard plastic chairs, the bed remote in her hand. She'd been hogging the thing for the past two hours, watching HGTV reruns. They'd traveled to Bora Bora and probably Timbuktu, and then segued into two home renovations in Toronto. Meanwhile, Tori had come and gone for x-rays, a CAT scan, and had been poked and prodded by a series of doctors and nurses. She was sore—very sore—but grateful her best friend had engineered her rescue.

"Gramps, they were little kids. They were dirty, they were hungry, and they were scared. I couldn't not do something."

"Yeah, well, don't ever do anything that stupid ever again." He moved his angry glare toward Kathy. "And do we have to watch another episode of drivel on that stupid channel?" Herb grumped.

"Kath!" Tori implored.

Kathy shrugged and tuned to the Rochester all-news channel, where the on-air weatherman blathered about temps for the upcoming week. "There are a few things I don't understand," she said, turning her attention to Tori. "Where did the smugglers get the spikes that they stuffed into poor Mr. Jackson's mouth?"

"From our shop," Tori said. "We saw for ourselves that the big guy picked the lock on your house." Kathy smiled at the reference. "He must have locked up when he left, and because Gramps was so preoccupied with losing grandma, he never noticed."

Herb nodded.

"And what about you, Mr. Cannon? I heard you talk to that fisherman, Larry. You warned him not to talk to the cops. Why?"

"That blowhard?" Herb asked. "I don't believe a word he says. If you'd heard the fish stories that guy has to tell, you wouldn't either. I figured he'd only mess up the investigation by confusing the issue. Biggie Taylor looks tough and talks tough, but I happen to know he's an old softie. He may have bugged Jackson for some of his worms, which is annoying, I'll grant you, but I've seen him get all panicky when there's a hurt bird or duck out on the water."

"Anissa sure had him cowed when she confronted him on the bay bridge," Kathy agreed.

"There's something I don't understand. Anissa and I looked at her father's journals and found pages missing from the last page. I wonder if we'll ever find out what happened to them."

"I've got a theory," Kathy said. "When I went to The Bay Bar to get help to rescue you, the Homeland Security guy nearly had a fit. He seemed prepared to let those guys get away with another murder—yours—in order to build a better case against them. I wasn't going to let that happen.

"And I'm damned thankful you stood up to him," Herb said.

A man with a blue bandana poked around the curtain. "Are you Tori?" he asked.

"What's it to you?" Herb asked.

"Mr. Cannon," Kathy admonished. "This is the man who saved Tori!"

"Oh. Sorry," Herb said. He offered Bandana-Guy his hand. "I'm Herb Cannon, Tori's grandfather."

"Nice to meet you. Dave Albright." They shook.

Kathy moved to stand beside the man. "Sorry I didn't have a chance to introduce myself earlier. I'm Kathy Grant, and this is Tori."

"Nice to meet you," Dave said, nodding to Tori.

"Mr. Cannon and I followed the ambulance here with Tori, so we don't know what happened back at the house. Are the kids okay?" The last time they'd seen them they were in the back of two police cruisers eating ice cream that Noreen had provided.

Dave nodded. "A social worker came and picked them up. They're somewhere here in the hospital getting checked out. They're from Indonesia and were probably stolen from their parents."

"They must be out of their minds with worry," Tori said, shaking her head.

"They've already found an interpreter. I think they'll be in good hands until they can get them all home, but God only knows what they've been through."

"Are we going to be arrested?" Kathy asked.

"Arrested?" Tori asked, aghast.

Kathy nodded. "That guy with the crew-cut was from Homeland Security. He forbad us to go and rescue you, but I'd hate to think what would have happened to you and those kids if we hadn't."

"My brother's a lawyer. I already talked to him," Dave said. "We may have disrupted an investigation, but we saved seven innocent lives. That's gotta trump any charges they can throw against us."

"Any?" Kathy asked.

"Well, most of them," he said and gave her a comforting smile.

Kathy smiled back.

Tori knew that look.

The cubicle's curtain was pulled aside and the resident, Dr. Patel, stepped into the small enclosure. "Sorry to interrupt," she said.

"I was just leaving," Dave said.

"Maybe I'll see you at the bar sometime," Kathy said.

He gave her an even bigger smile. "Maybe." He stepped away, and Herb cleared his throat, indicating they should listen to the doctor."

"Ms. Cannon, I'm pleased to tell you that although you have a strained ligament in your knee and an abundance of contusions and lacerations, you will make a full recovery. I suggest a number of hot baths and anti-inflammatories, such as aspirin or ibuprofen, and a little tender loving care from your family. In a couple of weeks you shall be feeling on top of the world once again."

"Thank you, doctor. It's a big relief," Herb said.

"I'll second that," Tori said and laughed.

"If you'll wait here, I'll get the paperwork started for your discharge." The doctor gave them a smile and they watched her leave.

"You're still not out of the woods with me, young lady. If you were just a few years younger, I'd ground you for a month," Herb said sternly.

"How about I paint the house instead?"

"With that bum knee, it's going to be weeks before you can climb a ladder."

"Maybe Kathy will help me?" Tori said, looking at her

best friend.

"Sure. I'll paint, and you can stand around and criticize my work."

Tori laughed, but Herb suddenly looked up at the TV. "Shhh! They're going to announce the winning Powerball number." He grabbed the ticket stubs from his shirt pocket.

"But I didn't buy you a Powerball ticket," Tori said.

"No, but I did," Herb said.

They listened as the announcer called out the numbers. "Ten; nineteen; thirty-seven; thirty-eight; fifty. And the Powerball number is twenty-eight."

"Damn," Herb cursed.

"Sorry, Gramps," Tori said.

"There's still Mega Millions," Herb said and fished out three different ticket stubs.

Tori shook her head, while Kathy attempted to stifle a smile.

"And the Mega Millions numbers are: two; thirty-two; thirty-five; fifty; fifty-nine, and three."

"Oh my God! I've got it!" Herb shouted.

Tori's mouth dropped, and Kathy looked just as shocked.

A nurse stuck her head around the curtain. "Sir, this is a hospital. I must ask you to keep your voice down." She disappeared.

"I won! I won!" Herb said in a harsh whisper. "Oh, my God, I won!"

"How much did you win? How many numbers did you get?"

"All of them!"

"All of them?" Kathy repeated.

"Oh, my God," Herb said once again. "I can pay my taxes."

"I think your tax bill just went through the roof," Kathy corrected him and laughed.

"Do you know what this means, Tori?" Herb asked, smiling.

"You're moving to Florida?"

SEVENTEEN

Never had Tori and Kathy had such an eventful summer—although they weren't sure they ever wanted to repeat it. The Lotus Lodge had not reopened. No matter what arguments Tori and Kathy had used, Herb refused to entertain the thought. He was too busy making other arrangements. Like buying a condo in St. Pete, Florida. He'd flown—first class—there on a number of occasions to seal the deal so he could begin his new life. Meanwhile, he'd made good on his threat and put the Cannon Bait & Tackle up for sale. He'd hinted that he'd spoken to a buyer, but hadn't yet settled on a final price.

Heartbroken, Tori had followed through with her promise to help spruce up the property. The house and boathouse had been cleared and painted. They'd sold off or ditched the last of her grandmother's treasures, and Tori had submitted resumes to every school district in a three-county area but had heard nothing. Her life was effectively on hold.

Not so for Kathy. The sale of the house had gone through, but it had taken almost ten weeks for it to happen. She'd spent that time bumming bed space from either the Cannons or Anissa, who'd found just enough handywoman jobs to stay afloat.

The lotus leaves were beginning to disintegrate into the bay, looking mushy and unsightly, but they'd be back next spring. The cygnets were just about the same size as their stately parents, and swam and ate near the marsh at the edge of the Cannon compound. On Labor Day, Dan Fisher made a mint from his launch when a glut of boaters hauled their craft out of the water for the last time that season.

Now, on the balmy first day of fall, Kathy finally closed on her house. Tori had accompanied her to the attorney's office, and they found Herb waiting for them upon their return to the Cannon compound.

"So, you're a homeowner," he said, giving Kathy a wide grin.

"Looks like it. Want to come over and see the wreck in person?"

"Why not?"

"When is the Dumpster due to arrive?" Tori asked as they waited for a car to pass before they crossed the road.

"Any minute now," Kathy said. "I've been itching to clear that place out and start working on it."

"I thought you weren't getting your inheritance for another two months," Herb said.

"What's sixty days? I'm broke for now, but I couldn't be happier," Kathy said. "Anissa and I have drawn up a list of projects I can start in the meantime. First on the list is clearing out the trash and calling an exterminator."

They stopped in front of the shabby old house. "Hey, someone cut the grass," Kathy said, delighted.

"That was Anissa. She came by right after you girls left for the closing. She borrowed my mower and went to town."

"Oh, that was so sweet of her."

"That's the last time she'll need to borrow it. Since I'm moving, I gave it to her," Herb said.

"But Gramps, how will I cut the grass in the meantime?"

"Oh, don't worry, honey. I wouldn't leave you stranded."

Did that mean he'd made arrangements for the grass to be cut until the property was sold? "Thanks," she said, but without much enthusiasm.

They walked up to the derelict house and climbed the steps.

"Boy, this really is a dump. Are you sure you can turn it around?" Herb asked.

"I'd better," Kathy said. She pulled the key from her pocket and inserted it into the lock. "Before the end of the day, I'm buying new locks for all the doors. I don't want squatters to ever show up again."

"Have you heard any news about those kids?" Herb asked.

Kathy nodded. "Dave called me just yesterday. He said they'd all made it home okay and are back in school and doing well. As well as can be expected, anyway."

"I thought you and that fella might be getting sweet on each other—although he's a little old for you," Herb said with what sounded like consternation.

Kathy shrugged. "Maybe, maybe not."

Tori knew the truth; Dave was only a part-time biker, but a full-time married man.

Oh, well.

"Shall we go in?" Kathy asked.

"Wait," Herb said. "He reached for his back jeans pocket and pulled out an envelope."

"Oh, Mr. Cannon, you shouldn't have," Kathy began.

Herb looked confused. "Shouldn't have what?"

Kathy looked at Tori for guidance. "Oh, I thought maybe you were going to ..." she let the sentence trail off.

"Give you a present? Gee, I hadn't thought of that. But you're right. I'm going to give you a housewarming present. Let me think on it for a couple of days and I'll get back to you."

"Oh, no, I didn't mean—"

"No, no," he insisted. "The work you did on the shop, the house, and the boathouse, you made them not only look presentable, but darn pretty. Made it look so much nicer for the new owner."

"Then you've sold the place?" Tori asked, panicked.

Herb nodded. "I'm just waiting for the new owner to sign the paperwork."

"And when's that going to happen?" Kathy asked.

"Any minute now." He handed the envelope to Tori. "I've decided to sell the place to Tori."

"Gramps!" Tori nearly shouted, and threw her arms around him. "I don't know what to say?"

"Just don't bad mouth me in the future when you come to regret it," Herb said.

"But, Gramps, I don't have any money. I don't have a job. How can I—?"

"Why don't you look at the sale agreement?" he suggested.

With trembling hands, Tori removed the paper from the envelope. She scanned the page, her mouth dropping open in shock. "But it says—" She couldn't go on, and passed the paperwork to Kathy.

"Oh, my God. You're selling it to Tori for the sum of one dollar?"

Herb nodded, grinning. "The lawyer said it was better if you bought it outright, instead of me giving it to you; that it would solve all kinds of problems in the future."

"I don't know what to say!" Tori exclaimed, breathless.

"How about thanks?" Herb suggested.

Again, Tori threw her arms around her grandfather, hugging him fiercely.

"We'll get this all registered in time for me to leave next week. Once I'm out of the picture, you can do what you damn well please with the place. Truth be told, I'm glad to get this monkey off my back once and for all."

Happy tears ran down Tori's cheeks. "Thanks, Gramps. Thank you so much. But what made you change your mind?"

Before Herb could answer, a car drove slowly past and honked. Irene Timmons waved. Once it passed, the car turned into Resort Road and then into the Cannon compound.

"Let's just say I had a little help coming to that decision," he said sheepishly. He cleared his throat. "I gotta get back to the shop," Herb said. "Another week and my next fishing will be in the Gulf of Mexico."

"I thought you wanted to trade fishing for golf?" Tori asked.

"Not until I get me a marlin," Herb said. He turned, and headed down the stairs and off across the yard.

Tori wiped her eyes. "Well, this is a day neither of us will soon forget."

"Right," Kathy said, smiling.

"I'm sorry Gramps stole your thunder about your own sale."

"Not at all. I'm just so happy for you, because best of all, we'll be neighbors. It's something I never thought would happen. It's the best thing that ever could have happened."

"Happy closing day," came a voice from the edge of the still-unruly hedges. It was Anissa, and bringing up the rear, holding a tray with four tall paper cups with plastic lids and straws, was Noreen.

"What are you guys doing here?" Kathy asked.

"We came to help you celebrate," Noreen said. She and Anissa climbed the steps and Noreen pushed the tray close to them. "We thought we should make a toast to you guys and your new businesses."

"Did Gramps tell you he's selling me the business?" Tori asked.

Anissa nodded. "Among other things." She nodded

toward the road. Across it, they saw Herb and Irene walking hand-in-hand toward the bait shop.

"Would you look at that," Kathy said, surprised. She turned to Tori. "Did you know they were hooking up?"

"No, but I suspected they might."

"How do you feel about it?" Noreen asked.

"Irene was my grandma's best friend. I think she'd probably be happy for both of them."

"Then it looks like we have something else to drink to," Anissa said. She took one of the cups. "I propose a toast: to business."

"Business?" Noreen asked.

"Yeah. Here we are, four smart women, and each of us has, or will have," she said, looking at Kathy, "a business of our own."

"I'm only part owner of The Bay Bar," Noreen said.

Anissa leveled a hard stare at the short-order cook. "Don't quibble. Now, where was I?"

"To business," Tori said, taking another of the cups.

"To our successful businesses," Kathy agreed, taking another of the cups.

Noreen picked up the last one, raising it in salute. "To us."

In unison, they touched cups and drank. Tori swallowed and coughed. "Wow! That's one powerful gin and tonic!"

"Glad you like it," Noreen said and smiled.

Just then, a big flatbed truck rumbled to a halt in front of the house. It backed into the yard to unload its cargo: a twenty-yard Dumpster.

"Drink up, ladies," Noreen said. "Kathy needs to start work today if she's going to have her business up and running in time for next summer's tourist season."

"Oh, I will," Kathy promised. "Lord willing and the creek don't rise."

They laughed. It felt good to laugh with friends. And

they drank. Tori had a feeling there'd be more of that in her future, too.

Anissa chugged her drink and then crushed the cup in her hand. "I'm going to christen your Dumpster with its first piece of trash, and then I'm going to grab some gloves and a mask and we are going to start cleaning house."

"Oh, thank you. But don't you have any jobs today?"

"I cleared my schedule so I could help a friend."

"Me, too," Noreen said.

"Make that three," Tori agreed. "After all, what are friends for?"

KATHY'S CHOCOLATE CHIP OATMEAL COOKIES

Ingredients
1 cup butter, softened
1 cup packed light brown sugar
½ cup granulated sugar
2 eggs
2 teaspoons vanilla extract
1¼ cups all-purpose flour
½ teaspoon baking soda
1 teaspoon salt
3 cups quick-cooking oats
1 cup chopped walnuts (can substitute pecans)
1 cup semisweet chocolate chips (can substitute raisins)

Preheat the oven to 325°F. In a large bowl, cream together the butter, brown sugar, and granulated sugar until smooth. Beat in the eggs one at a time, then stir in the vanilla. Combine the flour, baking soda, and salt; stir into the creamed mixture until just blended. Mix in the oats, walnuts, and chocolate chips. Drop by heaping spoonsful onto ungreased baking sheets. Bake for 12 minutes. Allow the cookies to cool on the baking sheet for 5 minutes before transferring to a wire rack to cool completely.

Yield: 3½ dozen

KATHY'S CUTOUT COOKIE RECIPE

Ingredients
1⅓ cups granulated sugar
1 teaspoon vanilla or almond extract*
1⅓ cups shortening
4 slightly beaten eggs
5½ cups all-purpose flour
1 teaspoon salt
3 teaspoons baking powder

Mix all the ingredients together until they form a ball. Place the dough in a plastic bag or covered bowl and refrigerate for 4 hours or overnight.

Preheat the oven to 350°F. On a floured board, roll out the dough to about ¼ inch thickness. Cut out shapes with the cookie cutters of your choice. Bake for 8-10 minutes or until the edges just start to brown. Cool on wire racks.

When thoroughly cooled, frost. If you wish to add colored sugars, do so before you bake the dough.

Yield: varies depending on the size of the cookie cutters.

* Feel free to substitute any flavored extract—they all work equally well.

Icing
4 cups confectioner's sugar (sifted, then measured)
3 tablespoons (or more) whole milk
½ teaspoon vanilla extract
Colored sugar crystals, sprinkles, and/or decors

Combine the confectioner's sugar, milk, and vanilla in a medium bowl. Stir until the icing is well blended, smooth, and spreadable, adding more milk by teaspoonfuls if too thick or more sugar by tablespoonfuls if too thin. Using a small icing spatula or table knife, spread a thin layer of icing atop each cookie. If using colored sugar crystals, sprinkle over cookies before icing sets.

ABOUT THE AUTHOR

The immensely popular Booktown Mystery series is what put Lorraine Bartlett's pen name Lorna Barrett on the New York Times Bestseller list, but it's her talent—whether writing as Lorna, or L.L. Bartlett, or Lorraine Bartlett—that keeps her there. This multi-published, Agatha-nominated author pens the exciting Jeff Resnick Mysteries as well as the acclaimed Victoria Square Mystery series, Tales of Telenia adventure-fantasy saga, and now the Lotus Bay Mysteries, and has many short stories and novellas to her name(s). Check out the descriptions and links to all her works, and sign up for her emailed newsletter: http://www.LLBartlett.com

You can also find her on Facebook, Twitter, Pinterest, Google+, and Tumblr.

If you enjoyed **Panty Raid** and **With Baited Breath**, please consider reviewing them on your favorite online review site. Thank you!

Made in the USA
Middletown, DE
15 June 2015